T0367304

The Coconut

Be Careful What You Wish For

Lesley J. Clay

authorHOUSE®

AuthorHouse™
1663 Liberty Drive
Bloomington, IN 47403
www.authorhouse.com
Phone: 1 (800) 839-8640

Published by AuthorHouse 06/09/2017

ISBN: 978-1-5246-9612-2 (sc)
ISBN: 978-1-5246-9613-9 (hc)
ISBN: 978-1-5246-9611-5 (e)

Library of Congress Control Number: 2017909106

Print information available on the last page.

This book is printed on acid-free paper.

I would like to thank God for blessing me with this gift to write.

Being able to tell my story to people around the world.

And I would like to give a Special Thanks to my two youngest sons, Jordan and Tristin for telling me Mom do not stop writing, just keep going. So I did keep writing and I will not stop writing!

INTRO -

Now, why am I laying here in a pool of my own blood? I am in disbelief saying, what in the hell did I get myself into? Help! Help! Somebody help me please! Mia! Marcus! I'm bleeding help me, call 911!

It started on an early Saturday morning; I decided to get up, get dressed and grab a cup of coffee at Cole's coffee shop. So I grabbed my keys and handbag and headed out the door. As I walked down the stairs to my car, I thought to myself, it's a nice day to just walk to Cole's. It was only two blocks away, so I began to walk. When I arrived at Cole's coffee shop; I was glad to see that there was no one in line, so I walked to the counter and ordered my usual - a large cup of black coffee. After paying, I grabbed my cup and walked over to the table by the front door next to the big picture window. I sat down and grabbed four packs of sugar and two creamers from the containers on the table. As I opened the sugars, I couldn't help glancing out the coffee shop window at the big bright blinking sign across the street.

Wow, that sign is bright, I said to myself while pouring my creamers into my coffee and stirring it. I just couldn't take my eyes off that big bright sign across the street: "Free psychic card reading with one free wish today only." I thought to myself while blowing and sipping my coffee. I've never been one to believe in that kind of stuff, but today that could all change. I guess it wouldn't hurt to go get my cards read for fun and make a wish. I have nothing to do today, and plus it's free; why not? So I finished my coffee and threw the cup in the trash. As I started crossing the street, I began to get light headed the closer I got to the psychic reader's shop. Wow, maybe I looked at the bright sign to long, I said to myself.

Finally, as I stood in front of the big bright sign at the window of the psychic reader's shop, I placed my right hand on my head, still feeling a little dizzy, but thinking that I would be alright. All of a sudden I started getting the chills, anxiety and butterflies in my stomach from not knowing what I was about to get myself into. I said to myself, "aw, maybe it's the coffee? No. Could it be my mind, body and soul sending me signals to turn around and just forget about this whole psychic reading thing, yes! Let me just go home.

As I started to go back across the street, I heard an old scratchy voice saying,

"Excuse me lady, are you coming for a free psychic card reading with one free wish today only?" "Well are you?"

I turned around and said, 'Uh yes, yes, I am good!'

She quickly grabbed my right hand and started squeezing it tightly.

"Ouch, that hurts!" I said pulling my hand away from her quickly. I noticed her black fingernails and her rough hands.

"I am so sorry, but I must get your vibes first before the card reading," she said, as she looked directly into my eyes without one blink.

She made me feel uncomfortable as she continued to look straight through the windows of my soul. I closed my eyes quickly and opened them slowly starring at her face. I couldn't believe it, her face looked so young, smooth and tight. It was like looking at a teenage girl, but wait! As I looked from her face down to her neck - aw, shit! She had the wrinkles of an 85 year old elderly woman playing bingo in a senior citizen home. Bingo, oh my god!

Her hair was like cotton so fluffy, thin and the color was dirty blonde. She is so fucking creepy looking.

"Did you say something?" She asked, catching me off guard.

I responded, "Huh, what, Oh no!"

"Good, because I must inform you that I don't just read the psychic cards, I am also a mind reader as well."

"What!"

With that said, I began to stop all my thoughts immediately!

"Welcome" She said, "come in and have a seat; I must set things up for your card reading. I will be right back. Oh, here's a pencil and paper dear. Write your full name and birthday down for me. I will need it for the card reading." She said.

"Okay, I'll write it now," Name: Latrice Baldwin, D.O.B: May 10, 1969.

After writing my name and birthday, I sat the pencil and paper down on the table. I then decided to take a look around seeing many different kinds of things, but it was the candles that caught my attention.

What kind of candles are these? I said to myself as I got closer to the shelf. A red candle with a man and woman figure stuck together side by side in wedding clothes. They looked as if they were having a wedding ceremony, and I was invited. 'Til death do us part, I do' and 'You may kiss the bride, I whispered to myself. I picked the candle up and held it close to my face, that's crazy I said as I put the candle back on the shelf.

Oh Shit! What in the hell is this? a big penis shaped candle! a big black one, and a big red penis shaped candle too! What the fuck! I don't even want to know what those candles are for -- Or do I? Ha, ha, ha. I laughed, maybe another time. This psychic reader is not only creepy; she is also freaky!

Man, I don't know about this, I said to myself as I continued to look around. There were herbs, incense and different shaped beads, shells, and even human skulls. What the hell! I also saw statues and many different colors of oils in this big glass case with a lock on it. I could see all the oils had different labels on them. Like um, oh here's one: *Bring your ex-lover back.* What? Go away evil. Oh wow, that sounds crazy; oh wait, wait, oh Shit! Look at this one here: *Make me wealthy.* Oh yeah, now that is my kind of oil, anything about getting money or having money. I swear, I would get butt naked and pour that make me wealthy all over my naked ass! Ha ha ha, let me go sit my crazy ass down before that creepy ass psychic reader comes back.

As I began walking back to my seat, I noticed a statue placed on the floor near the front door. Now instead of me going back to my seat, I had to be nosey, so I walked towards the statue on the floor and as I got closer, the image I saw looked unreal. This mutha fuckin statute had no body parts, just a big ass head with a straw hat on it. I squatted down in front of it to get a closer look. The face of it was so black, it had eyes a nose and a mouth made of small seashells. The statue was placed on a bright red circle shaped tray with a couple of things set around it; like a chocolate cupcake with sprinkles, a couple of suckers, a toy car and a big cigar half smoked. What the hell does this mean, this is some weird shit! I said.

Still, looking at this ugly ass statue, it is so ugly I just have to say it again. Damn, you're ugly and so fuckin black! What the fuck are you? a man or a woman? Where are your limbs? Why is there a cupcake and some candy on that tray for you, and you don't even have a stomach? Answer me! Yeah right, what am I saying? this ugly mutha fucka can't talk and it can't hear me. It's just a fucked up looking statue.

After I said all that shit, I swear that statue looked like it could understand every fucking word I was saying to it and it wouldn't stop looking at me! Naw, maybe I'm just paranoid, it's just a stupid statue. Let me touch it and see, go ahead touch it Latrice, I said to myself. So as I reached out to touch the statue my hair began to stand up from my scalp.

"Hey" "Latrice Baldwin!"

What the fuck and who said that? I was startled by that loud cracky voice.

"Never, ever touch! Understand. Now come have a seat, Okay?"

"Okay, I'm coming." So I stood up from squatting down by the statue and I began to walk over to the table. I pulled the chair out and sat down right across from this creepy ass psychic reader.

"So Latrice Baldwin, born May 10, 1969, place your right hand on this deck of cards on the table. Do it now!" she yelled while pushing my right hand down on top of the deck of cards. Then she took her hand off of mine quickly.

"Now concentrate, make your wish and take the one deck of cards and separate them into three sets. Do it now!" She said.

"Damn, Okay!" I said.

"Now, this first set of cards will tell of your past. The second set will be all about your present. And the last set will reveal your future. You have any questions?"

"No," I said.

"Then let's get started." She said.

As she reached for the first set of cards, I sat quietly watching her spread my past across the table in front of me. I really didn't want to hear about all the things that I had been through already. This is why I love that saying "leave the past in the past." She began to tell me things from my past that only I knew about. Damn! this is some crazy shit! I said, shh.

"Listen," she said, "I see so much sadness!"

As she continued to talk about things that happened in my past that I couldn't change. I begin to get teary eyed.

"You lived a very hard life back then."

With that said, it brought a lot of thoughts and more thoughts that weren't so good from my past. I swear, I couldn't take listening to anymore of my past! I just wanted to cover my ears and sing *lalala lalala*, until she was done talking about it. She watched the emotional struggle I was having with myself at the table. I just couldn't sit still as she continued to say more and more about my past!

"Oh, God!" I yelled!

"Okay, okay enough of your past!" She shouted.

"Thank God," I said under my breath while wiping the tears from my eyes and exhaling.

"Now let's talk about your present, the card show you're doing a lot better now than you were in your past, very good!" She said. "I see you have a new job, and an old lover from your past."

"Wait!" "What, what do you mean an old lover from my past?" I said.

"Just wait, not right now." She said. "You will see, now let me move on to your future. Oh! Wow! She said. "The future card is showing me that you are supposed to become rich, very rich. I feel that the wish you made has a lot to do with this card. Your wish was to become very rich, right?" She asked.

"Yes, I did wish to be rich!" I said.

"So, Latrice Baldwin, this one card I read shows you will need a little help from the Coco."

"The Coco, what is that?" I asked.

"The Coco is a very powerful spirit that can help you with your wish to become rich."

"Are you for real?" I asked.

"Yes, I am!" "This spirit, the Coco, has helped a lot of people for example; that famous actor / singer that is really big right now. Ah, ah what is his name?"

"Is it Tyrone?" I said.

"Yes, yes, Tyrone!" She said. "Look at him!" She yelled. "He is still one of the best actors and a great singer, right?"

"Well yes," I said.

"That is because of the Coco. The Coco worked very hard for him and now Tyrone comes by and pays his respect to the coco every month. There are even more and more people that have worked with the coco and requested help from the coco. So what do you think? Do you want to be another one of those people as well?" She asked.

"Yes, I do."

"Okay great." She said. "Now listen to me, Latrice Baldwin, in order for the Coco to help you. You must first believe in the Coco, never ever doubt the coco or you will be very sorry. Understand?"

"I guess", I said.

"Is that a yes?" She asked.

"Um, yes okay."

"Now, I'm going to give you a list of things you will need to do and things you will have to get and bring to me this Wednesday. You must have every single thing on the list and do what it tells you to do on the list before Wednesday."

"Why, Wednesday?" I asked.

"Well, because Wednesday is the day of the high winds and the night of the full moon! The ritual is done very fast on this day."

"Oh, okay" I said.

"Do you have any more questions?" She asked.

"Yes, how much will it cost me to get help from this Coco and how long will it take for this Coco to make me rich?"

"Well it will cost you $500 cash and the Coco's work will take up to 90 days once the Coco has been awakened. Now the Coco works at it's on pace and you will get results guaranteed. So I will see you Wednesday; with everything on the list and $500 cash right?" Latrice Baldwin, you do want to become rich now don't you?" She asked.

"Yes I do!"

"Okay then, here's the list."

I grabbed the list and said, "I will be back Wednesday with everything." I opened the list briefly and looked it over. "Shit, this is a lot of things." I said to her.

She started laughing "Ha! Ha! Ha! See you Wednesday Latrice Baldwin."

"Okay" I said, while folding the list in half and placing it into my handbag.

"So Wednesday it is!" We both shouted as I began walking out her shop.

"Oh wait, wait, Latrice Baldwin!" She yelled. "Before you go, I would like to introduce you to the Coco."

"Oh okay" I said.

As she pointed her nasty looking finger to the floor by the front door, I looked down by the door, and the Coco was that ugly ass, black, big head statue with the straw hat sitting on that bright red circle tray.

Holy shit! I said to myself. Is she serious, this must be some kind of joke, right? Yeah, okay, I'll just play along.

"Hey coco it's nice to meet you." I said with a big smirk on my face. "So I will see the both of you Wednesday. Oh, oh and Ms., I never got your name."

"Well, you never asked." She said. "It's Kwana - Kwana, the psychic card reader!"

"It's been a pleasure, Kwana."

"Likewise Latrice Baldwin, we will meet again Wednesday." She said.

As I walked out the psychic reading shop I headed home. While walking home, I decided to stop and take another look at that list; I wanted to read it so bad, but I was too excited! So I put the list back in my handbag. I'll read it when I get home.

As I began to walk home, my mind started racing with thoughts of becoming rich. I just couldn't shake those wealthy thoughts out of my head.

"Is this real" I yelled out loud, "the money, the mansions, the cars, clothes, champagne, caviar and the men?" The men, my god, the men! Looking and smelling so yummy, the money! Let me stop. I must respect the success. Oh yes, this shit better be real because I am so ready to take this world by storm. I can't wait.

I started to sing and dance the rest of the way home. I'm gonna be, I'm gonna be, I'm going to be rich. Watch out world, I'mma a be a rich girl.

I finally arrived in front of my apartment building and immediately stopped singing and dancing. Damn, reality just slapped me in the face. Smack, Ouch! So I grabbed my keys out of my handbag, opened the security gate and headed up the stairs to my apartment. I unlocked the door. Finally, I'm home and now it's time to relax. I took my shoes off set my hand bag on the coffee table.

Oh, the list, I said. So I took the list out of my handbag and sat down on the couch. Ok, things I need for the Coco, let me see now. Hmmm, okay 5 shot bottles of Bacardi, one bag of assorted gumdrops, Damn, is this mutha fucka human? Shit, I swear this better be real; got my ass paying $500. I could use that money to pay off my bills or just take a chance with lottery tickets and scratchers. I would probably have a better chance at becoming rich! Oh well, let me not complain. Besides, I'm curious to see the outcome with me and this whole psychic reading spiritual thing, plus who wouldn't want to find an easy way to get rich.

Let me finish checking out this list some more. Okay. One fresh coconut with the top removed and replaced. Don't throw the top to the coconut away, it is very important that you keep it for the main part of the ritual. The juice inside the coconut must be drained and then dried out, one picture of your face the size of the picture on your state identification card, 1 parchment paper the size of a US postal stamp. You will need to write your full name and birthday on one side, and your one free wish on the other side. Short and simple in pencil! Ok. I guess this isn't too much I have to get and do. Well let me get some sleep and pick up everything tomorrow morning. Wow! I can't wait! I can pick up everything from One Stop Shop it's only five blocks away from here.

The Next day.

"Excuse me where are your coconuts?" I asked the store clerk.

"There on aisle number 3" answered the store clerk.

"Okay, thank you"

"You're welcome."

The coconuts, okay aisle, here they are, got one. Now, let me go to the candy aisle. I see, aisle number 4, 5. Here it is, aisle number 6. Here's some licorice, oh an assorted bag of gumdrops, got them. Now let me get in the checkout line so I can ask the cashier to get me the 5 shot bottles of Bacardi and I'll pay for everything at the counter.

"Here's your 5 shot bottles of Bacardi"

"Thank You."

"You're welcome Ma'am, here's your receipt; have a nice day and thank you for shopping One Stop Shop."

Thanks. Now let me grab my bag. Where's my cell phone? Oh, here it is, let me call Kwana. Ring! Ring!

"Hello Kwana"

"Yes."

"This is Latrice Baldwin."

"I know!"

"Oh, okay I'm leaving the supermarket and I picked up everything."

"Good!" She said.

"I will have my picture Tuesday."

"Excellent!" She said. "The bag of gum drops is assorted right?"

"Yes."

"Very Good, because the Coco don't like the solid color gum drops at all."

"Oh really." I said.

"Yes really, assorted only, okay"

"Okay!"

"I picked up the assorted bag, hum, I really did. Now where can I get the parchment paper?"

"Don't worry about the parchment paper; I will have it for you when you come Wednesday" She said.

"Okay, thank you" I said.

"I have to go now." She said, "see you Wednesday. Oh Latrice, before I go, I must let you know that the coconut must be cut open gently in a circle at the top with a power drill. You cannot let it crack or break. The coconut is the most valuable part of the ritual. It is very important that the coconut does not crack or break. Oh, and make sure all the coconut juice is completely drained from the coconut, leave it out to dry." She said. "It will be dry by Wednesday morning. Don't forget, Latrice Baldwin, you have three days to have everything I will need for the ritual, so get that coconut open right away." Click.

"Hello Kwana, Damn!" She hung up on me.

Wow, now where and who can I get to cut the coconut open for me? I said to myself as I put my bags in the car and started it up to drive off still thinking about whom and where I can get the coconut cut open. I'll figure it out when I get home.

I made it home. As I was pulling into the driveway of my apartment building, I looked over to my right and saw my neighbor, Miguel, in his garage. He's always in his garage making and fixing on something. Miguel's garage door stays open 24/7. Honk! Honk! I honked my car horn and waved at Miguel as I continued to drive down the driveway of my apartment building. Finally, I parked and turned my engine off. I grabbed my handbag and my bag with the coconut in it, and closed the car door. Oh Shit! I forgot my keys. I opened the car door, reached in and got my keys out of the ignition and closed the car door and pressed the alarm on my key ring. Slow down Latrice, I said to myself while walking down the driveway of my apartment building. Now let me get up these stairs to figure out how to get this coconut cut open.

Oh, here comes Miguel walking down the driveway.

"Hey Latrice."

"Hi Miguel, how are you?"

I'm okay."

"That's good. So Miguel. What are you working on today in your garage? I asked.

"Oh. Nothing too much. Just a twenty part shelf for all my power tools."

Damn! I said to myself laughing in my mind.

"Really?"

""You want to see it?"

Um. I have to get some paperwork done for work tomorrow."

"Oh, come on Latrice. It won't take too long. Wait til you see it. It's nice, you will like it. Come on Latrice. Please."

"Oh. okay."

"Come on let's go," Miguel said.

So I grabbed my bag and put my handbag on my shoulder and walked over with Miguel to his garage and we both went inside.

"See Latrice, here it is, what do you think?

"Oh wow! Miguel that's nice."

"Why thank you."

"See Latrice, all of my power drills can go on the top shelf and my power saw's will go on the bottom shelf."

"Wait! Wait! I said. Miguel did you say your power drills?"

"Yes, I did. Why?"

"Oh my God, Miguel! Can I ask you to do me a big favor?"

"Why sure, Latrice. What's up?"

"Can you please drill a circle around the top of this coconut I have in my bag?"

"Why yes, I can do that for you, no problem, let me grab my power drill from my work table."

"Okay, thank you so much Miguel."

"Anytime, anytime," He said.

So I reached into my bag and gave him the coconut.

"Here it is," I said.

"Ok, now let me plug in the drill so I can get started."

He plugged in the power drill as we both stood at his work table, he set the coconut right side up on the table.

"Oh, Latrice, do you need the top once I cut the circle out on top of the coconut?"

"Yes! Yes! I do Miguel. I'm going to need it to put it back on the top of the coconut. You know like a cookie jar top."

"Oh ok." He said. "If you don't mind me asking, why do you need this coconut cut open like that for?"

"Oh, just a little project we're doing at work. My boss wants to see which one of his employees are the most creative with a coconut. Plus, you win $200 for the best looking coconut."

"Wow, that sounds fun," Miguel said. "Well I'm ready to gently drill the circle for you. I will make it very nice for you, Latrice."

"Okay thanks. Miguel." I said.

So as Miguel started to drill. I started thinking to myself. Shit! I hate lying to people, but I can't tell Miguel the real reason why I needed the coconut drilled open. He might think I'm a little crazy. No, he will think I'm LOCO!!

"Latrice, Latrice"

"Oh, Huh? Yes Miguel?"

"I'm done. Do you like it?"

"Oh yes, Miguel, I love it! Thank you so much."

"Sure, now what do you want me to do with the coconut juice? Just pour it out?" He said.

"Yes please." I said.

He picked up the coconut and walked out the garage with it to his front lawn. I stayed inside the garage watching him.

"Oh no," he said, "not on my beautiful lawn." So he walked to the side of his house and poured the coconut juice out on the ground and walked back into the garage.

I said to him, "Miguel you're funny."

I know," he said. "I love my beautiful lawn, here's your coconut Latrice."

"Thank you so much again Miguel."

"You're welcome. I really hope you win first place and that $200 at your job."

"Huh? I said. Oh! Oh! Yeah, me to Miguel."

So I took the coconut and put it back in my bag.

"See you later Latrice" Miguel said.

"Okay, bye Miguel."

I began to walk back to my apartment with the bag, my keys, and my handbag. I started walking upstairs to my apartment, I unlocked my door, went in and set everything on my coffee table. Then I went back to my front door closed it, and locked it. Now let me take this coconut out the bag and set it on my kitchen sink so it can dry out. I removed the top of the coconut that Miguel cut and set the coconut down on the kitchen counter by the kitchen window. Okay now, let me -- Ding! Dong! Ding! Dong! Ding! Dong! Who could that be? Ding! Dong! Ding! I'm coming, Ding! Dong!

"Who is it?" I asked. As I got closer to the front door no one said anything and the doorbell stopped ringing.

"Who's there?" I said.

Still no answer. I looked through the peep hole. I didn't see anyone, so I opened the front door. No one was there. I came out and stood on my doormat, looked to the left and I looked to the right, there was no one out there. I even began to walk to the top part of the stairway and looked down the stairs. As the wind began to blow, there was no one outside. That's weird, I said to myself, while crossing my arms, rubbing them with my hands and walking back into my apartment. Shit that wind is cold! I said as I walked back inside my apartment closing the front door and locking it. I know it wasn't my son or my daughter, they're gone for the weekend visiting my brother and his kids, they won't be back until tomorrow. This was strange I thought as I stood in my living room looking puzzled. Maybe whoever it was had the wrong apartment. Yes! That's what it was. I said.

As I begin to walk over to sit down on the couch, I heard a *Boom! Boom! Bam!* Oh! Shit! Now what the fuck! It sounded like something fell on the floor in the kitchen. Damn! I hope it wasn't that coconut. I quickly went into the kitchen to see what the noise was. When I entered the kitchen I started to look around and everything was still intact. Nothing on the floor, nothing in the sink and the coconut was still on the counter. Okay. Then what the fuck was that noise. Uh, wait. I still hear something. There's some taping over by my kitchen window. I went to look out the kitchen window, and I could hear the wind whistling through the crack of my kitchen window with that tapping sound on the window. I was scared as hell, but I still stood there at the window. Damn, the noise started to get louder and louder as I stood there looking out the window. I could see the tree branches from the big old tree in the front yard tapping the glass of my kitchen window from the wind. Wow, I said, feeling a sense of relief that it was just some tree branches tapping on the window. Thank God. Nothing was broken like that coconut. I was so scared, I thought I was going to come in the kitchen and find the coconut broken into little pieces all over the kitchen floor. Man! Just the thought of me trying to get another coconut cut open gave me a headache. Damn, it's starting to get cold in here. Let me go turn the heater on, sit down, relax and watch some t.v. I fell asleep.

The next day I'm up early in the bathroom washing my face and brushing my teeth. As I unwrapped my hair I begin looking in the mirror and telling myself I am so ready to be rich, the first thing I will buy is um??

"Hey Mom, we're home."

"Okay, I'm in the bathroom."

I guess I'll tell myself later, I said to myself as I walked out the bathroom.

"Hey kids, how was your stay at my brothers house?"

"Boring," Marcus said, "did you cook?"

"No boy I didn't."

"Mom! I'm hungry," Marcus said,

"and I'm thirsty," Mia said as she walked into the kitchen, "I couldn't wait to come home and pop me a cold can of soda open, let me get one out the fridge. Mom, you know that your brother and his wife and kids are still on some nuts and berries kick" She yelled. "They eat like squirrels. Ha ha! I mean they're still vegetarians. Your brother is crazy mom. You will starve at their house. Remind me next time we visit them to take our backpacks, and put a well done steak, a baked potato with sour cream and chives, and a ice cold soda. Oh, and don't forget a slice of German chocolate cake in me and Marcus' backpacks. Ha Ha Ha" Mia laughed.

"Stop talking about food," Marcus yelled! I'm still hungry."

"Boy go in the kitchen and find you something to eat." I said.

"Okay mom."

"Mom why is there a open coconut on the kitchen counter?" Mia asked.

"What coconut on the counter? Where? Can I eat it? Or are you making a coconut cream pie, even though I don't like that kind of pie? but I'll still eat it right now," Marcus said.

"No, boy," I said. "Don't touch it! You hear me."

"Well I know, I won't touch it." Mia said. "I hate coconuts, they look ugly and they're hairy. Yuck! And they taste nasty. The juice in it is so discussing. It's ugly and Nasty."

"I don't like coconuts either." Marcus said. But that coconut cream pie still sounds good."

"This coconut is here to make me rich."

"What do you mean make you rich?' Mia and Marcus said.

"Just what I said. So don't touch it!"

"Can it make me rich too?" Mia said.

"Oh sure. What you want to be rich?" I asked.

"Yes! I do," Mia said, "buy a big house on the hill; drive a big expensive car with diamonds, and diamonds on my fingers; a big purse and some big ass sunglasses on my face."

"Okay, I get it," I said.

"Come on Mom, who wouldn't want to be rich."

"Yeah, you're right Mia, but are you ready to get rich with the help of voodoo?"

"What? um, um, I'm not too sure about that," Mia said.

"You're not willing to call on a very powerful spirit to help you?"

"What?" Mia said. "No Mom"

"Well, I am. This coconut is a big part of a voodoo ritual. I'm not really too sure how it works yet. All I know is this coco in a coconut is a very powerful spirit that will get you whatever you wish for."

"How did you find out about that?" Mia asked.

"Well I went to a psychic reader shop."

"You what!!" Mia yelled coughing out her soda everywhere. "That's scary mom" Mia said while clearing her throat.

"Mom you're crazy!" Marcus said.

"I'm not crazy, Marcus. And what is so scary about it, Mia?"

"Mom you have to be very careful with voodoo and the spirits, it could become very, very dangerous, and sometimes deadly. You have to know what you're doing, and never doubt the spirit or the voodoo."

"Really? Now how you know so much about voodoo?"

"Well you know my friend Gabby?"

"Gabby?"

"Yeah, Gabriella O'Neal." Mia said.

"Oh yeah. The little pretty girl with the curly hair," I said.

"Yeah. Okay her mother, Geneva O'Neal a.k.a 'Ms. Gigi' is what everyone call her, Mom, she is the Voodoo queen! She knows everything about the Voodoo and will do anything with the Voodoo! Now listen to this".

"I'm listening." I said.

"Every Friday night at 9 p.m. or later, Ms. Gigi has a séance in her living room to talk to the dead!"

"What? Are you serious?" I said.

"Yes, Mom, dead serious," Mia said. "She burns candles on a altar in her bedroom 24/7. I seen the altar and the candles. While walking with Gabby to her bedroom, Gabby said, 'shh! Mia, look in mother's bedroom.' "

"Well did you?"

"Yes, You know I did Mom," Mia said. "Gabby told me to look as she pointed at the candles, 'you see the light color candles on mother's alter? those are to bring her whatever she feel is a need, and those dark colored candles on the floor, those are for the evil people she feel is out to get her.'

"Mom, there were more than a dozen dark colored candles on her floor."

"What! Now that's crazy, man."

"I know Mom." Mia said. "That stuck in my mind when Gabby was telling me and showing me those candles. But listen to this Mom. Now all of Ms. Gigi's neighbors say she's crazy. Shit, Mom."

"What girl!"

"Oops! sorry, I mean shu. I never thought she was crazy, I just thought she was a little different until I had to stop going over there for a while because my thoughts of Ms. Gigi being a little different had soon changed. It had me believing she was 51/50 after going over to their house three weeks ago to get a science project done with Gabby. That Mr. Brown, our science teacher just insisted that me and Gabby be partners. We had to do that project for extra credit. Plus Gabby bought everything we needed and told me to just come over. So I went to Gabby's house.

When I got there, I walked up the steps to the house and before I could knock on the door, Ms. Gigi said, 'come in Mia." So I open the screen door and walked in. I turned to speak to Ms. Gigi, and guess what?

"What?" I said.

"She was in a wheelchair!"

"What! shut your mouth! What happen to her?

"I'll tell you in minute. So I sat down on their couch, and Ms. Gigi started looking to her left laughing and talking as if someone was standing there, and no one was in the living room but me and her. So, as she continued to talk, I politely asked, 'Excuse me, Ms Gigi, is Gabby here?' 'Why yes she is, Mia.' 'Can you please tell her I'm here?' 'Hold on honey, she whispered, I will call Gabby in a minute. You have to wait a second, me and Charles are talking about something important.' Charles? I said to myself, what is she talking about. There is no one in this living room but me and her, And she ain't on no phone!

"What the fuck!" I mumbled under my breath as I sat on the edge of their couch. While waiting, I just couldn't sit still, I started getting scared because I didn't see anyone next to Ms. Gigi and she was still having a serious conversation. I just sat there listening to Ms. Gigi. I am really starting to believe her neighbors when they all said she was crazy. I said to myself, I better keep my eyes on Ms. Gigi. So I sat all the way back from the edge of the couch and continued to watch everything Ms. Gigi was doing.

Still waiting on Gabby, Ms. Gigi began to talk louder to this Mr.

Charles person. I look down at my watch and noticed that it was getting late, so I asked Ms. Gigi again if she could let Gabby know I'm here. 'Want a drink?' She asked. What? Who me? Mia said. 'No! I'm talking to Charles: 'You do baby? Me too.' Ms. Gigi said. 'Okay let me call Gabby to get us something special.' Gabby!'

Mom, I said to myself that this old bitch needs to be put in a straight jacket."

"Oh, Mia that's not nice to call her out her name."

"Well I was getting fed up mom, and plus she was scarring me," Mia said. 'Gabby! Gabby! Ms. Gigi,' yelled again. 'Yes Mother.' 'Can you bring two long stem glasses out and a bottle of my finest red wine for me and my man?' 'Yes mother.' 'Oh, and Gabby your friend Mia is here.' 'Oh, okay, Mother.' 'Hold on Mia,' Gabby said. Gabby went into the kitchen from the den to get Ms. Gigi the stuff she asked for. Gabby yelled, 'Mia! Come into the kitchen.' I said, 'okay.' So I got up off the couch and begin to walk to the kitchen. It got quiet. Ms. Gigi had stopped talking. So before I can step into the kitchen, I heard some kind of um, um, *smack smack,* um, noise.

'Now wait one got damn minute,' I said to myself. 'What the fuck is she doing,' I mumbled. When I turned around to look, I seen Ms. Gigi sticking her tongue out moving it around and puckering up her lips to the air as if she was tongue kissing someone."

"What! Mia are you serious?"

"Mom I am so serious!"

"Did you laugh at her Mia?"

"No mom. I was to scared too. So I quickly looked away acting like I didn't see that bullshit she was doing, and walked into the kitchen. That had to be some lonely psycho type shit, I said to myself, Mom."

"For real girl it is. I've had my moments before," I said laughing.

"Mom! I'm being serious!"

"Well baby I am too."

"What? Mom, come on.

"No, for real Mia." I said. "Maybe you shouldn't go back over there."

"Yes mom. I know. But hold on, as I entered the kitchen, Gabby told me to wait in there for her while she take her mother that stuff she asked for. So I waited. While waiting I can hear Gabby saying, 'Here you go mother, your two long stem glasses, one for you and your man, and your finest red wine right here.'

'Thank you baby. Oh, Gabby. Can you please open the red wine and pour it for me and Charles. We both would appreciate it.' 'Oh sure I can. Here you go mother and here's yours Charles. Now you two have fun! If you need anything else just holla.' 'We will baby.' Ms. Gigi said. I could not believe what I just heard! I stood in the kitchen in disbelief waiting on Gabby to come back in the kitchen to asked her what, when, and why.

"Okay," I said. "That's right baby get some answers before you be thinking you need a straight jacket yourself!"

"Yes, Mom I know." Mia said. "So Gabby finally walked back into the kitchen. I quickly grabbed her by her right arm, and before I could ask her what in the hell is going on over here, she quickly said come on, let's go to the den so we can get started on our project. 'What? No,' I said. 'What is going on Gabby?' 'Well Ah,' Gabby said. 'Come on Gabby, tell me, I'm all ears.' 'Well, um, Let's go to the den.' Gabby said.

As we started to walk out the kitchen down the hallway, Gabby led the way to the den. While walking down the hallway you could hear Ms. Gigi laughing loud and singing out of tune. Then she started screaming saying, 'me and Charles!! Charles and me and our babies!!.' I watched Gabby as she covered her ears with her hands as we walked down the hallway. I then looked back at Ms. Gigi and watched her make a toast with her glass to the air as if someone else was there toasting. 'To me and you Charles,' Ms Gigi said. Then she began drinking then crying and yelling, 'Charles, no come back!'

'Wow!' I said to myself as I turned back around. Gabby still had her hands covering her ears until we entered the den. Crash! Crash! 'What was that?' Mia said. Looking from the den quickly. Mom! It was Ms. Gigi throwing those two glasses and the rest of the red wine into the fireplace. 'What the hell!' I said. 'Come on Mia,' Gabby said as she finally uncovered her ears. 'Okay, Mia Let's get started on this project.'

'What, are you serious?' I said. 'What?' Gabby said, 'don't worry, I'll clean the wine and glass up later in the fireplace. My mother does this every day now. It's no big deal.' 'What? Gabby are you for real' 'Yes! I am,' Gabby said, 'come on, let's start this project.' 'No! No! No!,' I said, I need to know what is going on over here right now or I'm going to leave and we both will get an F on this project, and you will explain why to our science teacher Mr. Brown.' 'Okay, okay, Mia. I'll tell you what happened to my mother, but you can't tell anyone, okay? Promise me Mia.' Gabby said. 'Okay, I promise.' Mia said, with her fingers crossed behind her back.'

'Okay, Mia, do you remember when I showed you the candles in mother's bedroom burning on her altar?' 'Yeah' you said the light colored candles that she felt was a need,' I said. 'Yes, those candles,' Gabby said. 'Well mother worked with this guy on her job, his name was Charles Hudson Jr. She wanted Charles so bad she could taste him. Um! You know like chocolate! Melt in your mouth not in your hand type shit!' Gabby said. 'She didn't care if he had kids or if he was married. She just felt like this man was a need. So she started her voodoo on him. She began using the light colored candles first. In two days of the candles burning on Charles, he began to notice her and talk to her. That wasn't enough, Mother wanted more, so she began to wear this voodoo oil called "come to me," and he came. He didn't know why he came, but he wanted to be in her presence at all times. He was there and loving it. So things got real serious, he never went home. It was like he moved in with us. He was at our house every day and every night. My mother just knew she had him. Until one day he left for two weeks, he wasn't suppose to go anywhere. So she did more voodoo on him. She went hard on his ass this time. She started to burn a big red candle shaped like a dick to bring him back to her; for him to want sex with her only and with a need of a baby from him.

'What the hell, Mia!" I said.

"Yeah, Mom, Isn't that crazy,"

"Hell Yeah, that is real crazy," Mia said. "Oh, but wait, she also burned a big black candle shaped like a dick too. That candle was to make him where so he won't get aroused for anyone else but her, or have any desire for no one but her."

"OMG! Mia, wait, wait," I said, "Mia, when I went to that psychic readers shop, I seen those candles."

"What Mom?"

"Yes, I did. So did those candles work on him? I asked.

"Yes, Yes, they did. She did that voodoo on him with those candles. Charles came back to her and guess what?"

"What?"

"He got Ms. Gigi pregnant!"

"Pregnant? I said.

"Yes!" Mia said, "With twins!"

"What, get the fuck outta here!" I said.

"But he left her again Mom."

"What, Mia?"

"This time for a month. Ms. Gigi couldn't figure out why he left again. She told Gabby 'fuck this shit, I need to do a major love spell on his mutha fuckin ass! The kind where he moves in and don't go nowhere, just stay home and take care of me and our twins I'm having.'

"So what did Ms. Gigi do?" I asked.

"Gabby told me, 'girl she did a double whammy on his ass!'

"The double whammy? What the fuck is that?" I asked.

"Shit, Gabby said it was something where Ms. Gigi had to go under her bed and pull out a big old black trunk with a lock on it, and a whole lot of dust. Gabby said, 'Mother made me blow some of the dust off the trunk, whhh', while she went to go get the key. 'I got the key Gabby! I got the key!' Ms. Gigi yelled! 'That's right mother,' Gabby said as she watched Ms. Gigi get on her knees to unlock and open the big black trunk. Gabby said she got chills when her mother opened that trunk. 'Okay, now baby mother is gonna have to ask you to leave the room.' 'Why? Mother,' Gabby asked. 'Baby girl, this is some powerful shit I got to do to Charles Hudson Jr.' 'Okay. I'm leaving.' Gabby said. As Gabby begin to leave her mother's bedroom, she glanced into the trunk and seen a human skull, a open bag of graveyard dirt and some, um. 'Girl! get out of here now!' Ms. Gigi yelled, this mutha fucka, Charles Hudson Jr., is a got damn need!' She shouted!

Gabby said, 'Mia girl, she slammed her bedroom door behind me and I ran to my bedroom.' 'You did Gabby? I said. 'Yes I did. When I was in my bedroom. I could hear mother yelling words I didn't understand, dropping things, chanting, stomping on the floor for a whole hour. Then it got quiet. I heard her bedroom door open. Wham! Ms. Gigi swung it open so hard it hit the wall and knocked a picture from the wall to the floor in her bedroom. I could hear her coming down the hallway yelling, 'this mutha fucka, Charles Hudson Jr., is a got damn need! And he shall come back to me and stay this time.' Gabby,' 'Yes Mother, I'm gonna a step out for about 30 minutes. I will be back, come lock the front door.'

When I came out of my bedroom to lock the front door, Gabby said her mother walked up to her, gave her a kiss on her forehead. While holding two big black plastic bags in both of her hands. Sweating uncontrollably as she begin to walk to the front door.

Gabby asked herself, 'why is mother wearing all black? With a black hood over her head and a big wooden cross around her neck with a small red string tied in several knots tightly around her left wrist as if it was a bracelet.' Gabby yelled to her mother, 'Mother! Where are you going?' 'Don't worry about that. I'll be back. Baby you are too young to understand!' 'Well can I at least know what the red string is tied around your left wrist for?' 'Sure, baby,' Ms. Gigi said. 'This is protection, baby, to protect yo soul from all hurt, harm and danger in this life! Once you get of age I will tell you everything you need to know, and what you need to do. On how to protect yo soul. Understand?" 'Yes Mother', Gabby said. 'I will be back.'

"So where did Ms. Gigi go?" I asked Mia.

"I don't know, but Gabby said, wherever Ms. Gigi went, Mr. Charles Hudson Jr. was ringing her doorbell the next day!"

"What Mia, He came back?"

"Yes he did, Mia said, but Gabby told me he left again after receiving a emergency call on his cellphone. He said he would be back tomorrow evening. Ms. Gigi was fine with that. 'Is everything okay?' Ms. Gigi asked Charles. 'Oh, yeah.' Charles said. 'Okay. Call me Ms. Gigi said.' 'I will,' he responded. So he left.

"She really didn't have a problem with him at all leaving this time cause she knew the love spell she put on him was incomplete. She needed to get some of her bodily fluids inside of Mr. Charles Hudson Jr.'s system! Now being that Ms. Gigi knows her shit when it comes to voodoo, She said, 'tomorrow evening I will make a dinner date for me and Charles. All it will take is a tall glass of ice cold lemonade, with some of my fresh morning urine poured into the glass of lemonade and lot's of ice for Mr. Charles Hudson Jr. to drink. Ha! Ha! Tasty, and to keep his spirit locked to me where he don't hear no one, see no one, and speak to no one but me,' Ms. Gigi yelled, 'a bloody sanitary napkin from her heaviest day of her menstrual cycle squeezed into her famous spicy, tangy red meat sauce for her delicious spaghetti, such a delight don't you think? Once I squeeze my bloody sanitary napkin into the red sauce of my spaghetti and stir and stir and stir,' Ms. Gigi said with a wicked laugh, Ha! Ha! And serve it up to Mr. Charles Hudson Jr. Pow! Signed sealed delivered, I'm yours! Is what he will say to me,' Ms. Gigi shouted while laughing loudly.'

"Damn, Mia, she is crazy!"

"Yes Mom, I know. So Gabby said the next day Ms. Gigi called Mr. Charles Hudson Jr. over for dinner. Before dinner she will prepare that ice cold lemonade with the urine in it for Mr. Charles Hudson Jr. to drink, and the meat sauce and spaghetti noodles will be on the stove cooking."

"As a couple of hours went by, Ms. Gigi went into the bathroom to place a sanitary napkin in her underwear. She came out the bathroom ready for the blood to drip, drop, drip out of her. She couldn't wait to start cooking that spaghetti. Ring! Ring! The phone rang. 'I got it Gabby,' Ms. Gigi said. 'Okay mother.' 'Hello, oh hey Charles. Oh. Okay, bye bye.' Now Mr. Charles Hudson Jr. called Ms. Gigi to let her know he was still coming, but he would be running a little late for dinner she said to Gabby and begin to scream. 'Is everything alright Mother?' Gabby asked. 'Hell yeah! Baby girl, tonight the deal will be sealed with me and my man Mr. Charles Hudson Jr., and I will let him know I am pregnant with his twins and this love spell will be complete!'

"Oh, but wait," Gabby told me, "there was a problem Mia,' Gabby said, there is no way possible that love spell can be complete."

"Why? I asked."

"Wait, I'mma tell you Mom, right now."

"So Gabby said she watched as her mother went back and forth into the bathroom sweating while checking her sanitary napkin for blood. Ms. Gigi went into the bathroom at least four or five times. She begin cussing, and screaming, then hitting the bathroom door. 'What the fuck!' She said crying and yelling, this love spell will not be complete, fuck! There is no blood coming out of me!' Gabby told her mother, please calm down. 'But Gabby why won't I bleed? I need this man in my life,' Ms. Gigi said. 'Okay Mother, I understand that, but you are pregnant, you will not see any blood on that sanitary napkin no time soon.' 'Oh god! baby you're right.'

"Ding! Dong! Ding! Dong! Ding! Dong! 'Oh, no, he's here.' 'Don't worry Mother,' Gabby said, "just let me get the drink, and you tell him you're pregnant with his twins.' 'Gabby I can't! I can't!' Ms. Gigi said, if I don't complete this love spell, I will have bad luck!' 'No you won't Mother, just go answer the door and let him in. I'll go in the kitchen and get everything ready for you.' 'No! No! Gabby!' 'Go mother, trust me, I got this.'

"So what happened Mia?"

"Well, Ms. Gigi went to answer the door and she let Charles in."

'Hey Baby.' Charles said. 'How you doing? You look nice tonight.' 'Oh, um thank you Charles. Come in and have a seat. Dinner will be ready soon,' Ms. Gigi said.

"So they both sat down at the table. 'Gabby, can you bring our plates out please?' 'Oh, yes, Mother,' Gabby yelled from the kitchen. 'Hey Gabby.' 'Hey Mr. Hudson.' 'Can you bring me something to drink, Gabby, I'm thirsty?' 'Oh, sure I can Mr. Hudson, it would be my pleasure,' she whispered.

"Gabby stood in the kitchen laughing quietly as she grabbed the glass of lemonade for Mr. Charles Hudson Jr. with Ms. Gigi's early morning urine in it from the kitchen counter. She stuck her hand in the freezer grabbing a hand full of ice to put in Mr. Hudson's lemonade, then closed the freezer. She grabbed a spoon from the kitchen drawer and began to stir the lemonade before she brought it out to him. 'Here you go Mr. Hudson.' 'Thank you Gabby.' 'Oh, your welcome.' Gabby said as she stood back to watch Mr. Hudson drink the lemonade before getting their dinner plates out for the both of them from the kitchen.

"'Charles I have something to tell you," Ms. Gigi said. 'What is it Geneva?' Mr. Hudson said as he begin to drink the lemonade. 'Well... a... I'm a…' 'Wait, wait,' he said, 'let me drink this lemonade down first. Woo, this is delicious, nice and tangy. Was this made with freshly squeezed lemons?' 'Ahh, yes,' Gabby said as she quietly laughed to herself while she and her mother looked at each other. 'Let me go get the dinner plates for you and mother,' Gabby said. 'Oh, okay thanks, Gabby,' Charles said. 'So Geneva, what is it that you want to tell me?' Charles asked. 'I'm pregnant!' Ms. Gigi yelled, 'Charles, with twins!' 'Your what Bitch! I mean a your what?' 'You heard me,' Ms. Gigi said thinking in her mind, Oh shit, here it comes, the bad luck because this love spell was not complete, got damn! That drink he just drank is going to make him so fucking confused and angry. I don't have my blood to put in the spaghetti to regulate his feelings and emotions, or to calm his spirit down.' 'Oh no! Geneva, I gotta go, I got to get the hell out of here! I'm ah, ah, ah, going to talk to you later Geneva.'

"Gabby then came out the kitchen with the dinner plates in her hands. She watched Mr. Hudson as he was trying to get up from the table with fear all in his eyes. He knocked the chair over and headed for the front door. 'Charles wait! Don't do this to me!' Ms. Gigi screamed. 'No, Geneva! I can't! I have too much on my plate already! I got to go!' 'Charles No! Wait! Come back!' Ms. Gigi screamed again throwing herself to the floor crying. As Mr. Hudson walked out her front door. He didn't look back. And he never called.

"It's been 6 weeks now and Ms. Gigi hasn't heard a word from Mr. Charles Hudson Jr. She would sit in the house in silence thinking to herself, 'I should have did the love spell first on Charles and then burn the dick shaped candles on him to seal the deal! I did it backwards fuck! What is wrong with me? I know my shit.' Ms. Gigi shouted.

"Now Mom, listen to this shit Gabby told me. She said she came home from school and sat down at the dining room table to do her homework. It was just her and her mother. 'Mother are you okay?' 'No. Not really baby. Not really.' Ms Gigi said. 'Well I'm here Mother.' 'I know, thank you baby.'

"Ding! Dong! Ding! Dong! Knock! Knock! Knock! Knock! Ding! Dong! Ding! Dong!' 'Who is it?' Gabby said. 'Baby girl, it got to be Charles,' he's come back, he's come back to me!' Ms. Gigi said. She got up from her chair to answer the front door. She quickly opened the door, and Guess what, Mom?"

"What Mia?"

"Gabby said it sure wasn't Mr. Hudson,"

"Who was it?"

Mia said, "wait, wait, wait, mom, Gabby said to me, 'you'll see Mia, just listen.' So Gabby said she got up from the dining room table and walked to the front door and stood behind her mother as she stood at the front door. It was this woman standing at the door. 'Yes. How may I help you?' Ms. Gigi said. 'Um! I'm looking for a Ms. Geneva O'Neal.' The lady said. 'I'm Geneva O'Neal.' 'So your Geneva O'Neal, huh?' the lady said laughing with a smirk on her face and looking at my mother from head to toe. 'Mia, I ain't gonna lie, my mother is pretty,' Gabby said to me. 'Yeah, I know,' I said. 'But this lady was a bad bitch beautiful and dressed to kill, while smelling like two dozen of fresh cut roses when the wind blew in her fragrance as she stood at our front door.' Gabby said. 'This light skinned, platinum blonde, long hair, hazel eye, middle age bitch, was well intact, and showed no fear when she told my mother she was Mr. Charles Hudson Jr.'s wife.' 'What!' Mia said to Gabby, 'his wife?' 'Yes girl, His wife, and she never gave her first name. She just started pointing her finger in my mother's face. With a big ass five or six carrot diamond wedding ring that was shining so bright in me and mother's face.' 'What?' I said. 'Oh, and the lady had a red braided string tied around her left wrist like mother. But she also wore a yellow single string tied around her left wrist as well.' Gabby said. 'Okay, this woman does voodoo too!" Gabby said to herself. "Now that would explain why Mr. Charles Hudson kept leaving.'

Gabby said, the wife begin to get louder as she began to talk more shit to my mother. 'So he been fucking with your tired looking ass!' His wife said. 'What Bitch!' Ms. Gigi said. 'You heard me Geneva O'Neal!' 'Ah! Ah! yeah bitch, I heard you,' Ms. Gigi yelled. 'My ass is tired alright from being pregnant with your husband's twins!'

"With that said, 'shit got quiet,' Gabby said. 'That wife looked at my mother in her eyes showing no fear and no regrets.'

"Your what!" Mrs. Hudson yelled. "You will not have Mr. Charles Hudson Jr.'s babies bitch!!"

"Whatever!" Ms. Gigi said. "You fucking bitch! Get the fuck off my property now!"

"Oh. no problem," Mrs. Hudson said calmly, "but before I go, let me tell you something. You are not the first one, but I will guarantee, you will be the last!"

"Geneva O'Neal, are you making threats?" Ms. Gigi said.

"No honey, that is a promise." Mrs. Hudson whispered to Ms. Gigi. "You will never see or hear from my husband ever again!" She said.

"Whatever bitch! Bye! Bye!" Ms. Gigi said as she slammed the door in Mrs. Hudson's face Blam!

Gabby decided to walk over to the living room window and watch Mrs. Hudson as she thought she was about to walked down the steps... but she didn't. Instead, she stood at the front door and reached into her pantsuit pocket with her right hand and threw something out in front of their door!

Gabby said, "What?"

"What was it, Gabby?" Mia asked.

"Shit! I don't know. It looked like some kind of salt substance, but it was black!" Gabby said. She then walked away from the living room window after Mrs. Hudson started to walk down their steps not thinking to let her mother know that Mrs. Hudson threw something in front of their door.

"Can you believe that bitch!" Ms. Gigi said.

"No, Mother. Can you believe that Mr. Charles Hudson Jr. was married!" Gabby said.

"Oh Baby that shit didn't matter to me. Sometimes that happens." Ms. Gigi said.

"Mother, I think it could be a possibility that his wife might do voodoo too."

"What? Why you say that?" Ms. Gigi said.

"Because when she was pointing her finger in your face mother, she had a red string around her left wrist along with a yellow string.

"She what?" Ms. Gigi yelled, "goddammit! I didn't even see it! I was so mad! Come to think about it, why did Charles keep leaving? It wasn't just because of the love spell being incomplete. He was leaving before that love spell."

"You know your voodoo that you do mother!"

"Your right baby girl." Ms. Gigi said.

"So what happened after that," I asked.

"Well, anyway. Three weeks after that wife came over, Ms. Gigi got up one morning to get her newspaper from her front porch. As soon as she opened her front door, there was a big cow tongue rolled up real tight in a rope on her doormat in front of her door with a brown piece of paper with something written on it in blood!! Ms. Gigi bent down to pull the paper out of the tied cow tongue, she yanked the paper out and read what it said with blood dripping everywhere."

"What did it say Mia?" I asked.

Gabby said it read: "GENEEVA O'NEAL DEATH BE PUT UPON YOU," is what it said.

"Bullshit!! Mia," I said.

"So what happened?" I asked.

"Well. Gabby said, Ms. Gigi didn't think not to touch it until it was too late.

"Oh! Fuck. I touched it!" Ms. Gigi screamed. As she scrambled to get back inside her house with the blood all over her hands, she panicked. She reached for the door knob and slipped, bumped her head on the steps and fell into the rose bushes and laid there unconscious.

"When Ms. Gigi finally woke up, she was in the hospital." Gabby said. "She was delirious and she had broken her leg. And guess what?"

"I know Mia. Don't tell me," I said.

"Yes, Mom"

"She lost the twins!" Me and Mia yelled together!

"So when the doctor came in and told Ms. Gigi that she lost her babies, she was in disbelief crying and screaming: 'No! No! No! Not my babies!' She screamed! While hitting the doctor's chest. Saying he was lying to her! She could still feel movement in her stomach. Gabby tell him! She yelled. Please tell the doctor! Gabby! Baby! Please!' Ms. Gigi yelled. 'I can't mother. It's true! What Dr. Gold is telling you.' 'No! No!' Ms. Gigi screamed! At that time the nurse was called in to give mother a sedative. So she could get some rest. She slept until the next day. I stayed there with her Gabby said.

"The next day, she woke up in better spirits as she asked me to pray with her, and I did" Gabby said.

"Amen. Thank You baby, I love you so much, you're the best daughter in the world."

"I love you too mother."

"As soon as Gabby said that, two of her mother's co-workers walked in holding flowers and balloons and a card signed from everyone. Except Charles. 'Wow, thank you guys.' Your Welcome Ms. Gigi. Her co-worker Irene said. Ms. Gigi I'll put the vase with the flowers right here by the window and set the get well card on the table for you. Her other coworker Helen said. 'Thank you ladies,' Ms Gigi said.

"Gabby took the card from the table and she begin to read the get well card for her mother. She asked Irene and Helen why Charles Hudson Jr. didn't sign the card? 'Well. Girl! You didn't hear what happened to him'. 'No. What do you mean? What happen to him?' Ms. Gigi said. 'He died!' Irene said. 'He What?' Ms. Gigi yelled as she started shaking and reaching for Gabby's hand. 'Are you sure' Gabby said as she grabbed her mother's hand and held it tightly. 'Yeah,' Helen said. He died 5 days ago. In a bad car accident.

'What' Gabby said. 'Yes Mia! Irene told us that before that happen. Charles came to work and asked if he could take two weeks off. He told the supervisor he needed some time off for a um. Ah. Ah. Hey man! Are you alright Mr. Hudson? Yeah. I just got a bad headache. Charles said to the supervisor. Charles never gave a reason why he needed the two weeks off. And every time Charles would talk he wasn't making any sense the supervisor said. 'Which supervisor did Charles talk too?' Ms. Gigi asked with tears in her eyes. Was it Steve? 'Yes.' Irene said. 'Steve Phillips. You know Mr. P.' Irene said. 'Yes,' Ms. Gigi said. So Mr. P. said Charles was saying he felt bugs crawling all over him and he keep seeing black dots in front of his eyes, and he said Charles was sweating so bad to where he had to give him a towel out the lounge and a glass of water that Charles ended up dropping on the floor. 'I'm so sorry Mr. P'. 'Don't worry' he said, 'I'll clean it up. You just go home and get yourself some rest'. 'Okay. Sir I'll do that' Charles said. As Charles walked away Mr. P said to one of his other employees, 'I hope Mr. Hudson isn't using drugs.' Mia! Me and mother looked at each other.

"Irene continued telling us about what happen to Charles, 'Hey wait!' Mr. P yelled, 'Here's your time off paper for the two weeks you asked for'. Charles grabbed the paper and started twitching and was still, sweating, scratching and talking to his self while walking away. See you after two weeks. Mr. P said. Take care of yourself Mr. Charles Hudson Jr. Yeah! Yeah! I will Mr. Charles Hudson Jr. said.

"After the two weeks was up no one had seen or heard from Mr. Charles Hudson Jr. He never came back to work. Irene said. So two days ago. A detective came up to the job asking questions about Charles he informed us that Mr. Charles Hudson Jr. had died in a violent car crash and there were no drugs or alcohol found in his blood. When tested, His car was taken for investigation. During the investigation they found a black bag with some kind of nude male doll inside of the black bag under the driver seat of Mr. Charles Hudson's car. The doll had pins stuck in the head! The hands, arms, legs, feet, ass and penis! Girl! And it had black duck tape covering the eyes and the mouth of the doll. Irene said. The detective said what was really so weird was that, the doll they recovered from under the drivers seat in that black bag, the head had been twisted around to it's back! And when Mr. Charles Hudson Jr.'s body was removed from the driver seat of his car his head was twisted around to his back too, just like the doll!

"What!" Mia screamed, "Gabby now you're scarring me" Mia said. "I've heard enough! Gabby."

"Wait, Wait, Mia listen. After Irene and Helen told us that, my mom told them she was tired and needed to get some rest. So they both said 'okay'. Hope to see you soon Irene said. Yeah. Everyone misses you at work Helen said. I miss everyone too. I'll see you girls later. Ms. Gigi said. Okay. Bye. Ms. Gigi. Bye. So they both left.

Gabby quickly got up and closed Ms. Gigi hospital room door. Omg! Mother I thought they'd never leave! Yeah. Baby. I know. Ms. Gigi said with tears in her eyes. Aw. Mother don't cry. But she killed him and my babies! Ms. Gigi yelled. I know mother. I know. Gabby said. As she started to cry too. And hugged her mother tightly. I'm here for you mother. I'm here. Gabby said. As Ms. Gigi continued to cry.

"So that's what happened to Ms. Gigi, and this is why I say be careful what you wish for."

"Oh Mia, I'll be fine," I said. "Plus, I'm not trying to take anyone's husband, I'm just trying to get rich. So I'm going to bed, I have a big day ahead of me. Goodnight, see you guys in the morning."

"Goodnight to both of you crazy ladies," Marcus said laughing loudly.

"No, you're crazy, boy," Mia said to Marcus.

"You crazy," Marcus said "with your hoodoo voodoo story,"

"Marcus, go to bed," I said.

"Okay mom. See you in the morning mom." Mia said.

The next day. Good Morning today is the big day. Let me get up get dressed and get the coconut and put it in a bag. With the rest of the stuff I have to take with me. Okay I'm ready to go. I'll stop and get a small copy of my ID picture first. Then be on my way to the psychic reader's shop. "Mia! Marcus! I'm leaving have a good day at school today! Don't be late and make sure to lock the front door when you guys leave."

"Okay. Mom. Hey mom I change my mind about becoming rich at least not with voodoo. I'm to scared! I don't want to get rich that bad." Mia said "It's always a price you have to pay. Dealing with the spirit world." Mia said.

"Oh girl. See you later! I am going to get the ritual done today with this coconut! Shit! I'm not scared to get rich!" I said. "And I'm sure not scared of no spirit! That I paid 500.00 too. Whatever it takes to get me rich. I'm going to do it! Now Bye! Bye!"

"Bye mom." Mia said. "Hey mom!"

"What Marcus? Don't forget to bring us back a evil spirit! Ha. Ha. Ha."

"Boy very funny."

So I grabbed my bag along with my key's and my handbag and left. As I started up the car to leave I couldn't stop thinking about what was going to change my life forever the coco. Okay. I'm here let me park right in front of the psychic reader's shop. Oh good I see her she's there. She just open the door and put her sign out. Let me grab my stuff! Okay. Now Latrice before you go in. Take a deep breath then let it out and say. Oh God I'm asking you to forgive me for what I'm about to do. I pray. I'm not making a wicked wish. I just want this to come true so bad! Oh! Yes! Champagne wishes and caviar dreams right around the corner for me! Okay let's go Latrice is what I said to myself.

I walked to the front door. "Hello! Hello! Good morning."

"Latrice Baldwin". "Come in."

"Good morning Kwana." I said as I walked in. I looked down on the floor and there was the coco. On that bright red tray. But wait! What is this I see a new straw hat. New toy car. Wow! A convertible sports car. Really. Damn, more candy, and look at this a whole cigar not smoked. Next to a red velvet cupcake. So you bossed up! "Big head." I whispered to the coco so Kwana couldn't hear me.

"Come have a seat Latrice Baldwin." Kwana said. Okay. Coming I said. I walked over to the table. And we both sat down at the table. "Do you have everything for the ritual?" Kwana asked.

"Yes I do. Oh! Wait! I said. "Let me go get my picture out of my glove compartment in my car." I stepped outside to the car and got the picture.

When I walked back inside, it felt like I was being watched. I swear! That coco gives me the creeps. But I can't show any fear. So I walked back over to the coco and gave it the middle finger. That was for you coco, trying to make me feel uncomfortable when I came back in here.

"You ugly mutha fucka! I whispered. You better give me what I got coming! Money! Money! Big Money! Make me rich! Ugly."

"Latrice! Come now! We must get started."

"Okay, coming Kwana."

"I'll see you later blacky," I said as I walked away.

Blam! A voodoo masked fell from the wall, scaring the hell out of me.

"Latrice, come have a seat, I need you to take everything out of the bag and set them on the table."

"Okay," I said.

"Oh, wait it seems like the coco is a little upset. I don't know why. I will deal with that issue later"

"What? I said to myself. "Here's the coconut with the top cut. 5 shot bottles of Bacardi assorted gumdrops."

"Yes," She said. "The cocos favorite."

"And here is my picture and the $500 cash."

"Very good! Okay. Now here's the parchment paper Latrice. Write your full name and birthday on it then turn the paper over write down that wish you made days ago." She said

"Oh. Okay."

As I begin to write my name, she took the top off the coconut. Then she opened the bag of assorted gumdrops. I had stop writing and began to watch her stick her nasty looking hand into the bag of gum drops pulling out a handful. She was dropping the gum drops all over the floor, picking them up popping them in her mouth. As she grabbed the topless coconut she dropped some of the gum drops inside of the coconut. As she still stuffed the last of the gum drops into her mouth. "Um! Um! Um! These are so delicious." She said.

"Now, What kind of shit is this." I said to myself. As I continued to watched her.

She then set the coconut on the table and grabbed all five shot bottles of Bacardi with one hand and started rubbing the bottles of Bacardi all over her body!

"What the?" I started laughing.

"Shh, Quiet" She said. I then held in my laugh.

"Here's the paper" I said. "I'm done."

"Just set it on the table, and be quiet" She said.

I set the paper on the table and sat quietly still just watching her. She begin to wipe the saliva from her mouth with her left hand as she still held on to those shot bottles of Bacardi in her right hand. Then she immediately opened one of the shot bottles with her left hand wet with saliva, wetting the bottle as she quickly poured the Bacardi into the coconut. Then she opened the second bottle poured that one straight into the coconut real fast with it splashing all over me and her. I wiped my face off on my shirt. Now she opened The third bottle. And poured it all in the coconut not getting a drop on neither one of us that time. Okay. There goes the fourth shot bottle she opened it real slow. Putting her nose up to the rim of the bottle smelling the drink. Hmm! She said. Then looked at me and began to sip a little of the Bacardi. Then she screamed. Oh! Oh! Oh! Scarring the shit out of me! I literally felt I needed to check my pants! This is some crazy ass shit!! I mumbled while holding my right hand over my heart as it pounded fast onto my finger tips. After she screamed she picked up the coconut and held it in her left hand and continued to pour the rest of shot bottle number four into the coconut. I asked her was she okay.

"Quiet!! She said. "I'm fine! Let me finish!"

"Okay. Okay. Forgive me for asking," I said. With a puzzled look on my face. So she grabbed the last shot bottle of Bacardi opened it and just drunk it!!! She swallowed the whole bottle in one shot. Then grabbed the coconut with both hands placed the top on it stood up from the table and faced me. And began starring at me, with not one blink and not moving a muscle! Just looking straight possessed!! With the coconut top slightly open as she held it. Damn! Am I seeing things! I said to myself or is that something peeking at me from the inside of the coconut? Shit! Now I'm scared! What should I do? Get up and run out of here! Or just pick up one of these statues in here and hit her creepy ass in the head with it! What to do Latrice! What to do! Oh. God! There's nothing to do.

She said, "Huh."

"What?" I mumbled.

"Let me finish this ritual! She yelled."

"Okay" I said. "Shit! I forgot. She read minds also," I mumbled to myself.

Kwana finally sat down rolling her neck around. Then she began looking up at the ceiling. Then she slowly moved her head down to look at me. Now give me your picture. Here you go. She took my picture and spit on the face and stuck it upside down in the coconut.

"Now. Give me the parchment paper with your information on it and your wish!" She said. I passed her the parchment paper she snatched it from my hand.

"Damn!" I said. As she began to ball up the parchment paper and threw it in the coconut.

"Now give me both of your hands! Place them over the hole of this coconut." She said while removing the top of the coconut off. "Close your eyes and concentrate on your wish. Believe it and it shall be." After she said that she placed her hands on top of mine. Then she began talking. In another language!

While listening to her talk. It gave me chills. And the feeling of her hands on my hands felt like her flesh was releasing graveyard bugs on to my flesh. It felt so nasty, it was so hard to concentrate. I swear!

"Okay. Enough!" She said. "Open your eyes." I was to scared to open my eyes. But I finally did. She got up and grabbed something from her shelf. What did she get? I said to myself. I see a long thin white candle in her hand and a box of matches and the biggest cigar I ever seen in my life! What's next I asked.

"Do you smoke?" Kwana asked.

"No."

"Well you do today."

"What?' I said.

"Yes. You must inhale and blow smoke into the coconut five times." She said.

"But Kwana, I don't know about this!"

"What do you mean," she yelled. "You want to become rich, Right?"

"Well um, yes." I said.

"Then open your mouth wide, and put this cigar in your mouth, close your lips tightly on the cigar, and I will light it,". She said. "Um. Um. Don't waste my time Latrice Baldwin! We are just about done with the ritual. So What are you going to do? SMOKE?" \

"Yes! I'll smoke!"

"That is what I like to hear."

"Okay, let's smoke!" Kwana said. "I will hold the coconut with one hand for you and light the cigar with my other hand."

"Okay." I said. So I picked up that big ass cigar and placed it in between my lips. And she lit it quickly.

"Now inhale and blow into the coconut! Now!" She said.

As I began to inhale the smoke from this fat ass cigar, I couldn't stop fucking Coughing! Cough! Cough! Cough! And I damn sure can't concentrate.

"Stop coughing! Kwana yelled. "You must smoke, and concentrate!"

"I can't! Stop fuckin coughing! Cough! Cough! "And I can't concentrate with you yelling at me! Okay."

"Well. I guess you don't want to become rich," She said.

"Yes I do!"

"Then inhale dammit! And blow the fucking smoke in the coconut right now!"

"Look lady you ain't gonna keep yelling at me, I got this!" I said. Okay, Latrice concentrate is what I told myself. Inhale, exhale into the coconut. Alright I can do this. Just stay calm.

"You ready to try again." She said.

"I'm ready." So I grabbed that big ass cigar. Now blaze it up! Kwana! Ha! Ha! Ha!"

"Okay! Latrice." She laughed. "Smoke it! Smoke it! Ah! Ha Ha Ha!" Kwana kept laughing.

I quickly inhaled the big cigar without a single cough! Huh! And blew the smoke into the coconut. Did it once. Did it twice. Then three times. Woo! Now here I go! Blowing and blowing in that coconut like crazy thinking about that wish. Of becoming rich, wanting it so bad keep blowing Latrice! I said, I'm blowing! After the third inhale. Shit!

I started feeling real dizzy and very light headed.

"I can't inhale the smoke anymore!" I yelled.

"You must smoke in order to finish the ritual!" She yelled. "Your almost done!" Come on Latrice Baldwin! Do it! Just two more inhales!" She shouted.

"Okay! Okay," I said. As I coughed. I put the cigar between my lips again and closed my eyes. And held my stomach with my right hand. And started inhaling the smoke and blowing straight into the coconut for the forth time. I can feel the smoke burning my eyes as I kept them closed tightly. And my throat was on fire!

"Okay, last one Latrice Baldwin" Kwana said. Now inhale real deep and hold it! Concentrate on that wish you made. Concentrate! Concentrate!" Is all I kept hearing. While being so damn delirious. The word concentrate begin to sound like it was slowing down in my mind, like Satan was saying 'concentrate!' real slow and laughing at me at the same time. Ah! Ha! Ha!

"Now blow that shit into the coconut now!" Is all I heard. Okay Latrice, you got this is what I said to myself as I started to inhale deeply. I'm holding it and concentrating without one single cough!

"Now blow!" she shouted. I then opened my mouth and started blow, blow, blowing into that fucking coconut!

"Yes! I'm done" I said as I start coughing. Cough! Cough!

"Excellent! Excellent" She said as she clapped her hands and laughed loudly. Ha! Ha! Ha! "Now it is my turn to smoke to seal the deal with the coco! Once sealed! It can not be taken back, reversed or undone! This is for life no matter what the outcome shall be! Understand! She said.

"Oh yes. Sure." I said as I coughed.

"This is real! Latrice Baldwin." She said.

"Okay! Okay."

"Now I am just about finished with the ritual." She picked up the big cigar from the floor remembering it was still lit. She quickly put it in her mouth and inhaled it and blew the smoke all over the coconut and inside of the coconut for the last time. Man she blew that last smoke out like a American Indian smoking in a sweat lodge! Not one cough! Blowing from a peace pipe slow and serious! How! Then she took the cigar out of her mouth and put the tip of it out by squeezing it with her finger tips. And also squeezing it with her hand.

As she uttered, Um! Um! Oh! I love that heat from the cigar it is so soothing"

"Oh. Hell no!" I whispered. Now I know why her hands are so gray and her nails are so black! Okay. She said I must seal the coconut. She grabbed the long white candle from the table. She gently placed the coconut on the table. She grabbed the lighter and the top to the coconut. She lit the candle and began to hold it downward as the hot candle wax started rapidly dripping. On the table, the floor and on her fingers I just sat quietly watching her. She placed the top to the coconut back on the cocnut. And began moving the candle over the top of the coconut letting the hot wax drip into the coconut's open cracks sealing them closed. She moved her hand slowly and whispered the words to the ritual, over and over until the hot wax had completely filled and sealed the coconut's openings.

She then raised the coconut up towards the ceiling with both hands, and said, "It shall be coco! It shall be!"

Then she brought the coconut down slowly to her mouth, then kissed it. Muah! Leaving saliva all over one side of the coconut. Yuck!

"The ritual is complete!" She yelled as spit flew in my eye when she said that. So I wiped my eye. As she set the coconut down on the table. Let the wax settle and dry.

She said, "while we wait, Latrice Baldwin, I must let you know a couple of important things about the coco: #1 The coco isn't fond of babies, kids or teenagers! Never put the coco in the same room with children and never speak of children in the coco's presences. If you do. The coco will get very angry and very jealous! Angry and jealous?

I said, "wow!"

"Just don't do it!" She yelled.

"Okay. I heard you". I said.

"This is very serious Latrice! Now #2, never treat the coco like a child. Don't ever scold or verbally abuse or physically destroy the coco. Or you will be sorry! Understand!"

"Yes." I said. Oh! My God. She is really serious about this ugly rock! I mumbled.

"The coco is a very smart spirit." She said. "Not handsome, but fun loving, and also known in the spirit world as one of the most powerful! And hardest working spirit's in the spirit world for the living. The coco is capable of getting you anything your little heart desire's in this human life. Now #3, If the coco feels like your not sincere. You will have a big problem! Never forget this Latrice Baldwin. Don't get me wrong the coco can also be a prankster. Then again the coco can become deadly! Latrice Baldwin."

"Okay. I won't." I said. So the coco can become deadly. I mumbled under my breath laughing. That's so funny. What the coco will run me over with the toy car on that bright red tray, or just head butt me with that big ass head. Ha! Ha! Ha! She's drunk! I said. Telling me that. That must be that fifth shot bottle of Bacardi she drank. Talking! You know the drank from the ritual. Yeah! That got to be it.

So she begin to pick the coconut up and started looking at the top pressing down on it with her finger tips. I take it she was doing that to make sure the coconut was sealed.

"Good. She said. It is sealed nicely!" Then she put her face close to the coconut and started whispering to it as if someone was in there. Now she's laughing as she reached for a brown paper bag from under the table we were sitting at.

"Open this bag for me."! She said. I opened the bag as she gently placed the coconut down inside the bag. Then she rolled the top of the bag down tightly.

"Here you go Latrice Baldwin. And oh, here take this envelope it has the instructions and the prayer you will need to do at sunrise and sunset not missing a day for 90 days. Understand!"

Yes. I said. Oh! And before you start the prayer you must turn on some music. Not just any.music. The coco loves to work to oldies but goodies. Never turn the music off or change the radio station. Because if you do! She said.

"I know. I know. I will be sorry right."

"Correct!," She said.

Now you have up to 90 days for the coco to show you some result's. The day you begin the prayer is the first day of the 90 days that the coco will start to work for you. You must have patience. The coco works at it's own pace. It could be fast or it could be slow. So whatever you do don't worry you will get some kind of result! During the 90 day period. The coco can see and hear you once awoken. So you watch what you say and do! Any questions? No. Now grab your bag! And go! You have my number. Just call if you can! I mean when you can!"

Aw. Okay I will. I said. Thank you so much Kwana. Anytime! She said. Anytime! So I grabbed the bag with the coconut in it. And began to walk to the front door.

She yelled, "Latrice! Latrice!" I turned around and said.

Yes. Kwana. Oh! Have a nice day! And remember! Be careful what you wish for!" She said laughing loudly!

"Oh. Okay! I will" I said. I didn't understand what was so funny I thought to myself. She must still be tipsy. Whatever. I said. As I begin to walk out the door. I opened the door and before I could step out. I look down on the floor and begin to look in the face of the coco Oh. Hell no! I mumbled under my breath. I could of sworn the coco was looking at me laughing too! Let me get the fuck out of here! I walked to my car quickly and opened the passenger door and placed the brown paper bag on the seat. Closed the door and walked around the car to get in. I put the important envelope on the dash board. Then put on my seat belt and started up the car and said come on to the coco let's go. So I begin to drive.

While driving I turned my head to look at the bag in the passenger seat. And said I am so glad your black ugly face is inside of the coconut! That big ass head under that dumb looking straw hat. I begin to laugh Ha! Ha! Ha! I turned my head back to pay attention to the road! Oh! Shit! I quickly pushed my foot on the brakes! As the brakes made a loud screeching noise until the car finally stopped! In the middle of the road. What the fuck is this! A black cat crossing my path. Starring at me as if it could say bad luck! That's what cha got! That's what cha got! Bad! Bad! Bad! Bad! Luck! Shit! Finally it crossed the street. But it still was looking at me. Wow! This shit is spooky! Oh shit! Did the brown paper bag with the coconut in it fall on the floor. Nope! It didn't, it stayed in the passenger seat like a person in a seat belt. Buckle up! Okay. I begin to slowly drive off. While driving I looked into my rear view mirror. I could see the black cat still looking at me!

Let me get the hell from over here! So I drove home. Saying to myself that was some crazy shit! I pulled up in my driveway feeling somewhat safe. So I pulled into my parking stall. Turned the motor off. And grabbed the envelope with the instructions. I just want to take a glance at it. A large red vase a live plant and a pound of soil. What does this mean? A small bottle of pesticide. Let me just sit here and read all of the instructions. Okay. A small garden shovel, and gloves. You will take the coconut out of the brown paper bag and place it at your front door. Coco I am going to take you upstairs and set you by my front door. I'm going to leave you out here by my door. I have to pick up everything for the ritual, come on black and ugly, I said, let's go upstairs.

I began to walk up the stairs and started to think. I need to get to the nearest 1 stop house and gardening shop. Let me see. Oh! There's one five blocks from my apartment. Okay. So I placed the brown paper bag on the ground in front of my door with the coconut in it. I got the instructions. Now let me head down the stairs to my car. I open the car door got in and put my handbag and the instructions in the passenger seat. Started up the car and drove off. Two more blocks. I see the sign. Here it is. I pulled up in the parking lot of the 1 stop house and gardening. Here's a parking. I hope this place have everything I need for the ritual. I said while grabbing the instructions and my handbag out the passenger seat then locking my car door. Let me get a basket and go in.

"Hello, Welcome to 1 stop house and gardening shop," the store greeter said at the entrance of the store.

"Oh. Hello' I said.

Now let me open the instructions. Okay. Big red vase. Vases? Vases? Aisle #2. Wow! Look at these vase. They are so pretty. Here's a red one. I love it! I'm going to get this one. I carefully set it down in my basket. Soil and pesticide got both of them. Their on sale. Good! Gloves aisle #7. Found them. I need a pair in large. Got the large pair and threw them in my basket. Okay what else. A small shevel and a live potted plant. These two things I can find in the outside gardening area in the store. I believe that is in the front part of the store near the check out stand. Excuse me. I said.Yes? One of the workers said. Can you direct me to the shevel's in gardening sure Miss. The worker said. Straight down this aisle on your left at the end of the aisle. And your live potted plants? I said.

"Your potted plants will be right next to the exit doors in the front of the store."

"Okay great. Thank you so much." I said.

"Your welcome." The worker said.

I begin to push my basket down the aisle with the shevels. I see the shevel I want. This small neon yellow one right here. Now last but no least the live potted plant. Let me go to the front of the store exit. Okay. Here's the plants. I see all kind of weird plants. Oh! There's a full fat ficus plant. I'll take it. Now I have everything. I need. Let me get over to the check out stand. While placing everything on the counter I started thinking the rich thoughts again I went into a daze, while the cashier was adding everything up. You said the price of my two Furcci purses are \$10,200, Yes. Oh! Is that all? I said as I snapped back to reality!

"Miss! Your total is 102$^{\underline{00}}$."

"Oh. Okay," I said and smiled. Giving the cashier 105$^{\underline{00}}$.

I then grabbed the vase and my bag and began to walk out.

"Oh! Miss! Your change."

"Oh! Oh! Thank you."

"Your welcome. Thanks for shopping at 1 stop house and gardening."

I grabbed my change from the cashier and walked out the store. Saying to myself I am so ready to get this show on the road! I open the trunk of the car and put the vase and my bags in. Then closed the trunk. Got in the car with my handbag and the instructions and left. I got to get home to get started with the coconut.

I finally made it home. I pulled into the driveway. I look to my right next door and who do I see my neighbor you know. Miguel. What is he doing today in his garage? He see's me. And begin to wave at me I wave back and continue to drive to the back of my apartment building. While driving to the back I see Miguel in my rear view mirror flagging me down. Oh god! What does he want to show me today. I said. As I parked my car. I turned the motor off and got out the car. Before I could get my things out the trunk of the car. Miguel begin to call my name.

"Latrice! Latrice!" He walk down my apartment driveway. I close my car door and met him as he walked up to me.

"What's up? Miguel".

"Oh nothing to much. I was just wondering did you win?"

"Did I win? Win what? You know Latrice."

"No. I don't. That contest at your job with the coconut".

"The coconut?" I said. "Oh! Oh!"

See this is why I hate lying you always have to remember what you lied about. I said to myself.

"Oh. No. Miguel I didn't win. Actually I came in last place."

Here's another lie. I said laughing to myself.

"Oh! No! Latrice. What a bummer!" He said.

"Yes. I know. It was fun. My co-workers were very creative. Really. Well if I was a judge in that contest. I would of made sure you won 1st place, because making that top to the coconut into a lid was quite creative."

"Aww! That's so sweet Miguel. Thank you"

"Oh your welcome. I was glad to help. Well I don't want to hold you up any longer," He said. "Plus I'm making a dog house for my dog Louie."

"Oh. Okay. Miguel. So I'll see you later Latrice. Okay. Bye Miguel. I said. As he begin to walk back into his garage.

I then walked back to my car to get my stuff out of the trunk. I gently picked up the big red vase and put my bags inside of it. And closed my trunk. Then I begin to walk to the stairs slowly. I didn't want to drop it. So I went up the stairs slowly and set the vase down on the ground next to the brown paper bag by my front door. Then took my keys out my pocket and unlocked my front door. I went in set my handbag on the coffee table along with the instructions for the coconut. Now let me change my clothes. I said. I really need to get started with the coconut. I mumbled to myself as I walked to my bedroom. Okay. Let me grab a T-shirt and a pair of sweatpants. I know I'm about to get dirty. I got my T-shirt from the top drawer and my sweat pants from my bottom drawer of my dresser and got dressed.

So now I'm ready! To get started with this ritual shit! I begin to walk to the front door and go outside as I walked out damn! I forgot the instructions on the coffee table. I quickly went back inside and grabbed the instructions from the table. As I began to walk out the front door again. I heard a loud noise. Blam! Blam! Huh! What the fuck was that! I said loudly. I looked in the dining room where the noise came from. And it was the window being blown back and forth by the wind making the mini blinds hit the wall. Shit! Could it be something trying to warn me not to work with the coco. Ha! Ha! Ha! It better not be.

"I'm trying to get rich!" I yelled. So back you go! I yelled! Then I closed the window's and locked them. Now let me get outside and get started. I went back outside and closed my front door and sat down on the ground and took the bags out of the big red vase. I begin to take everything out of the bags and set the stuff on the ground next to the vase. While taking everything out of the bags, I noticed something strange. There was no type of high or low wind blowing outside at all. So how did my dining room window's blow open like that? Wow! That was creepy. Anyway let me read these instructions. Okay. Take the vase and make sure it's empty. Put your gloves on keep gloves on until your done. Open the bag of soil and begin to scoop the soil out with both hands. Fill the vase to a halfway mark. Take the pesticide and spray the soil inside the vase 3 times. Then get the coconut out of the brown paper bag and place it inside the vase right side up. Now you will need to scoop more soil out of the bag again with both hands. Get enough soil to cover the coconut completely. Spray pesticide again 2 times. Take your small shevel and dig the dirty out from around the live potted plant it should be lose enough to take the plant from the pot and place it in the vase on top of the soil with the coconut underneath the soil. Okay. I'm transferring the ficus plant into my big red vase. Cool! I did it. Scoop the last of the soil from the bag with two hands again and make sure the soil holds the plant in the vase tightly as you add the soil and fill it to the top of the vase. Okay fill it to the top with the last of this soil. Oh! Shit a water bug! And two worms. In the last of this soil. Oh! God I hate bugs! But I have to put the last of this soil in this vase. Okay. Latrice! Put the soil in the vase! I said to myself. I scooped up the soil with my hands and being screaming! Shit as I threw the last of the soil in the vase. I then got up feeling itchy and dirty! As I watched the worms move around in the soil in the vase and Oh! The water bug running out of the vase too.

What's next on this damn instruction paper. Spray the pesticide 1 last time in the soil under the live plant. Hell yeah! Let me spray these mutha fucka's! Yuck! Once I sprayed the pesticide. I stood back and watched the two worms move around quickly fighting for their lives. Sticking their heads in and out the soil until they both collapsed to their death! I can't lie, I felt a sense of relief shit a sense of victory! I don't know where the water bug ran to. It must of sensed death was near. Anyway I took my shevel and scooped the two dead worms out of the soil. Screaming again as I threw them down the stairs. I walked back over to the vase and sat back down and crossed my legs. And continued to read the instructions. Okay smooth the soil out with the shevel. Make sure the plant is in the vase. Standing real still.

Now your ready to take the coco into your home. The coco must be set on something up high like a shelf or a mantal. And make sure no one can touch it. Especially! Children! Remember the coco isn't fond of children! Never forget this. Once the coco is placed up high and away from others you will be ready for the awakening the next morning at sunrise. You must pray to the coco face down. What? Face down! Yes! Face down. The instructions said. And never, ever look up at the coco when praying! Or Something bad will happen! Now you must believe in order to receive. Once you get your results. You must reward the coco immediately! Here is the list of the offerings for the coco.

1 dozen red roses
2 metallic balloons with long red strings
1 shot glass of Bacardi

Set the roses behind the vase. Put each metallic balloon on the right and left of the vase. And the shot of Bacardi place it in front of the vase. Now I must warn you. Never ever reward the coco before the work is complete. If you do. The coco will feel all work is done. The coco will pull a couple of pranks. And the ritual will fail. If you have any further question call me Kwana your psychic reader.

Okay after reading this shit it should be easy. I know just where to put the coco. In my living room on my glass stand by the big picture window away from everything and everyone. Now let me get my ass off this ground and get the coco inside.

So I open my front door and picked up the big red vase with both hands. Oh! My god! This vase is heavy! I put that heavy ass vase back on the ground. I need to put something by the front door to keep it open so I can carry the vase in quickly to my living room. I walked in the house and looked around to see what can I put by the door to keep it open. Oh! My handbag I grabbed it off the coffee table and dropped it on the floor in front of my door. Now let me hurry up and bring that heavy ass vase inside. Okay let me try this again. Both hands Latrice! I said. Oh! Oh! Shit! I think I got it! I said as I brought the big vase in. I looked down at my handbag on the floor. Thinking that was a big No! No! I set the heavy vase on my living room floor. I couldn't stop thinking about how important it was not to put my handbag on the floor. I was told growing up putting your handbag on the floor was bad luck. I remember putting my handbag on the floor years ago at my drunk ass verbal/physical abusive ass great grandmother's house in the middle of the hood! She had just came from the kitchen checking on her peach cobbler. With a hot bowl of gumbo in her right hand. She seen me! I put my handbag on the floor. Now why did I do that! Put my! Watch out Latrice! My Aunt Margo screamed! What? I said. Then I ducked! Shit! From getting hit with a hot bowl of gumbo! Bitch! Is what my great grandmother called me. As a matter of fact she called me bitch! So much til I really started to believe that was my name! That sounds crazy but it's true! Don't you ever put yo handbag on the got damn flo! Yo ass will never ever have any money! And you'll stay having bad luck! You Understand! Now pick it up! So I did still ducking. While my aunt Margo sat on the couch shaking her head. No. At me.

Now My great grandmother was no joke! May God rest her soul. She scared me so bad. I grabbed my handbag off her floor and ran out of her house! And didn't look back. I remember that shit like yesterday! So this will be the first time in years and the last time sense that day I did that. Let me pick my handbag up right now. From the flo! I mean floor.

When I went to pick my handbag up from in front of my door. I looked around and felt I needed to duck! But I didn't hear no one screaming. Watch out Latrice! So I tossed my handbag onto the coffee table. Now enough of that. Let me go get the step ladder out of my hallway closet. Okay here it is. Shit! I hope I can stand on it and put that heavy ass vase on the top shelf of my glass stand. I opened the ladder in front of the glass stand. And walked over to the big red vase. Ou! I have to pull the vase over to the stand. It's just to heavy. Is it all the soil in it. Or did that big head spirit come to life before the awakening prayer. Ha! Ha! Ha! Man! Let me catch my breath! I am going to put this vase on this stand! Fuck this shit! I'm trying to get rich! So I grabbed the vase and pulled and walked the vase over to the ladder quickly. Then used both hands and lifted the big vase over my head. Ou! Ou! And finally put it on the top shelf of the glass stand. That's right Latrice you did it! I said to myself. While out of breath! Thank God. Okay let me make sure it's up there sturdy enough. Um! Um! Here we go! Okay. It's sturdy!

My phone rings. Ring! Ring! I jump from the ladder to answer the phone. Ring! Ring!0

"Hello"

"Hey mom."

"Hey. What are you doing? Mia said. Oh. Just cleaning the house. Why? I asked. I have someone right here that wants to speak to you. What?

Mia. Come on. I'm busy. Where are you Mia? Mom hold on! Mia! Who is it? I asked. Hello! Hello! Mia. Hey beautiful. Hello. I said. Do you know who this is? Um. Maybe. Maybe. He said. I mean. Um. Yes. I do know who you are.

"Who am I baby?" I paused. "It's Tim."

"Timothy Rose."

"That's right baby! How have you been sexy? I missed you." He said. Oh. Really. Really baby! He said. So are you still single? He asked. Um. Well I thought to myself should I tell the truth for the first time? Um. Yes I am. What about you? I said. Are you single? Tim? That I am. So with that said. How about dinner? He said. Well? Okay. I said. Good baby we got alot of catching up to do. I'll get your phone number from Mia. And I'll call you tonight. I'm going to be out here for 3 weeks on business. So we have plenty of time to hook up. Okay. I said. I'll call you tonight. Oh! And Latrice. Yes Tim. I really do miss you and can't wait to see you again. You hear me baby. Tim said. Yes. I do. I said. Okay. Here's Mia. Okay. Chow baby. Tim said. Hello mom. Yes Mia. Me and Marcus will be home in about a hour. Did you cook anything? No I didn't. Your famous words Mia said. What? Oh! Nothing. I'll stop at John's Burgers and get me and Marcus something to eat. Did you want anything? Yeah! I want to know where did you find Tim?

"Oh. Mom don't worry about that just go out and have fun! When you two hook up. But Mia.

Bye mom gotta go. Mia Wait! I yelled.

Wow! My daughter just ran into one of the most romantic young sexiest single guy on this earth! The kind of guy when he's away you look at his picture and lick it and keep licking it mmm! Ha! Ha! Ha! I am so serious! He has no children. But he is a good man! The kind you bring home to mother. And even mother tries to sit in front of him in a dress with her legs open. With no panty gurdle on! That's another story. My ex. Timothy Rose. Is a workaholic. His job keeps him on the go. Just traveling around the world. For million dollar business deals. Shit! He couldn't settle down and start a family if he wanted too. The money is to damn! good. But you know what after the coco make me rich. I'll go back to the psychic readers shop and purchase that oil I saw in that glass case. Um a what was it? Bring my ex lover back! Yeah! That's it! No! Wait a minute. Maybe I won't go get that oil. I really don't want to be tied down with my riches. I wanna have fun! Plus after hearing what happen to Ms Gigi kind of scared me just alittle bit. Okay enough of that. Now the coco is safely in place. Let me grab the instructions again. Here it is on the coffee table. Okay where's the prayer. Right under bow your head and concentrate. Never look up at the coco when praying. I remember that. That's crazy. But if that's what I have to do to get rich then I shall. Now what does it say about the prayer. Okay begin to chant to the coco in a whisper 3 times coco, coco, coco, again getting louder! Coco, coco, coco, now begin the prayer.

Coco, Coco, fulfill my desire.
I offer you. What you require.
Coco, Coco, let it be.
Make my wish reality.

You must chant and pray at sunrise. And pray and chant at sunset for 90 days. Okay. I will make sure I remember this too. Now the first sunrise you begin will be the first day of the 90 days. You must have patients. The coco works at it's on pace. Sometimes fast and sometimes slow. Either way there will be an outcome no later than the 90th day got it. Now let me get my tired sweaty ass in the shower. I said to myself. After lifting that heavy ass vase and talking to that sexy ass ex of mine. Shit! I'm sweating from head to toe. And I worked up a appetite. I'll make my famous shredded cheese, ranch dressing noodle. When I get out the shower. So I walked to my bedroom to get my things together to take a shower. While in my room I heard the front door. Mom! Yes! I'm in my bedroom! Oh. Okay. Mia said mom. Did Tim call you yet? No not yet. He will. Mia said I know, I said. Knowing him he'll call late night, early morning. Interrupting your dreams.

Oh mom. Mia said. I know him. I said Anyway where's your brother?

He's in the living room.

Hey Marcus! How was your day?

Good! Marcus said. Just in here about to do my homework. You know I have to keep up with school work and home work. Being on the high school's basketball team and travel team.

Yes. I know.

Hey mom! Where did you get that big red vase from? It's huge! Marcus said.

What vase? Mia said.

In here in the living room on top of mom's glass shelf. You can't miss it. It so big! What. Like your head! Mia said.

No! It's bigger Marcus said. Let me see it. Mia walked into the living room. Wow! That is big and bright. What's in it? Oh just my ficus plant. And the coco.

What! Mia said. Ah man not that voodoo stuff again!.

Mom! Marcus said. I'll tell you when I get out the shower.

Okay mom we'll be out here waiting. Mia said. Okay. I said as I walked into the bathroom and turned the shower on.

Oh! And don't touch that vase! I yelled. Did you hear me? Yeah. Marcus said.

I went back into my bedroom and grabbed my things for the shower. Before going back into the bathroom. I stepped out my bedroom and looked in the living room and Mia!! I yelled. Don't ever touch that vase ever!

Why? She asked. Is the coco gonna bite me! She said. Laughing looking at Marcus as he laughed too.

Listen to me it's not funny! Don'tever touch that vase! You understand!

Okay. Okay. Mom. Mia said.

You either Marcus. Okay mom. He said as he stop laughing.

After yelling at Mia. I headed to the bathroom to finally get in the shower. Mia Come on. Mom is serious about that coco make her rich thing. I'm not touching that vase.

Marcus said. Are you Mia? Oh! No. Sure. Marcus said.

I'm not! Mia said.

When walking into the bathroom I couldn't see shit! Damn I left the shower on! The steam was so thick. Oh! Well.I got to wash myself up. So I closed the door and took my clothes off. And got in the shower. I grabbed the body wash and lathered myself up. Saying to myself I will be filthy rich 90 days from tomorrow. I can't wait. I said as I begin to wash the soap off me. After washing the soap off. I turned the shower off and grabbed my towel and got out the shower. I started to dry myself off. And said to myself, should I tell my kids about the whole damn ritual? Or just alittle bit mixed with a couple of lies. Yes! A little bit mixed with lies! So I put my gown on and grabbed my tooth brush and tooth paste off the sink. Turned on the water and started dancing in the mirror and brushing my teeth. After I finished brushing my teeth and dancing. I started writing with my finger on the steamed mirror. I will soon be rich! Bitch! Laughing when grabbing my dirty clothes. Walked out to put them in the washer on my service porch then walked into the kitchen.

"Mom! Can you tell us now?" Mia said. About the vase in the living room.

Sure. I said. Hold on. Let me make me some noodles in a cup. Real quick.

Aw mom! Mia and Marcus said. Come on mom you can tell us while you make a noodle. Marcus said. We need to know if you brought a evil spirit home with you Marcus said laughing. Yea! Mom Mia said.

Okay! Okay! Come in the kitchen. Now listen to me don't ever touch that vase. It will give you bad luck! Only I can touch the vase.

Really mom. Yes I'm serious. Ding!

Mia get my noodles in a cup out the microwave. Pour the water out of my noodles too. Okay mom.

Now if you see or hear me praying to the coco either morning or night. Do not disturb me! Understand!

Yeah. Okay. Sure. I'm serious you two. Plus the coco is not fond of children. What! I'm not a child! Mia said I will be 18 in a couple of months.

I'm not a child either I'm a teenager Marcus said. I'll be 16 this year.

You both are still under age so that's being a child. Now pass me my noodles, the shredded cheese and the ranch dressing. I don't know why the coco don't like children. Shit maybe a child stole the toy car or bit the cup cake on the tray. I said. While mixing and blowing my noodles in the cup.

What? A toy car. Mia said and a cup cake Marcus said what kind chocolate or vanilla? He said laughing

Oh! Kids that's a whole nother story. I'll tell you about that another time. Anyway just don't touch the vase. And Oh! I have to keep music playing for the coco at all times. So don't touch the radio either.

Come on mom are you serious? Mia said. Ha Ha Ha!Hey

Mom the coco like hip hop? Marcus said

No! Mia said. The coco like R&B. No! No! I said. The coco likes to work to oldies! Oldies but goodies. I said while snapping my fingers. So we have to listen to that kind of music mom all the time?

Yes you do!

Oh God! Mia said. I'm glad I have my earphones. Marcus said.

Mom that's not fair Mia said.

Shit life isn't fair! That's why I'm doing this voodoo with the coco in the first place. But mom! Mia said. I don't want to here about it no more! Mia!

Ring! Ring! Ring! Ring! I'll get it Mia said.

Hello. Is your momma home? Yes. Is she busy? No. Tim. Hold on. Mom! It's for you!

"Okay. Coming. Here mom it's Tim.

"Guess you don't know him that good anymore or he changed."

"Girl shut up!" I said.

Now pass me the phone.

"Hello."

"Hey baby. What are you doing? Oh. Nothing to much just talking to the kids. Why. I asked. What's up?Well. You want to go to dinner? Sure I said. When? This Friday night. What's today? I said. Tuesday. He said. I will be closing out two big business deals this week.Tim said. One Wednesday and a very big business deal this Thursday so I want to go celebrate! With you baby. This Friday night on my yacht that is stationed out in Marin Shore not to far from your apartment. You can board my yacht and have dinner by candle light. Pop a couple of bottles. Dance until our feet get tired. Take off our shoes and relax and enjoy each others company. Then both of us get butt naked and let me lay you on your back and give you a full body massage with that hot taka oil. You use to love that! Didn't you? He said. Oh.Yes. I said. You thought I forgot? Tim said. Well. It's been so long. I mean that was long time ago. I said. So is it a yes? Tim asked. Well um um. I think I have something to do. Friday. Night. Yeah! Me! He said. As he laughed. I thought to myself. Shit he read my mind! While thinking about what he use to do to me butt naked on my back with that hot taka oil. OMG! I need that right about now! Hell yeah! I'm free Friday night! I screamed to myself. I could be sitting in the living room Friday night butt naked in my long trench coat on the couch watching the time on my watch until his driver arrives. I want to tell Tim this so fucking bad! But I didn't want to seem desperate.

So are you busy? Hello! Hello! Latrice! You there? Tim asked

Oh! Oh! Yes. I'm here.

So are we on Friday night?

Yes. It's a date under one condition.

"What's that baby? You have to have me home by sunrise".

What! Why baby? No breakfast in bed. He said.

"No. I have to be home before sunrise."

Why! Are you a vampire? If so you can bite me and suck on my neck until the sunrise. Ha! Ha! Ha!" He laughed.

If I was a vampire you would have to wear a wooden cross around your neck while holding a bible and chewing on garlic like gum. Really. He said. Yes. Really. I said. Okay. Now. Why do you need to go home so early? I um. Well um. I started to think of something to tell him. Come on Latrice. Tell me why will you have to leave me so early. He said. You are really single. right? Um yes! I couldn't tell Tim that I have to make it home at sunrise to pray to a big head spirit inside a coconut buried in a big red vase on a glass shelf in my living room with the oldie station playing. Oh! Hell! No! He'll probably sex me up real good. Then as soon as we get back to Marin Shore. He will have the people waiting for me with a cream color straight jacket! Fuck that shit! You know what to do Latrice I said to myself. Start lying. Okay. Here I go.

Tim! It's Marcus! What about Marcus baby? Is he okay? Yes! He's fine. He has a basketball game early Saturday morning. It's his damn travel team. We have to go to Oakwood City. So I have to get a early start on the highway. Oh! Okay. He said. You will owe me some breakfast in bed next time we get together. And I mean real soon. He said. Okay. I said. Latrice baby I've been thinking about taking this position that was offered to me out here. What do you think? He asked. I think that sounds good. I said. We'll see you know the offer got to be big for me to take it. I'll let you know and then we can celebrate a whole weekend together. If I take that offer. Okay. I said. So I'll have my driver pick you up Friday at 8:30pm. 8:30pm? I thought to myself the coco and praying. Um can your driver pick me up at 9:00 pm instead. Sure baby. The yacht leaves the shore at 10:00 pm. So 9:00 pm it is. I still have my same driver Mr V. You remember him? Yes I remember Mr V. Okay he can stop and get the kids something to eat. Just before he picks you up. Okay. I said Marcus still love fried chicken with waffles? Tim asked. Yes! He does. I said. Mia too. Tim said. Yes. Okay I'll have Mr V. bring them some Ricks Waffles and Chicken with plenty of syrup and hot sauce! Okay. Sounds good. I said. And for you my beautiful. I'll send you something special 30 minutes before he arrives. Okay. Dress to empress me baby! He said.

"Don't worry. I will".

"Thank you baby I'll call you later on tonight. Chow baby".

"Bye Tim". Click! Now if Tim's driver picks me up at 9:00 p.m. I will have time to pray to the coco. Before he get's here. Yes! And then go and enjoy myself!

"Mom" What did Tim say? Are you guys hooking up? You know Tim got alot of money. If you guys get back together you don't have to do that voodoo stuff with that coocoo.

You mean the coco! I said.

Yeah! Whatever you call it. Hold on young lady! It is the coco! And yes we are going out Friday. And that's his money he work hard for. And his job keeps him in and out of town. I don't like that Mia! That's why we broke up. He did say he was thinking about taking a job position out here. But who knows. We'll see. I said. But in the meantime I am doing my voodoo with the coco. But mom! Mia my mind is made up! Okay. Okay. Mom just be careful. I will I promise. Hey mom! Yes. Marcus. Is he sending us some food when he have you picked up? Yes Marcus. Good. That's what I'm talking bout! What bringing you something to eat? Like some Fried chicken and waffles! I said. Oh! Hell yeah! What! Boy calm down! Oops! Sorry mom. That's the hunger inside of me talking Marcus said. Oh and mom I almost forgot I have a basketball game Sunday morning in Oakwood City don't forget. We have to be out there early. Okay son. That's crazy I said to myself. So I really didn't lie to Tim about a basketball game. Good now let me take my lying ass to bed. I'm tired. Plus I have to go to work tomorrow. And be up at sunrise to pray to the coco. Goodnight you two! I yelled as I walked to my bedroom. Don't stay up to late! You both have school tomorrow!

Okay mom. Mia said. Goodnight mom Marcus said. See you in the morning. I said as I sat on the right side of my bed. Then I started thinking to myself, I can't wait to wake up the coco at sunrise. The prayer, the chanting is so exciting to me. Shit! I'm more excited about the voodoo I'm doing with the coco then my date with Tim. I said as I laughed while setting my alarm clock to wake me up at sunrise. So the clock is set. I put it on my night stand. Got in the bed and turned my lamp off and fell asleep.

I began dreaming: Madam! Oh. Huh! Did you want me to pop two bottles for you? Ah. No. Just one. Please. I said to um. Who is he? Your butler madam. My butler? What the fuck! Now that's what I'm talking about! Please don't wake me up. I am dreaming. Just let me sleep! I shouted in this dream. Madam. Yes Mr? Mr. Bentley. Mr. Bentley Yes. He said I heard that name before. Hum? Your lobster tail with a side of hot! Butter sauce is coming right up. Madam. Okay. Thank you. I said got my mouth watering! Mr. Bentley! Oops! Didn't mean to spit on your suitcoat when I called your name sir. I mean Mr Bentley I understand madam. Would you like a napkin? A napkin Ha! Ha! Ha! I laughed. Yes. As you wish madam. Here's a napkin for you.Thank you. Your most welcome madam I will return with your lobster tail and your bottle of platinum ice. Do you want me to get anything else madam. No. I'll just sit back and relax by this pool and catch some sun. Okay madam. He said. As he walked away wiping his suit coat off with a napkin. Oh hell yeah! This is the life! It is going to feel good to be rich! I yelled while laying in the sun closing my eyes with my $500^{\underline{00}}$ designer sunglasses on my face. Some nice black colored lens with gold trim. Some Tucci's. Oh yes. I must exhale to all thoughts of my bullshit 9 to 5 job! They got me over worked and under paid! Paying my bills, bills, bills! Shit I barely can pay them bills on time every month I got a headache just thinking about it. And me eating those noodles with ranch dressing and shredded cheese taste good! But aint good! Ahhh! Madam! Oh! God! Huh! Yes! I apologize madam. I didn't mean to frighten you. Oh that's okay I said. I was just thinking about something's that really don't matter right now. So what do you have for me on that lovely tray your holding. Yes madam I have your nicely cooked lobster that wouldn't stop screaming! Once it was dropped in the hot pot. What? And your bottle of dizzy dew! My dizzy what? Enjoy madam. Mr Bentley said as he popped the bottle of champagne and poured some into my glass and said enjoy as he started to walk away. Did he just say that weird shit to me? No maybe I've been sitting in the sun to long. Yeah or this dream is coming to an end. Anyway. Would you look at this lobster tail! I can't wait to dip it in this butter sauce. Oh wait a minute! I must sip some of this very good expensive drank first. I picked up the glass to sip. But before I took a sip. I said fuck this shit, I looked around and then set the glass down on the tray and grabbed that bottle of platinum ice champagne and said I'm about to take this whole bottle of P.I. to the head! Now let me make a toast! Here's to the riches for you broke bitches! I turned the bottle up quickly and begin drinking it. I drunk it like a thirsty camel in the desert dropping down on its front knee's! In the hot ass desert sand! Ha! Ha! Ha! Awh! Burp!! Got damn!

Ring! Ring! The phone is ringing! Ring! Ring! Mr. Bentley! Ring! Ring! Shit! I'll get it. If I can stop my head from spinning! So I got up and stumbled to the patio area and grabbed the cordless phone. Hello fuck I woke up! It was a fuckin dream!

"Hello! Who is this?"

Hey baby. It's me. What time is it? I said. Ah just 3:00 am in the morning. Tim! Yes baby. I see you still haven't changed. What do you mean? He asked. Always the dream wrecker and never the dream catcher.

What! He said. Never mind. I said. Where you sleep baby?

No! I was up reading a book! Oh yeah.What are you reading?

The Coconut. Be Careful What You Wish For!

Sounds good.

Yeah! I'm sure it does!

Tim! I was sleeping! Oh.

Okay. Baby. I'm sorry. I didn't mean to wake you from your beauty sleep beautiful. I just got off of work and couldn't stop thinking about you. Tim said. So I had to call and say goodnight. Or should I say good morning. And give you a kiss muah! Oh really I said. I can't wait to see you Friday. He said. I can't wait to see you too. Well baby I'm going to let you go back to sleep I'll see you Friday okay chow baby. He said. "Bye, Tim."

Click! Now I'm up I can't go back to sleep. I swear! If Tim wasn't so got damn fine and financially stable! I would of cursed his ass out! Shit. I didn't even get to taste that lobster tail in my dream. That Mr. Bentley said wouldn't stop screaming in the hot water in the pot. That was crazy! I wonder what did that dream mean? I feel it was a good sign. I guess. Well I'll be staying up now. I just have a couple of hours to sunrise anyway. I'm going to get up and make me a cup of coffee and go watch some tv. Oh and I can't forget to turn my radio on. For the coco. Then pray and chant. Come on sunrise! I yelled. Cough! Cough! Shh! Latrice I said to myself. You don't want to wake up Mia and Marcus. I heard one of them coughing. So I quietly walked into the kitchen and made me a cup of coffee. You know my usual black with four packs of sugar and two creamers. After pouring in the sugars and creamers I took my cup of coffee and a spoon and begin stirring it while walking back into the living room. I sat down on the couch. Then grabbed the remote and turned the tv on. I flipped through the channels as I blew and sipped my coffee. I wasn't really interested in what was on tv. Because I couldn't stop thinking about that dream I had. Wow sunrise please rise I said. I am so excited to wake this big head spirit to change my life forever! Shit! Let's do this shit! I said as I set my coffee on the table and reached for the instructions to see the prayer. Okay. Here's the prayer. I started to read it. As I grabbed my coffee again and begin drinking it. As I continued to read the prayer. Don't forget Latrice you must say the prayer and chant face down never look up at the vase when praying and chanting. That is some bullshit! I said. But who wants to look up at that ugly mutha fucka anyway. Even if it's buried inside a vase. I said to myself. As I begin getting mad as hell! Whatever I said. Throwing the instructions with the prayer back on the coffee table. And drunk the rest of my coffee up and slammed my cup on the table! I better get what I wish for! I said. I got off the couch and went to the living room window to open the curtains. I opened the curtains turned and looked at the clock on the wall.

Okay 30 minutes to sunrise. Now let me go turn my radio on low and find the oldies station. As I turned the radio station looking and looking for that oldies station I could see the sun peeking out alittle bit more from behind the hill. Fuck where is that radio station. Oh. Wait! Wait! I think this might be it. A blast from the past. That's it! With the lyric's to take your breathe away and the artist to die for! With the music that will make you dance to death! We'll be back after these few commercials. That is a weird ass radio station. I mumbled to myself. Anyway.

Now I can see the sun coming up. I looked at the clock again. Oh my god! I have 5 minutes to begin the prayer. Let me go to my hallway closet real quick and grabbed a pillow to put under my knee's so when I pray to the coco. I won't hurt my knee's. I set the pillow down in front of the vase on the floor. I have 3 minutes left. Let me turn the radio up just alittle bit. Hey! That's my jam. Smiling faces, smiling faces they lie! Shit! I started dancing and snapping my fingers to the music. Okay! Okay! Stop this Latrice! I have 2 minutes to pray. I'm ready I said I begin stretching and taking deep breaths and then asking God to forgive me for being desperate for material things in my life. As I'm about to get on my knee's and look down the stairway to hell and make a wish to the devil, I can't say I don't know what I'm doing. If I did. I would be telling one of my biggest lies I'm all so famous for. I do know you are a forgiving God and with that said. I am down to 30 seconds to pray to the coco and I shall.

With the thoughts of the bad things way in the back of my mind, I begin to get down on my knees, without saying Amen. Feeling that would be a sign of disrespect. If I did.

10 seconds left I begin to bow my head down towards the floor not looking up at all. As told in the instructions. 5 seconds 4, 3, 2, 1. I can hear the music playing as I begin to chant in a whisper to the coco. Whispering. Coco, Coco, Coco, again. Louder. Coco! Coco! Coco! Now pray. To the coco.

Coco, Coco fulfill my desire.

I offer you, what you require.

Coco, Coco. Let it be

Make my wish reality! I shouted!

"Mom!"

"Oh shit!" I whispered.

"Mom, is that you?" Mia said.

"Uh. Yes."

"Are you okay?"

"Yes."

"Why were you shouting?" Mia said.

"Yeah Mom, who you in there yelling at," Marcus said. "You woke me up out of my dream. I was at an all you can eat Sam's buffet about to sit down and start grubbing, as soon as I raised my fork to my mouth I heard you yelling, and I woke up," Marcus yelled.

"I'm sorry kids, it's just that I was trying to kill a big water bug in here."

"Oh Okay. Did you get it," Mia said.

"Uh! Yes. I did," I said smiling shaking my head as I got up off the floor. 'There goes another lie,' I said to myself. 'I know one day my fantastic lies will catch up to me. But until then I will keep lying until they do,' I said, laughing to myself as I picked the pillow up from the floor and put it back in the hallway closet. Now I have to get ready for work. I turned on the shower, got my clothes and quickly in got out and got ready. Okay, I'm on my way out the door feeling good after doing the first prayer to the coco today. After tonight's prayer, the coco will go to work for me. Yes!

"Mia! Marcus! Get up for school, don't be late. I'll see you two later. You hear me?" "Yeah mom, we're up," Mia said.

"Okay, love you."

"Love you too mom"

Off to work with the thought of one day soon I can say to my boss take this job and shove it! Ha! Ha! Ha! Or just take a 100.00 bill and wipe my ass with it and stick it on my bosses forehead. Smack! Ha! Ha! Ha! That's funny too. Well until that day comes I better make it on time. I said as I started driving out of the apartment building's driveway.

Now before I make a right turn out into the traffic. I look to my left then I was about to look to my right. But instead, I looked again to my left and who do I see in his garage early in the morning? Miguel, there he go building something. I honked my horn at him. Honk! Honk! He looked up at me and smiled then waved. I waved back then quickly made a right turn, and shouted, "Adios Amigos!" I don't have no time this morning to stop and look or listen to Miguel telling me about another project he made. I have to get to work. Let me see, if I stay on this street, Winco Blvd, I should make it to work in about 10 minutes. And as soon as I get there, I'm going to clock in fast. Shit every second counts. Plus, I left so much paperwork on my desk that needs to be filed.

Okay I made it. I made it to work on time. Good. Now let me get inside and clock in. Now where is my card to clock in? Um um. Here it is. Okay let me stick it in this machine right now. Click! Now I'm officially here for 8 long hours. I swear today at sunset I am going to chant and pray with all my energy to the coco. 'I have to get rich', I said to myself as I pushed the elevator button to go up to the office, ding. The elevator doors opened, so I got in and there were a couple of people on the elevator, so I pushed the 17th floor button and road the elevator quietly. I thought to myself, 'after 90 days, I won't be on this elevator or at my desk piled with files', and I won't be' um, um… 17th floor. Well that's me. So I stepped out the elevator and walked right into the office door where I work. I begin to walk down the aisle to my desk.

"Top of the morning Ms. Baldwin"

"Huh? Oh Good morning," I said.

"Hey Latrice"

"Oh, Hey," I said with a puzzled look on my face.

"Hey! Hey! Ms. B."

"Girl you want some coffee?"

Some what? I said to myself. Oh, No thank you. Shit! Hell no! I don't want no coffee. I don't even know her! I thought to myself. Or the rest of those co-workers that spoke to me. Let me hurry up and get to my desk. That was strange. They act is tho they knew. I am going to be rich soon. Well the most I can say is let these mutha fucka's keep being fake in this place of business. While I'll have my ass in Paris on that famous bridge placing my lock on that famous gate. Yelling! And Screaming! "I'm rich bitch!" Just before throwing the key into the water below the bridge. I said. As I sat down at my desk. Laughing to myself.

As I begin to file the paperwork on my desk. I looked at the clock on my desk. Shit! It's still early. I'll just keep filing until my co-worker/ friend get here in about 30 minutes. Her desk is right next to mine full of paperwork too. That's because we spend so must time gossiping. "Debbie" is her name. Debbie Romono. She was born and raised in Brooklyn New York. I can't wait until she get's here. She is so funny she keeps me laughing! I love her. We file papers together go to lunch together and at the end of the day we gossip about everything and everybody. She comes from a close knit family. Their always in church and Bible study faithfully. One time she told me. She killed two ants on her sink because they were crawling to her fruit bowl. Do you know she went to the confession booth and confessed about killing the two ants. And asked for forgiveness. Saying she really didn't mean to kill the ants. But they were about to crawl all over something she eats. So that following Sunday she went to the early morning church service and sat in the front role. When everyone bowed their heads to pray and closed their eyes. Debbie said. She just couldn't do it. Because there was this priest sitting on the pool pit starring at her. So she begin to look him in his eyes. And he started to make faces at her and started opening and closing his eyes while looking at Debbie. Then he sat very still starring at her. Debbie said. So what did you do? I asked. Girl! Got mad and said to myself shit! God forgive me for getting up leaving and cursing in your house of worship! But I got to get the fuck out of here! What! I said. Yes! Honey! I politely excused myself from the front role of the church. And didn't look back! I started laughing! Latrice don't laugh! That shit ain't funny! Debbie said. I'm serious! Okay. Okay. I said. Thank You. Debbie said. Now I believe to this day that he was the priest in that confession booth. When I admitted to killing those two ants on my sink! He thinks I'm crazy! Latrice! But I'm not! So fuck him! I'll pray to God at my own house on my own time. Debbie said. Ha! Ha! Ha! I started laughing again. Now this is why the other co-workers don't talk to me. Because they say birds of a feather flock together. Which that is not true. As you can see outside of church she swears like a drunkin sailor. Or should I say like a Captain sinking with his ship. Yelling. All bitches in first class abandon the fucking ship! Jump now! You rich ass hoes! I mean. Ladies can you please jump. Ha! Ha! Ha! There are a couple of co-workers that say she's to loud and she's very rude! I don't care tho. Me myself. I just say she's straight with no chaser. She tells the truth! You know how some folks can't handle the truth! Oh. Well. I love her for being straight out. But at the end of the day. When we clock out. We laugh about all the shit that goes on and talk about so many people and then when it's time to clock out. We both say see you tomorrow. And then she go her way and I go mine. We never call each other on the phone unless there's a meeting or some kind of holiday office party. That's crazy. Huh. But it's true. She should be walking in soon. I can't wait. I got some juicy gossip for her about me and my ex Tim. Timothy Rose. We are hooking back up tomorrow night! She is going to scream! And say my name and say bitch! Your crazy! Then the gossiping begins. Debbie knows so much about me and Tim's past relationship. And she never even met him. I remember I use to come to work talking about Tim so much to her! Just like that fast talking man at a public auction! Do I hear? Timothy Rose! Is the best man in bed! Going once! Going twice! Sold! To the lady with her mouth open and her eyes closed sliding down the wall in the back of the room! Yes! That would be me! He's mine! Need I say more! Ha! Ha! Ha!I laughed.

I really wish I could tell Debbie about the coco. But I can't. Because

Debbie has a big voodoo phobia. Now listen to this. She wears 5 gold chains on her neck. Each one with a gold cross on it. She keeps a bottle of holy water in the bottom drawer of her desk and a bible open on top of her desk on 91st. Psalms page in front of her baby sister's picture. Oh! And she carries garlic in her purse to keep all evil away she said. PU! Oh! Here she comes right now! I hear her loud ass mouth!

Excuse me Debbie! Yes! You have 30 new files you will have to file today.

What! Well put the mutha fucka's on my desk! Shelia! Oh! My God! That's right bitch! Call on God! Because you need him! Debbie yelled. Well I never! Shelia said. And your ass never will! Debbie said while walking to her desk. Good morning. Debbie. I said. Oh. Hey girl. Guess what Debbie. What? Me and Timothy Rose are hooking back up tomorrow night! Debbie screamed! Latrice! Bitch you crazy! See I told you. She was going to say that. So he came back to open your legs and put his face in your pussy. And yell in it and hear a echo! Right? She said. Ha! Ha! Ha! Debbie your funny! Funny! Girl. It's the truth! Yeah. Yeah. Your right. I said. I know I'm right! Debbie said. But have fun Latrice! Oh! Believe me I will! Just don't get in to deep. You be careful with Tim. It's a reason why it didnt work out the first time girl. You never know. What these men be into. You know. What I mean. No what do you mean Debbie? Girl I mean like putting voodoo on your ass! What? Come on Debbie. I said. No way! Really. I said. What! You don't fucking think so Latrice? Debbie said. Well um not really. Oh! Wait! Wait! What time is it? Debbie asked. After 9:30 am. Oh! Girl hold on! Let me read my bible and wipe my desk down with my holy water then I'm going to tell you. Why. I have a voodoo phobia and why I'm single and don't trust men. Debbie said. Okay. I said. As I watched her throw holy water all over herself. Even between her legs and then rubbing it on her ass in a circular motion. She put some holy water on a cloth and rubbed it on the top of her desk. Then she prayed. Amen! Debbie said. Then she sat down at her desk. And started telling me to much information! Now Latrice about my voodoo phobia and why I'm single to this day girl with three neon color vibrator's in my closet. No wait! I mean two vibrator's in my closet and one under my mattress! So when I get the urge to wanna splurge! What the fuck I said to myself. She is crazy! Latrice! Huh? I am so afraid of being with a man! After what happen to my baby sister Tina! Debbie said. Girl! She lost her fucking mind! My baby sister be on the corner of 7th Street and Rosebud Blvd. Dancing! Girl! In a yellow poke a dot bikini and some 7 inch high heels! Just sweating! And you know what! It don't be no fucking music playing!

"What? Shut up!" I said.

No! I'm serious Latrice! Just dancing with her hair all over her head! And oh my god! She stinks! Her fucking pussy and ass stinks very very bad! She won't come home. My poor mother cries everyday and pray every night that her baby girl will come home. Wow I said. I know Latrice. She's fucked up!

That's sad." I said. Yeah! Sad. Even my mother has full custody of Tina's 1 year old daughter. My sister's baby's dad did that shit to her! What? What did he do? Get her hooked on drugs! Hell no! I wish at least she could of got some help. Well what did he do to her? I asked. Girl he fucking went to the neighborhood fortune teller a gypsy put a got damn curse on my baby sister! Come on Debbie are you serious? Hell yeah! Listen to this. Latrice. I'm listening. Okay the baby's dad. Anthony Greco aka Tony. Is what everyone calls him. He's well known in our neighborhood. He took good care of my baby sister. She had everything with this guy. Until she had the baby. That's when the arguing started and he became abusive. Telling her that she don't pay attention to him anymore sense she had the baby. He gave her a black eye before he busted her lip and broke her arm. My big brother Danny wanted to snap his neck! But Tina kept going back to Tony until this last time.

I was staying at my mother's house for a couple of days while my apartment was being exterminated for ants. We had just finished eating dinner. I took the plates from the table into the kitchen and started to wash the dishes. My mother went in her bedroom. While washing the dishes I heard my grandma calling my name from her bedroom. Debbie! Debbie! Coming grandma! I dried my hands and went to see what she wanted. I got to her door. What's up? Grandma. What do you need? Well a. Um. I need a slice of ice cream crunch cake. And a um! Tall glass of man!! What? What did you say grandma? Oh shit! You heard me! Yeah. I heard you. Well go get those things for me Debbie! Well I can go get the cake for you. But the tall glass of man? We don't have any of that. I said. Laughing! Latrice I couldn't stop laughing. It made my grandma so mad. She said. What's so funny Debbie? You silly bitch! Oh. Well excuse me grandma! Debbie said. Your excused! And next time go to the bathroom! What? Grandma. Oh! Go to hell! Debbie! Latrice I walked out her room still laughing. Now I see where you get that bad language from. I said laughing. You think so Latrice. Yes! Yeah me to girl Debbie said. So I went back into the kitchen and cut my grandma some cake and got her a tall glass of milk not a man. Grabbed her a fork on the way out the kitchen. Then went back to grandma's room and gave her the glass of milk and the slice of cake. And walked out fast before she could start saying something crazy to me again. So I'm on my way back to the kitchen and the doorbell rings. Ding, Dong, Ding Dong! Now who could that be at this time of night. Ding, Dong, Ding, Dong. Coming! So I got to the front door and opened it. And it was my baby sister, Tina she was holding my niece and a couple of duffle bags. So I quickly opened the door and grabbed my niece from her arms.

And continued to stand at the front door holding my niece and the front door open for my sister until she came in from finished paying the cab driver. My mother came out her bedroom asking who was at the door. She seen me holding my niece and grabbed her from my arms and gave her a kiss and asked me what was going on. I don't know mother. I said. Here comes Tina. Ask her what happen. Okay. Debbie I will, mother said. Tina walked into the house. I closed the door behind her as she put her duffle bags on the floor by the front door. Hey Tina is everything okay? Mother said. I swear Latrice. I will never forget that night. Debbie said. Now before my baby sister could answer my mother. She took her jacket off and walked back to the front door to get her duffle bags. She bent over to pick up the duffle bags. And girl! I said what the fuck! To her. Got damn girl! Tony really kicked your ass out! Or should I say kicked you in your ass! Then put you out Debbie said. Latrice. My sister had a Doc Carter fresh boot print with blood stained in the crack of her ass. And she had on white jeans. Oh! My god! My mother yelled. Call the cop's! No fuck the cop's go get me my gun! And call your brothers! Oh! No! Please mom don't! Tina said. As she started to cry and say I'm okay. Mom. It's over! Me and Tony are threw! I told him the truth! The truth? What do you mean Tina? Mother said. That I was cheating on him and my daughter wasn't his. Tina said. What! We all yelled. Well she's not. Tina yelled. Well. Thank God! My mother said as she kissed my niece all over her face. Saying she never liked that Anthony Greco anyway. Mother that's not why he kicked me in my ass. Well. Why did the asshole do that to you Tina? Debbie asked. I told him that I was tired of faking the moaning while having sex with him! And he never satisfied me! With his little bitty dick! Tina said. Latrice. I screamed so loud, and so long girl. I was horsed for two weeks. I said to my baby sister you mean Tony has the biggest balls on the streets. But in his pants he packs the smallest dick! No fucking way Tina! Debbie said. What! Did you say? Grandma shouted! You got poked with a stick! Ha! Ha! Ha! I laughed! Latrice. And said no grandma! Oh! Well fuck you too!! Grandma yelled. This shit was crazy! Debbie said. It sure was. I said to Debbie. So what else happen? I asked. Well. Hold on. Let's go to lunch. Debbie said. And I'll tell you the rest.

Okay. I said. Look at my desk! Girl. I sure got alot of cases filed today. I said. Listening to that crazy shit! Yeah! I did too Debbie said. Can you believe it? No. I said. While Sitting here running my mouth! Now I'm hungry! Debbie said. Are you? Yes. I am! I said. We have a 1 hour lunch break. So where are we going to eat? Debbie said. Well. Um. I was thinking. Let's go to Rick's Waffle and Chicken. I said. Oh! Hell yeah! Debbie said. That delicious golden fried chicken and those big fluffy waffles! Let's go Latrice! Okay. I said. That's what Tim's driver is going to bring the kids tomorrow. When he picks me up to meet with Tim on his yacht. Tim said he's going to send something special for me. Girl! What if it's an engagement ring! Debbie said.

Oh! Hell no! I said. Shit! You never know. That mutha fucka know's what he's doing. He know your kids don't give a damn about a lobster dinner. But you do! You damn right I do! I said. I bet you do! Debbie said. He will have some lobster. Fresh from the sea. Nice lobster plates for you'll on that yacht by candle light. Debbie said. He better! If he want some of this dessert this sweet cherry pie! I said. We both laughed. While clocking out for lunch. Then we got in my car and left. Good afternoon ladies are you ready to order.

Yes! I am! Debbie said. Let me get the #5 Ricks pick for the chicks! Okay. Breast or thigh? I'll take the breast Miss Lady! Debbie said. And for you miss? Um. Um. Girl get what you want Debbie said. It's my turn to pay for lunch! You better eat girl!You ain't eating none of that noodle, ranch dressing, shredded cheese bullshit you be eating! Debbie said. Yuck!

Girl! What you talking bout, that taste good! I said as I laughed. Come on Latrice! I'm hungry! Order your food! Okay! Okay! I'll have the #1 Rick's breakfast in bed. Okay. Miss did you want a side order of grits with that? Yes Please. I said. Okay ladies does this complete your order? Yes! Okay. I'll be back with your drinks. Thank you I said. Your welcome Oh! Excuse me! Debbie said. Yes. What's your name? Michelle. Okay Michelle. What comes on that plate? That #1 Rick's breakfast in bed. Oh! A extra long all beef sausage link between your waffles. What the fuck! Oh God! Debbie said. Michelle girl the way that sounds. I don't know if I want to eat it! Or just get on top of this table and have sex with it! Girl your funny! Michelle said. Laughing as she went to get our drinks. Latrice! What are you doing ordering something like that! Are you getting yourself ready for tomorrow night with Tim? What? No! You said order what I want! Oh yeah your right. Debbie said. Okay ladies. Here's your drinks. And I'll be right back with your food. Okay. Latrice I want to finish telling you about what happen to my baby sister. But I'm so fucking hungry girl. And we only have about 25 minutes left for lunch. So. I will tell you the rest when we get back to work. Debbie said. Okay ladies lunch is served! Michelle said. Oh! Thank you! Debbie said. Mmm! Thank you I said. Your welcome ladies enjoy. Mmm! Look at my breast so big and juicy! Crunch! Mmm! delicious! Yeah looks good I said. Wow Look at my plate. That extra long hard cooked beef sausage between my big soft golden waffles. I said. Debbie dropped her chicken breast on her plate she quietly watched me open my waffles and pour maple syrup all between my waffles and all over that large hard cooked long beef sausage link! Her mouth begin to water, she couldn't stop looking as I slowly picked up the long large shiny wet sticky beef sausage from between my soft golden waffles with both of my hands. As it dripped the sweetness onto my plate and ran off my finger tips. Mmm! I'm about to open my mouth and you know. Bite it! Mmm! This is delicious! Good choice. I said. Debbie! Are you okay? Huh? What? Oh yeah girl I'm sorry. Debbie said. Shit! Watching you eat that big beef sticky sausage got me hungry! And horny! What! Now Debbie. I think you better start dating again. You think so Latrice! Hell yeah! I know so girl! I don't know Latrice. I still have to tell you what Tony did to my baby sister Oh. Oh yeah I said. Well I'll be right back. Debbie said. Where are you going? I asked. I need to go to the restroom. I think I had an accident on myself. Are you serious? I said. Hell. Yeah but don't worry Latrice just finish your food. I'm going to ask for a doggy bag. Debbie said.

Is everything okay ladies? Michelle said. As she put the bill face down on the table. Yes! I said. Oh can I get a doggy bag. Debbie said. Sure let me go get it. Michelle said. Debbie picked up the bill. Michelle! Debbie yelled. Yes. Here's the money sweetie for the lunch bill. Debbie said. Okay Michelle said. Thank you. Debbie said. Latrice. Debbie whispered. I'll be in the restroom. So Debbie got up and headed to the restroom. Excuse me miss! Michelle said. To Debbie. Yes! Here's your change and your doggy bag. Okay just put it on the table. Okay. Well ladies you have a nice day. And come again. Michelle said. Oh girl that is what I am about to do in your restroom! Debbie said and laughed. Excuse me! What do you mean? Michelle asked? Oh nothing! Debbie said. Excuse me! Waitress. Yes sir! I'll be right there. Okay. Ladies I gotta go. Okay here's your tip. I said. Oh thank you kindly Michelle said. As she walked away. Latrice! Fuck that bitch! Debbie said. I was about to tell her. I'm going into your restroom and I'm going to come again and again! Debbie shhh! Stop that! Will you just go to the restroom and hurry back! We have to get back to work. Okay! Okay! Latrice. I'll be back in two and two. Hey are you going to eat the rest of that big sausage? Why? I asked. Well I was wondering if I could take the rest of that beef sausage in the restroom with me! Girl! Hell No! Alright! Alright! I'll be back. Debbie said. She quickly walked into the restroom.

While waiting I sat there looking around at the people eating in this rundown hole in the wall place we call a restaurant with a grade "B"! In the window. I said to myself as I watched a roach crawl on the floor making it's way into the kitchen area. Fuck! I just lost my appetite and pushed my plate from in front of me. Thinking. Tomorrow night my kids will be eating this shit! While me and Tim will be on his yacht eating lobster. Now what kind of mother would I be to let him get the food from here for Mia and Marcus. Oh no, I know! I'll call Tim tonight and tell him to have his driver pick up some burgers from Big Burgers. I'll do that as soon as I get home from work. And I must make sure I make it on time to pray to the coco. Believe me I will be ready before sunset. On my knee's with my head down and my ass in the air! Praying! I don't ever want to eat here or at any other nasty ass place they call a restaurant around here! I will have my ass on the other side of town with a nice clean glass of ice and a bottled water.

Once the coco grant's my voodoo wish. I will not be here ever again with piece's of length floating around in my glass of soda! I said to myself. Oh my God. I said. Oh! Yes! Yes! Yes! What the? Or who the, fuck is that? Sounding like one of those shampoo commercials! Oh shit. I whispered. Got damn it's coming from the restroom. It got real quiet in the restaurant. Everyone being looking towards the restroom. I already know who it is! Let me go get her. As I got to the restroom door I begin to knock! Knock! Knock! Debbie! Are you alright in there? Debbie! I shouted. Now you see. Do you really think I should go somewhere with her when I get rich. Yes! I am. For entertainment purposes only! Like going to a male strip club! I would give Debbie one thousand dollars in one dollar bills and just sit back and watch every male stripper from a African American shaking his colla greens with his chicken wing while giving her a lap dance and a Hispanic dancing in front of her with his flour tortilla's and his pinto bean and of course the Asia, popping his sweet and sour pork in her face! Leaving her stumbling, and broke as she walk out the club feeling like she just been raped and robbed! Ha! Ha! Ha! Debbie! Yeah Latrice. Come on out of the restroom! I said. Okay. Okay. Here I come! Debbie said. She opened the restroom door. And when she stepped out that restroom, her hair was all over her head mascara ran down her left eye when she said I'm okay. Her blouse was hanging off her right shoulder, zipper unzipped on her black slacks. Damn! And she was barefoot holding her high heels in her right hand. Just standing there as if she just came back from a night club dancing and drinking all night. Girl! What happen to you in there? Come on let's go look at everyone looking at you. I said. Oh God, I know. Debbie said. Excuse me folks the toilet is flooded in the ladies restroom. Debbie said while walking back to our table to grab her doggy bag. Michelle! Yes. You might want to put a out of order sign on the ladies restroom. It's a mess in there. Okay. I will. Michelle said. Okay let's go Latrice. Debbie said. I'm right behind you. I said. While walking out of Rick's Waffles and Chicken I started thinking to myself. Debbie is really crazy! She is really looking like some man climbed in the restroom window and raped her! And really she was in there rapping herself! I just shook my head as I walked behind her. I unlocked my car and we both got in. And headed back to work. You think I'm crazy Latrice? Debbie asked. Well! Ah! Yes! I said. Oh! Fuck you Latrice! Debbie said. Next time can you just order a fucking salad! Debbie yelled. We both looked at each other and laughed. Then I pulled up in the parking lot at our job. We still had a few minutes left before clocking back in. We sat in my car. I started laughing again at her as she fixed her hair and make up in the mirror. Stop laughing Latrice! I can't! I said. Well I rather be safe then sorry. Debbie said. These men now a days are snakes. Debbie. Not all of them. I said. Oh! Really. You don't think so Debbie said. Okay let's clock back in from lunch. Debbie said. So I can tell you the rest of this shit about my baby sister. Okay. I said. So Debbie put her heels on and fixed her clothes. And we walked in our work place. Clocked in. And walked to our desk. No one spoke to us as we walked to our desk. Well hello to you too! You tired ass co-workers! Shh! I said. Fuck them. Debbie yelled. Let's just talk about your baby sister and the voodoo. Latrice! Don't say that word! What word? That word you know! Debbie said. What voo! Yes! That! Debbie said as we both sat down at our desk. Okay. Before I tell you this shit! Let me put some of my holy water on me again. Okay. I said. So I sat at my desk and watched Debbie put the holy water all over herself again but this time she made a cross sign on her forehead. Amen! Debbie said. She sat down and put the holy water back in her desk draw. Okay. Latrice. Listen to this. Remember I said my sister's baby's dad kicked her in the ass and put her out. Yes. Well we thought he was done with my baby sister Tina. Girl! That mutha fucka Anthony Greco aka. Tony. Was in the making of getting even with my sister Tina. She stayed at my mom's house for three weeks then she started leaving and not coming back for weeks. Leaving my niece with my mom and not calling. To check up on her baby. Latrice girl! We had got word that Tina was seen a couple of times with Tony But when she finally came home no one questioned her. Shit! We felt she's grown she know's what she's doing right? Right. I said. No! Wrong! Debbie said. That fucking asshole Tony! Went to the neighborhood fortune teller. You know where I live we call them gypsy's. Debbie said.

Gypsy's? I said. Yeah. The people that can't read or write! And they have a gift to make a curse worse! They take all your money! And by the time you realize nothing is getting better. You go back to tell them and guess what! What? I said. They are gone like the wind! On your ass leaving you holding the shit bag! Debbie said.

"Damn that is crazy," I said. "So Debbie how do you know your sister's baby daddy went to a fortune gypsy or gypsy teller?" I said.

"Latrice it's a fortune telling gypsy."

"Well I don't know", I said.

"Good, and don't try to find out or do any business with those fuckers! So this is how we found out about Tony going to the gypsy. My mother's friend Mrs. Mancini came by a couple of days ago. Trying to tell my mother that she seen Tony go inside the fortune tellers shop just before she went in. Mrs Mancini has been going to the gypsy for 3 months now. She go there to get white candles to burn in her home for her husband that died 6 months ago. And she goes once a week to talk to the dead. She talks to her mother and her husband. What? I said. Yes one time she told my mother her husband Mr. Mancini said hello! No way! I said. No really Latrice. But my mother is convinced that Mrs. Mancini lost her mind after her husband died. My mother is a strong believer in God. Anything else she don't believe in. So anyway Mrs. Mancini was waiting to talk to the dead and pick up her white candles for her husband the day she seen Tony there. He was behind the curtain with the gypsy. Madam Yvette is her name. And she talks very loud when your behind the curtain with her and when she's doing a reading in her crystal ball. Mrs Mancini said she wasn't trying to be noisy but she couldn't help but be all ears. She said she listened as Madam Yvette being to ask Tony what did he want. But before she could do any work she must give him a reading. So she begin to read him. Mrs Mancini said. It was her and a old blind guy waiting to be seen. While waiting the old blind man leaned over and whispered to Mrs Mancini saying he can't wait until he can go behind the curtain and put a hot sexy spell on his-self so his new young in home care nurse will undress him and give him a sponge bath butt naked three to four times a day. He said laughing then coughing and farting at the same time.

Ha! Ha! Ha! Debbie your funny! I said.

No! I'm not being funny girl! Debbie said. These people don't care they go to these kind of places to get their way! Yeah. I know. I said as I looked at my watch to see how much time was left before we have to go home.

Okay we have 1 hour. Little do Debbie know I'm one of those people to not trying to hurt no one. Just trying to get rich.

Latrice!

Yeah! I said.

So listen Mrs Mancini said she had to get out of her seat and walk around in the gypsy's shop, to get some fresh air from that farting ass customer. She begin to walk closer to the counter near the curtain. And stood there and listened. Madam Yvette started to read Tony. Oh! Wait! Madam Yvette said. You have a serious problem I'm picking up on. So she got up from her chair and told Tony to please stand up and raise his arms and spread his legs apart. As she walked around him. At that time Mrs. Mancini had gotten closer to the curtain and begin peeking inside as Madam Yvette's fan blew the curtain open just enough to look in at what was going on in there. And Latrice what I'm about to tell you is some crazy shit! Debbie said.

Tell me Debbie! I said. Okay now Madam Yvette never knew that Mrs. Mancini was watching. Well at least she thought she didn't know. So Mrs. Mancini said she watched as Madam Yvette stopped walking around Tony and stood in front of Tony. And said. Can you please take your pants off. So Tony said sure okay. With the thought of Madam Yvette was getting fresh with him. Tony placed his pants on the chair and stood back in front of Madam Yvette smiling! Mrs. Mancini said she looked at his face and said to herself Oh my god! That is Mama Romono's daughter Tina's boyfriend. She thought what the fuck is he doing here. So she stood there and watched as Madam Yvette told him to spread his legs part again while in his boxer shorts. As Madam Yvette got on her knee's in front of Tony telling him to close his eyes. And begin to put her face on Tony's dick and balls. She started inhaling deeply and opened her mouth! As Tony stood there in his boxer shorts. What! Debbie. I said. Yes! Debbie said girl! Mrs Mancini said she thought Madam Yvette was going to give him a blow job!

What! I said. Mrs. Mancini said she wanted to turn her head but she couldn't. So all of a sudden. Madam Yvette exhaled. And said to Tony I smell damage in your dick and balls! Let me see. Madam Yvette said. Keep your eyes closed. She said to Tony. As she begin to take her right hand and gently rub and hold his genitals in her hand outside of his boxers. Mrs. Mancini stood there watching in disbelief. She said. Madam Yvette then looked in the opening in the front of his boxers at his dick and balls and immediately put her right hand inside of his boxer's and held his dick and balls in her right hand with a soft but firm grip. She closed her eyes and started humming low. Hmmm. And then she got louder Hmmm! As she begin moving her hand back and forth in his boxer shorts.

You got to be kidding me. I said.

No! I'm not Latrice! Mrs. Mancini said it look like Madam Yvette was jacking Tony off! And the look on Tony's face he thought the same thing. Until Madam Yvette pulled her hand out of his boxer shorts quickly and then screamed! And fell back on the floor. And hit her head. Then turned her head and looked right in Mrs. Mancini's eyes! Scarring the shit out of her! Mrs. Mancini said she ran back to her seat. She could here Madam Yvette telling Tony open your eyes and get dressed. Please quickly! Okay Tony said. Mrs Mancini said she had to go back to the curtain to see what else Madam Yvette was going to do. So she did. Sit down Tony. Madam Yvette said. As she took her right hand with Tony's bodily fluids on it and rubbed it all over her crystal ball for a theral reading. Madam Yvette closed her eyes and placed her left hand on her crystal ball as well. Mrs. Mancini said.

Latrice. I know it's almost time to clock out so I'm going to try to make this short and to the point. Okay. Plus today is our last day at work. Sense were going on Christmas vacation.

Yes! I know. Latrice said. We won't see each other for 3 weeks. And I hope when we get back Debbie. We can gossip about you finally kissing somebody under the mistle toe! I said. We both laughed.

Okay. Okay. We'll see. Debbie said. So Latrice listen to this after Madam Yvette closed her eyes. She started laughing! Then opened her eyes. And asked Tony. Who are these women that sit and laugh at your genital problem. Mrs. Mancini said she being to describe to him everyone of us that was at my mother's house that night. That was laughing at what my baby sister Tina said about Tony's dick! Shit! She even picked up on my crazy ass grandma! When she said did Tina get poked with a stick! What!

Debbie that is some crazy shit! I said.

Yeah that's fucking crazy! Now how did Mrs. Mancini know about that. She wasn't at my mother's house that night when we were laughing about that. Yeah that's true! I said. So Madam Yvette said to Tony. Who is the youngest one I see very pretty girl with a beautiful baby girl in her arms? It's Tina. Tina Romano. That beautiful little girl isn't yours. Madam Yvette said to Tony. So the little girl isn't mine! Tony said. With tears in his eyes. I'm so sorry Tony. No she's not. Tony started to cry. That fucking Bitch! How could she do this to me! I can see you loved this girl and her beautiful baby very much. I did. Tony shouted! And She has hurt you really bad! Madam Yvette. Said. Don't cry my son. I will help you. But as far as doing any type a spell on your genitals and penis. I can't help you on that. That is something passed down to all of the men in your family. They all have the same problem with their penis. But, What I can do is make that pretty girl laughing in my crystal ball suffer for the rest of her life! Really! Tony said. Yes! Really! Madam Yvette shouted. Okay. Do it! Please do it! Tony said. Okay. Okay Madam Yvette said. But Wait. I will need to know Tina Romano's date of birth. Madam Yvette said. Okay. It's July 26, 1996! Tony said. Okay. Tina Romano born July 26, 1996. Perfect. Madam Yvette said as she grabbed a pencil and paper on her table and wrote it down. Now I can put a curse on Tina. A really bad curse! If you want me too. Yes! Yes! Please Tony said. Wait. Wait. Wait. Tony! I must warn you, once I do this to Tina the curse can not be reversed! Or removed it will be a done deal! For the rest of her life. You understand? Oh yes! Tony said. As Mrs. Mancini listened at the curtain. Whispering to herself Oh my God! Please don't do it you asshole! I must tell Momma Romono. She said as she continued to listen. Now Tony are you still seeing Tina? Well. No! Okay. I will have to give you something for her to come back to you. Like what? Tony asked. Ah a couple of oils and a candle to burn. Okay! Okay! Tony said. That's nothing to much for you to do. But as for me. Madam Yvette said. I will do the major part! I love it! She said. Let me see! How about I make her lose her mind! Ha. Ha. Ha. I will need some of her hair. And also can make her feel hot and sweaty for the rest of her life! Sounds good! Tony said. And last but not least! I WILL FUNK HER PUSSY UP! FOREVER!!! She will never I repeat never beable to open her legs up for sex with anyone ever again! It will be to STINKY! I will give her the curse of the SKUNK! Yes! Madam. Yvette skunk her ass! Tony yelled. Okay. I will. So you must call her. Then meet up with her. And have these two voodoo oils. I'm going to give you to put on your body. Make sure your wearing these oils when in her presence. Their called. Come to me and Hot sex! Oh okay. Tony said. Now pass me that black pussy shaped candle from that shelf over there. Okay. Tony said. Now here take these oils and this pussy candle. Once you get her in your presents the oils you put on your body will capture her soul. She will go home with you and rip your clothes off! She will want to suck and fuck you so bad! And she will all fucking night. Madam Yvette said. And you better let her! Understand!

Oh hell yes! Tony yelled. Just make sure you have that pussy candle ready to light when you get her ass in your house. Don't waste time! This will all happen very quickly! Oh! On that pussy candle you must write her full name and birthday above the wax clit of the candle. Then you can write every fucking thing you want her to do with her pussy for you! Make it Snap! Crackle and Pop! Ha! Ha! Ha! They both laughed. But whatever you do Tony! Do not eat her pussy! At all no matter how good it looks to you or how great it feels to be inside of her! Understand! If you do you will be very sorry! Now after the fun time and it being a one night stand. She will spend the night with you. So make sure to cut me a piece of that beautiful hair of hers to complete the curse. I will start preparing the curse on her today. So remember Tony you must never ever touch or stick your little dick in her ever again! So enjoy! Oh! And don't forget to steal her funky panties and put them in a ziplock and bring them to me! Madam Yvette yelled. And the curse will be complete!

No problem Tony said. Okay now take these things with you. You will need all these things to use. And when your have everything I need for the curse, bring me 500$^{\underline{00}}$ cash! And the curse is done! Instantly! Madam Yvette said.

Okay I will bring you her funky panties! And some of her hair. Oh! And here's the 500$^{\underline{00}}$ cash right now. He said as he pulled the five one hundred dollar bills out of his pants pocket and slammed the money on Madam Yvette's table. I see your serious Tony! Yes I am! Good! Now go. I will see you in a couple of days. Madam Yvette said. Oh shit! Mrs. Mancini said. I have to go tell Mama Romono. Before this asshole get's to her daughter Tina. So Mrs Mancini backed away from the curtain and whispered. I'm sorry my darling husband. I can't stay to pick up my white candles for you today or stay for the seance to talk to you and my mother I have to get to Mama Romono's house.

So Latrice. Mrs. Mancini said she got out of there quickly! Debbie said. Heading to my mother's house. When she got to my mother's house she knocked on the door. My sister Tina answered the door and left out on her cellphone waving at Mrs Mancini. Pointing telling her my mother was in her bedroom. While on the phone with guess who? Debbie said.

Tony! Latrice said. Yes! That mutha fucka called my sister as soon as he stepped out of Madam Yvette's shop! Debbie said. What! Latrice said. So

Mrs. Mancini walked in and went to close my mother's front door. As she closed it she fucking seen Tony pulling up to my mother's house she didn't close the door all the way she left it cracked open and watched my baby sister Tina get in the car with Tony. While Mrs Mancini watched she said that when Tina got in his car and closed the car door Tony gave her a hug and looked at the front door with a evil smurk on his face. As if he knew Mrs Mancini was watching them she said it scared her! And she slammed the front door quickly with chill's! Mama Romono! Mama Romono! Yes! I'm in my bedroom. Mrs. Mancini! Oh! Oh! Okay! Hey Mrs Mancini. How are you? Mama Romono said as Mrs. Mancini entered her bedroom. Shaking! My mother said it look like Mrs. Mancini had just witnessed a murder! Debbie said.

What! Latrice said. Mama Romono! Please call your daughter Tina! And tell her not to leave with that guy! What do you mean? Momma Romono said. Come and have a seat Mrs Mancini.

No! I can't! You must save your baby girl Tina! She just left with the guy I just seen down at Madam Yvette's today! He is going to do something very bad! That will mess your daughter up for life. What guy? Um a! Her baby dad. Oh Tony! Yes! Yes! Mrs. Mancini said. Oh just settle down Mrs. Mancini more than likely she's trying to patch things up with him. No! Momma Romono! He is out for revenge! He was at the fortune tellers shop for a couple of hours. Getting things ready to destroy your daughter Tina! Please you have to listen to me! Momma Romono! Mrs. Mancini! Calm down! Now what is it that Tony is going to do to my daughter? Something real horrible! Is what she said to my mother Debbie said.

So Mrs. Mancini begged and begged my mother to please call Tina. If she didn't she will be sorry.

So what did your mother do? Latrice asked.

Well. She told her to go home and take two, get some rest and call her in the morning. Then my mother got out of her bed put on her house coat and begin to show Mrs. Mancini to the front door. Oh. My God! Please! Please! Call your daughter before it's to late! Please she's such a beautiful girl so young, she has her whole life ahead of her. You must listen to me! Momma Romono please! I'm listening and what I just heard is the call to God you just yelled. Momma Romono said. Please Mrs. Mancini go get some rest. And maybe tomorrow you can go down to the church and pray and get your white candles lit for your dead husband there. And stay out of those fortune telling shops! I don't believe in none of those places. Anyway! Momma Romono said.

As she opened her front door to see Mrs. Mancini out. I will see you tomorrow. Momma Romono said. No! Please listen to me! Mrs. Mancini yelled. As she walked down the steps. Tina will be walking dead soon! If you don't call her. You still have time!

"No!" Momma Romono said. As she slammed the screen door closed. Waking Tina's baby up! Cries cries! Now I must go Mrs. Mancini! Good day! Momma Romono said. Before slamming her front door. You will be sorry! Mrs Mancini yelled as she walked out of Momma Romono's yard. Voodoo is real!!! You hear me! You will hurt! Momma Romono! Mrs. Mancini said. As her voice being to crack and her eye's begin to water knowing in her heart that Tina will be a lost soul soon.

"Wow Debbie, your mother did not want to here her" I said.

"No! And to this day she hurts. She don't talk anymore". Debbie said. "She cries and cries herself to sleep behind the shit over what Tony did to my sister". Debbie said.

Oh shit! It's almost time to clock out. Debbie said.

We still have time Latrice said. So how did you all find out that your sister was out there on the streets. Girl there were people in the neighborhood coming to my mother's house. Knocking on the door. Saying Tina was on the corner. Doing some strange things. Maybe one of us should go and get her.

My mother still did not believe it. She wouldn't go. So I went. And that's when I seen her out there, and my God smelled her too! I tried to talk to her while holding my nose but the smell was to strong and she wouldn't listen. I even grabbed her hand and she pulled away. So I left. I went back to my mother's and told her it was true about my baby sister and we have a problem. A big problem! Mother she is fucked up! Debbie said.

"No Debbie please! What happen to her?" Momma Romono said.

"I don't know but I am going to find out," Debbie said.

Mrs. Mancini came here telling me something I told her to leave and I didn't want to hear it.

Why? Mother. What did she say. She said she heard that boy Tony went to the fortune telling place up the street and put a spell on Tina.

What! What fortune telling place? Debbie said. Are you talking about Madam Yvette's! I think so, Momma Romono said. Mother don't worry I'll be back. Debbie said. Where are you going? Momma Romono asked. Up the street! Debbie said. So I left Latrice I went up the street to find Madam Yvette's shop. And guess what the bitch and her shop was gone! No way! Latrice said. Yes! Way. Debbie said. With tears in her eyes. How will I tell my mother this shit! My baby sister will never be the same! She will never ever come home! Debbie said. So I went back home and broke the news to mother and she cried and told me to call our church. So someone can get over there to Tina and pray for her. So I did. It wasn't that easy. They went and prayed and they prayed for her even put holy water on her! It was to late. That mutha fucka Anthony Greco got his wish. And to this day my fucking baby sister is still out there on the streets fucked up. So this is why I say be careful Latrice you don't know what these men are capable of doing to us. Wow! I said to myself. That's some fucked up shit! Latrice said. Well it's time to clock out. Debbie said as she grabbed some tissue out of her desk. And begin blowing her nose loudly. I'll see you after Christmas vacation. Debbie said. Yes! Latrice said. So I grabbed my handbag and pushed in my chair and gave Debbie a hug. See you next year. Okay you be safe. You too. Latrice said. So we both clocked out and left. Well me and Tim are not like Debbie's sister and her ex boy friend. Beside's Tim's package ain't small! So I'm not worried about him trying to put no voodoo on me! I said to myself laughing as I got in my car and headed home. I pulled into the driveway got out the car and rushed upstairs. Ready to pray to the coco. Can never be late or miss praying to this big head spirit. So I set my things on the table and got in prayer position with my head bowed down to the floor never looking up as I begin to pray. Okay done. Now let me get on the phone and call Tim to let him know to pick the kids food up from Big Burgers instead of Rick's Waffles & Chicken. Hello Tim. Yes baby what's up? I was calling to tell you can you change the. Change what? You cancelling out on me? What did I do? What did I say? Tim said. You don't want to see me.?

No No! I mean yes! I was trying to tell you to pick up the kids food at Big Burger's instead of Ricks Waffles & Chicken spot. What! Marcus no chicken! He'll be okay. Just pick up two big burger combo's with cheese. Yes baby! Tim said. Thank you. My pleasure. And I can't wait to see you tomorrow. Girl. Tim said. I can't wait to see you too. Be ready baby you remember what time my yacht leaves. Yes I do. And my driver will be there in front of your apartment on time with the food for the kids. And his hand out to help you into the car. Okay. Yes see you tomorrow. Okay. Until then chow baby! Tim said. As he hung up.

Now I will be up early in the morning ready to hit the mall for this hot date tomorrow night. Shit! Let me check my credit cards and see what I have available to spend. Hell! I might just purchase a dress for tomorrow night then return it the next day. Ha. Ha. Ha! You know what I mean. Got to keep it clean! I just might do that. Once the coco get me rich. Fuck this wear and return shit! I will have designers in my living room measuring me so much you would think I'm a world's famous book writer. Ha Ha Ha! That's funny. Well I'm off work for the Christmas holiday. So I have all day to shop and get ready. To finally see this sexy ass ex of mine. You know my great grandmother used to say never go backwards, cause if it didn't work the first time the shit wasn't meant to be. Mind you. This is the same grandmother that felt a certain way about putting your handbag on the floor. Watch out Latrice! Well I don't think it will hurt anything taking a couple of steps backwards to Tim. Plus he was the best ever in bed. I can just image what he can do now! I'm in! Cellphone rings! Hello. Hey mom. Hey. Are you at home. Yes Marcus. Okay. My basketball practice will be over in one hour. Coach Tez. Said he will drop me and Mia off at home. Okay. I'm here. Okay. Oh and mom! What? I said. Did you? Did I cook? No! Oh man! I'll tell the coach to stop at the taco stand. Okay. I said. Bye mom. Now let me check my credit cards. Balances. I have just enough credit available to have a good time. Tomorrow. Good! I said to myself. As I got up to go turn the water on in the bath tub. So I can finally take a bath. I grabbed my things off my bed that I need. And went into the bathroom and turned the water off in the tub and took my robe off and hung it on the hook and got in the tub and laid my head back and being to relax. I began to go into a deep thought about this whole getting rich with the coco. The stories I have heard about doing voodoo was all a negative out come. Hopefully mind will not be the same. No it won't be the same why should it. I'm going to be rich I said as I blew bubbles from my hand. Laughing out loud while taking my bath. Are you alright in there mom! Huh! What. Yes. Mia? Yes were home. Oh. Okay. I didn't hear you come in. I'm sure you didn't. You were laughing to loud. Mia said. Really. I said. So there goes my relaxing in the tub. Let me get out. So I got out of the tub grabbed my bath towel and begin to dry off and get dressed for bed. I still couldn't stop thinking while getting dressed about all the negative things that I was told about the voodoo. Well I'll be alright. I'm not doing any voodoo on anyone mine is different. I said to myself as I reached down into the bath tub and let the water out. Then I walked out the bathroom and went to my bedroom and got in the bed. Hey mom! Hey Marcus. I ate a couple of taco's the coach bought me. Oh okay I will talk to you two in the morning I am tired and need to get some rest. Okay mom Mia and Marcus said. Turn the tv off before you go to bed. Okay mom. Now let me get some shut eye. I have a big day ahead of me. I have to look delicious enough for Tim to throw me on the table and eat me up! Ha Ha Ha! I can't wait! It's been a long time! I said to myself as I pulled the covers on me and turned the lamp off. Next day. Hello. Welcome to Sassy's. May I help you with something. Um. Yes the red dress in the window. Okay let me get it for you. Here you go. Good choice she said as she gave me the red dress. The devil's blood. Is the name of this dress. She said. Wow okay I said. Can I try it on? I asked. You sure can. Thank you I said. What is your name, I might ask. Abby. She said. And yours. Latrice. Okay Latrice the dressing room is at the end of this aisle to your left. Okay. I said. So I took the bright red devil's blood dress to the dressing room and tried it on. And it fit perfect! It had the best cleavage cut and it fit my body like a glove. As I turned around in the mirror in the dressing room. Hey Latrice! How's the fit? Abby asked. Like a glove! I'll take it! I said. Can I see. Abby said. Sure. So I came out the dressing room. And did alittle spin for Abby. Girl! You are on fire in that dress! She said. You have shoes to go with the dress. No. I said. Let me get you some. What size you wear? A seven. Okay. I'll be right back. Abby said. So I stood around the dressing room waiting for Abby to come back with the shoes. While waiting I started thinking about Tim, and me wearing this dress. Shit just the thought of Tim taking me by the hand and walking me to the dinner table then pulling the table cloth off the table and picking me up as I straddle his waist with both legs. Then he lay me down on top of the table and start to kiss my forehead my nose, my lips, and my chest. He just can't stop kissing my body as he continue to kiss lower and lower and lower. I can't help but say to myself when he start kissing all around and below my belly button. Shit! Dinner is served just before he kisses my! Latrice! Latrice! Huh? I said. Look at these shoes. Try them on! Abby said. Okay. So I put the shoes on. They were beautiful! These shoes were hot! Red hot! So what do you think? Abby said. I'll take them. Okay great Abby said. So I took the shoes off and took the dress off. And gave them to Abby from the dressing room. Okay Latrice. I have one more thing for you these nice tear shaded diamond earring to complete your outfit. Come on Latrice. Let me show you. Their up here at the checkout counter. Well okay let me get dressed I said. So I got dressed and walked out the dressing room to the front counter. Abby took the earrings out of the glass case and put one up to my ear. These earrings were so nice I couldn't resist. Okay Abby. I'm sold! Okay Latrice! Now I have one red devil's blood dress one pair of walking with the devil red five inch heels. And one pair of the devil's tears diamond earrings. Wow I said to Abby. What's wrong. Abby asked. Oh nothing except I feel I just went shopping in hell! What! Your funny Latrice! Abby laughed. Am I really. Yes! Your the first person that ever said that. Is she serious I said to myself. Now your dress is $500^{\underline{00}}$ shoes are $300^{\underline{00}}$ and don't forget the earrings they are $200^{\underline{00}}$. So your total is $1{,}000^{00}$ out the door with no taxes added. Cash or credit? Abby said. Credit please. Okay Abby said. So I reached into my handbag and gave Abby my credit card. As she swiped my credit card in the machine. I waited to sign on the dotted line. I couldn't help but think of becoming rich soon. As I signed my credit card receipt. Just to be shopping with a black card. And not this shiny neon color credit card that I have to keep track of my balance and make sure I don't go over my limit. Okay! Latrice your card has been charged. And thanks for your autograph. On the signature line.Your done! Okay. I said. Here's your bags. Thank you. I started to walk out the front door of the clothing store. Oh! Wait! Wait! Latrice! I forgot to give you this. What? I said. Your invitation to the devil's ball in hell! Are you serious? I said. Yes! Abby yelled. I'm just kidding it's a 75% off coupon on your next purchase. Oh okay thank you. That coupon ain't nowhere near hell that's heaven! I said. As me and Abby laughed. Enjoy. Latrice see you next time. Okay bye. Bye Abby said. Now let me calculate that was $1000^{\underline{00}}$ all together now I have $510^{\underline{00}}$ left on my credit card. I still need my feet and nail's done a Brazillin wax. Ouch! And my face made up. Let me call.

Um! Um! Ring! Ring! Ring! Ring! Who is this calling me. Mia! She knows I'm shopping! Hello! Hi mom. Hi Mia! What's up? Well I was calling to let you know that Tim had your surprise delivered to the house all ready. Aw! Really. Yes mom Tim sent so many! I don't want to know yet! Just wait until I get home and let me be surprised. But mom! Your not suppose too. Bye Mia. I'll see you in 2 more hours. Okay but mom! Girl. Got a go. Click! Now let me call. The Place For Your Face. To get my face made up. By a make up artist. Ring! Ring! Hello. Place for your face to be made. Twinkle speaking! Yes. Twinkle. I would like to make an appointment for tonight at 7:30 pm. That would give me time to pray to the coco. I thought to myself. 7:30 pm. Um! Um! Twinkle said. Hold on let me see who's available. Okay. I said. So as Twinkle put me on hold I was hoping maybe he could make up my face. For me tonight. Okay! Hello! Hello! Yes. I said. I can do it for you Twinkle said. Oh great. Thank you so much! It's my pleasure. Twinkle said. So I will see you tonight at 7:30 pm. Okay. Text me your address. Twinkle said. Here's my number 555-556-555 I will call you when I'm on my way. Okay. I said. I'm texting you my address now. I said. Okay um! I got it Twinkle said. I'll see you tonight. Make sure to wash your face with warm water. What's your name? Twinkle asked. Latrice. Thank you Latrice I'll see you tonight. Ta Ta! Bye. I said. Well that will give me time to go get a Brazilion wax. That is scary! When you're hairy. I got to get my hair straighten real quick. And finally get my feet and nails done! Then go home and take a shower and wait for Twinkle to come do my make up. And then pray to the coco and get dressed for my date with Tim. Wait for his driver. Then go get some of that good, good! Yes! I look at my watch time is ticking so let me get out of this mall I will be in here shopping soon enough once the coco grants my wish so I left Hello. Miss. What do you need done today? Well. Um. I need a full brazillion wax. Okay. Come right this way. So I begin to follow the lady down the hall. Hey go in there, door number 8 to your left. Okay. I said.

So I walked in and she begin to sanitize the table. Okay now you get naked she said and lay on this table. Oh. Okay. I said. I will be right back. Let me go get everything I need for the waxing. She said. So she walked out. I started taking my clothes off and begin to think shit I haven't had a wax in along time. Before getting on the table all my clothes were off and I walked over to the full length mirror and said to myself. What the fuck!

I turned myself all the way around in the mirror and say damn Latrice! Are you sure you need a brazillion wax or a weed wacker wax. I had so much hair on my pussy and growing out the crack of my ass. Bushy underarms and I had the nerves to be growing a mustache with a mini beard on my chin. Shit! If I would of waited any longer. I probably would of start barking at the next full moon like a werewolf. Now this is embarrassing. I said to myself as I quickly grabbed the sheet from the table and wrapped up in it tightly. I have to have this done. I can't go out with Tim like this! Okay! I'm back Ms. Lady. Alright let's get started. Okay. Well um. I need to um. Tell you that I. Go ahead and remove the sheet and lay flat on your back and raise your legs. Um okay. But I must let you know that I um. Here let me help you she said. So she pull the sheet back and screamed! What, why, why! You let the hair grow like that on your body! Why? Well because I'm single. What! No Excuse! No Excuse! That is discussing. Now Wait! Let me call the front desk. She said. Oh My God just nasty she said to someone on the phone. I need help! She screamed then smiled at me. Then she started whispering on the phone. Saying we have a scary hairy lion, tiger and bear in here. Oh my! The person at the front desk shouted on the phone. I'm in room 8. She said. Really. Yes! Come right away! Okay. Miss now you are going to need more than just a full brazillion wax. We are going to have to give you the weed wacking wax! What? What is that? I said. Don't worry we'll fix you up. Okay. Um. Well I guess. I said. So in walked two more women with their masks and gloves on, with scissors and a big hot bowl of wax and a big roll of tape. Shit! While laying there all I could think about is did I owe someone some money and I didn't pay. So they sent someone to cut me, then burn me! And duck tape me and throw my hairy ass out the back door of their business! This shit is crazy! Next thing you know one grabbed my right leg and the other one held my left leg. While the one that called them in. Put her mask on and her gloves and begin to tell the other two ladies to open my legs just a little wider and hold them tight! She said. I'm going in! So she started opening my pussy lips. Then she, Oh! Ah! OOOUCH!!! Thank you. Come again they said. As they watched me limp out from what just happen to me in there. I'm in pain! Yeah right come again I said. As I slowly got in my car ouch, ouch. Now let me get to Jaya's hair salon and get my hair straightened let me park in the back of the hair salon. I am really in pain from that stupid weed wacker wax! I walk into the hair salon slowly. Hey Latrice! Hi Jay thank god your here today. Are you booked up today? Well somewhat. Why? What you need girlfriend. Oh just a straighten. Okay don't worry I got you. Come on over and have a seat in my chair. Okay I said as I still had a slight limp. You okay. Latrice? Ah yeah. Did you fall? Yeah I fell alright. I said. As I limped to sit in her chair ouch! ouch! I fell right into that wax shop. Called It's Scary When It's Hairy! What! I heard about them! When you come in with to much hair on you. It's serious! Jaya said. Girl! That aint no lie! Mine was serious! What! Latrice your crazy. Well you can stand up girl while I straighten your hair. Thanks Jay. No problem. So who you getting all dolled up for? Um. Tim. Tim! Timothy Rose! Jaya yelled. Yes girl. So are you two serious this time. I wish. Jay. I remember he was a workaholic! And still is. I said. All work and alittle bit of play. Oh wow I'm sorry to hear that. Jaya said. Well whatever happens with it this time around I wish you the best of luck. Oh. Thank you Jaya. Your welcome you deserve it. Aw. You are so sweet Jay. Yeah Latrice I know, I know. Okay. Girl. I'm done let me grab you a mirror. Here you go. Is it straight enough? Yes. It is. I love it! Jay. Okay well let me wrap it for you so it will be nice and straight. When do you meet up with Tim? Tonight I said. Guess where Jay. Where? On Tim's yacht! You go girl! His driver is going to pick me up in a couple of hours. I heard that! Well go have yourself a ball. A ball girl? Shit! Two balls tonight! I will be holding in my hands. What! Girl you still crazy! Jaya said. Shit crazy! No Jay I am serious! And I got to go! I said. Okay. Well. I'm done wrapping your hair. So how much do I owe you? Don't worry it's on the house Jaya said. You sure? Yes. Girl. Go have fun! Okay. Yes I said. Thank you Jaya so much. Now I got to get over to Nail Town to get my feet and nails done. And I know over there I have to sit on my ass in pain! So I'll call you Jay. Yeah let me know how everything went on your date with Tim. I will. See you later. Latrice. Bye. Bye, Bye. Jaya said. Now the last stop nail town. So I got in my car and drove to the end of the block and pulled in the parking lot of Nail Town. Got out my car and walked in. Hi. How may I help you? I need my feet and nails done. Oh. Okay. Come have a seat in spa chair. We take care of you. Okay. Okay thank you. Oh you go pick nail polish over there on the shelf. Okay. So I walked over to the shelf and picked red. Ruby red! Okay thank you miss. You sit down right here in spa chair. How you like you nails? A Short set please. Wow! I love this color ruby red!I said to myself as I picked the nail polish up and looked at it. Delicious! Okay I finish you nail's miss come sit by the fan so they dry completely. Oh okay. I take your handbag for you. So I got up and sat down at another nail booth and put my fingernails in front of the fan. Where to put your handbag? The lady. Asked. That just finished my nails. On the floor? She said. Oh! No! No! No! I said. We already know about that floor shit. I said to myself. No just put it right here on my lap. Please. Thank you. Your welcome. Okay now Casey will do your feet. Now I am just about ready for tonight with Tim. I'm kinda nerves but I am ready! Let me look at the time. Oh! Shit! It's getting late. So I touched a couple of my fingernails to see if they were dry and guess what they are dry! And Casey just finished polishing my toes. Now let me get up out of here and head home. Oh god I almost forgot to pay. I opened my handbag and took the money out and paid, here you go miss. Oh thank you lady. Took my car keys out and walked out smiling and saying I have to get in this traffic and make it home to take my shower get dressed, get my face made up and pray, pray to the coco. Then be ready for Tim's driver to pick me up to meet with Tim on his yacht. Damn! Latrice. Let's go! Is what I said to myself. So I got in the car and got right into traffic. Rushing home. Shit! These people driving to slow! And I'm getting caught at to many lights! Honk! Honk! Go the light is green stop texting! Honk! Honk! I got a hot date tonight! Drive dammit! I shouted. Shit finally traffic started to move Now that's more like it! I'm two blocks away from my apartment. Hurry up Latrice! I screamed smiling, thinking about me with Tim tonight. I finally turn onto my block. As soon as I made a left into the driveway I begin to drive to the back of my apartment building to park. And Guess who I see. Miguel in his garage of course. Smiling and waving at me with a couple of people in his garage with him. So I smiled and waved back as I kept driving to the back of my apartment building. I can't let Miguel make me late for my date! I said. So I pulled up in my parking stall. Turned the car off and quickly grabbed my handbag and bags and closed and locked the car doors and headed up the walk way to get upstairs to my apartment to go get ready. But before I stepped up the stairs I heard music playing and people laughing and talking. It was coming from Miguel's garage. Shit. Let me go be nosey I said. So I began to walk to the side of Miguel's garage. And peeked in. Miguel had company! Alot company! What! I couldn't believe it! People laughing and drinking, dancing and yelling! Go Miguel! Go! Go! I looked at Miguel and he was playing limbo getting real low! Where people started shouting Miguel get low, go! Go! Get low go! Go! As they clapped their hands in such a rhythm. I just stood there and watched Miguel as he made it under without touching the stick. Yeah! Miguel you did it! Someone said. Somebody get this man a beer! Some lady gave Miguel the beer and a hug and a kiss thank you! Miguel said. As he looked right at me. Oh! Hey Latrice! He said. I put my finger up to my lips and said shh! And gave him a thumbs up. And he looked at me and smiled and gave a thumbs up back. And begin talking to the lady that gave him that beer. So I headed to the stairway of my building saying to myself. Look at Miguel having fun. That is what I will be doing having fun in a couple of hours! Yes! Butt naked fun! Ha! Ha! Ha! I got to my door and took my keys out my pocket. And unlocked my front door and walked in stop dropped all my bags on the floor. I just stood there looking around. Then I started screaming! This is so beautiful! The balloons, and all of the roses! Just beautiful! Oh my god! Let me call Tim and tell him. Thank you! Hey mom your home. Oh Yes! I said. Mom I tried to tell you when you were at the mall. What? Wait! Mia. Let me call Tim. To tell him thank you for this beautiful surprise. Aw. Damn. It went to voice mail. I'll just tell him tonight. Click! I hung up not leaving him a message. Okay. Tell me what? Mia. About this surprise. Tim sent you. Oh. I'm so glad you didn't tell me. Cause I am so surprised! It's beautiful! Hey mom! Marcus said. Let me pick your bags up for you. Okay son thanks. Oh and there's nothing in my bags to eat. Aw! Mom. Don't worry Tim's driver is bringing some food from Big Burgers in about an hour. Big Burgers! Marcus said they don't have no fried chicken! So what! Mia said. They have the best burger's in town! Boy you will be alright with a big burger combo! I said. Especially after me and Debbie ate at Rick's Waffle and Chicken House. And I seen a roach crawling to the kitchen! Like it was going to ask for a extra waffle or something. What! Yuck! Marcus said. Are you serious mom? Mia said. Yes! Very serious! I said. Wow! I still can't believe Tim sent all these beautiful full bloomed red roses. Give me one. Mia. I want to smell it. Here mom. Mmm! Smells good! Here put this rose back in the vase with the rest of the dozen. Tim sent. Shit! I'm still looking around. It is about 15 vases with 2 dozen roses in each vase. Oh. No! Look at the time. Oh! God. I have to get in the shower like now! And get dressed! That make up artist will be here soon. Plus I have to pray, pray, pray! To the coco and be ready to get picked up by Tim's driver. So let me go turn the shower on! So I begin to walk down the hallway to the bathroom. Went into the bathroom and turned the shower on and then went to my bedroom to lay my clothes out on my bed. Mia! Come see what I bought to wear. Okay. Mom coming! I started taking everything out of my bags. Aw Mom! That is so pretty! What that dress. Yes. I know! I said. And those shoes! Mom what are you trying to do to Tim. Girl be quiet! Oh Mom I hope you enjoy yourself tonight. Yeah mom me too! Marcus said. Don't do nothing I wouldn't do. Boy like what? Not eat! Mia said. Laughing! Oh no I'm gonna eat! All that fresh lobster I'm sure we'll be having by candle light. No noodles tonight with shredded cheese and ranch dressing! Yuck mom! Mia said. Stop it! I said. Oh Mia. What where you trying to tell me when you called me at the mall. I asked while tightening up my hair scarf. Um Oh, Oh Yeah. Mom didn't you say that the psychic reader said that the coco is not suppose to be in a room with red roses or balloon's and any kids. What! Well um a yes. Oh My God! I forgot! With that said. I ran into the living room! And Mia followed me. Where, what and how to move all of these balloons, and roses! Mia I have to get in the shower and get dressed. I have a make up artist coming in about 20 minutes! Okay mom don't worry me and Marcus can put some of the roses in your room and close your door. And the balloon we can take to our bedrooms and put some on the back porch by the washer and dryer. Okay! So go get ready mom. We got this. Oh okay! Are you sure? I don't want to call it off with Tim. You wont have to we both got this mom! Marcus said. Don't worry you get ready to go have a good time tonight. Yeah mom the coco can't even see those red roses or these creepy looking metallic colored balloons. Mia said. I love balloons plus I'm hungry you better not cancel Marcus said. You better let that driver bring my Big Burger combo. Marcus shut up! And grab a vase full of roses and take it into mom's room. Mia said. Thanks kids. So I grabbed my clothes off my bed and quickly walked into the bathroom. As the kids started to move all the vases full of red rose and all those shiny balloons into the bedrooms and on the service porch. I could hear those two laughing and yelling at each other. As I got into the shower. Alright out there! I yelled. Be good! Okay mom! They both said. Now as I begin to lather up with the body wash I started thinking about what the psychic reader Kwana told me. About the roses and balloons. Aw. I don't really think that little bit of time around the roses and balloons will hurt anything. I said to myself.

While washing the soap off me in the shower. Those are alot of beautiful red roses and very shiny balloons. Tim sent me. Wow! I said to myself. But still thinking about what Kwana said. Never ever reward the coco before the job is done! Because the coco will think your wish has been granted. Understand! Oh! And Latrice the coco isn't to fond of children, children, children, echoed in my mind. Oh okay! I said to Kwana. I remembered. As I turned the shower off. I quickly grabbed my towel off the towel rack. And thought to myself. Now the roses and balloons are not any type of reward or offering! Right. Their for me! Shit! that big head mutha fucka knows that those red roses are mine! And so are the metallic balloons. And the coco not being found of children. I don't have no damn children in my house. Just a couple of teenagers. So I should be just fine. I dryed off and started getting dressed. I wish I could of went back to the psychic shop and grab me some of that voodoo oil to put on me tonight for my date with Tim. Ha Ha Ha! I had to laugh at myself saying that shit While loosening my hair scarf in the mirror. Ding Dong! Ding Dong! I hear the doorbell that must be twinkle the make up artist. He is right on time! Mia, Marcus get the door please! Okay mom I got it Marcus said. Okay son! Thank you. I yelled while I opening the bathroom door. Mia walked pass me going to the front door to see who was at the door. Hey mom looking hot in all that red! Mia said. Why thank you Mia! I hope Tim thinks so too. Oh He will. He will! Mia said. Marcus who's at the door? Um! Um! Someone by the name of Twinkle! He said. Laughing. Twinkle! Mia said. Stop playing Marcus! Mia said. As she got to the front door. Oh! Honey! He's not playing! My name is Twinkle and I'm here to do Latrice's make-up is she home! Oh. Yes. Come in please and have a seat. I'll go get her for you Mia said. Thank you. Twinkle said. And you young man. Here take my make up case and set it on the table please. I would appreciate it! Twinkle said. Okay Marcus said. I must sit down and take my shoes off. I been making up faces and performing miracles all day! Twinkle said. Oh. My aching feet! Twinkle said as he took his shoes off.

Marcus went to set Twinkle's make up case on the dinning room table. While watching Twinkle take his shoes off. Marcus started frowning. Then his eyes got big! Latrice! Are you ready! For me to make you glamorous! Girl! Twinkle yelled. As he stood up and opened his purse and pulled out some house shoes. Marcus eyes were still big! As he tapped Mia on the shoulder. What boy. She whispered. Look he got bright yellow polish on his toes! What? Mia said. Uh. He sure do. And a flower design on both of his big toes! Mia said. With hair growing on both of his big toes! They both begin to look and laugh at Twinkles toes. I'm almost ready. Twinkle I'll be out in 2 minutes. I said. Okay! Twinkle said. While putting his feet in his house shoes. What's so funny? Twinkle asked. Mia and Marcus. Oh. Nothing. They both said. Yes it is. You guys keep laughing at something! Twinkle said. As he started setting up his make up kit. What is it? Just tell me. I won't get mad. I see you two looking down at my feet. Oh! Okay I know. The polish is not my color? Or is it my two big toes, that have hair growing out of them. Right? Mia and Marcus didn't say anything. And they both stop laughing. Well I didn't get a chance to wax both of my big toes. Because I been making so many people glamorous that I haven't had the time to glamorise myself. So excuse my toes! Twinkle said. Can you please! Well um! I didn't say a! Mia said. Say what! Twinkle said. Okay I'm ready. Latrice said. Okay. I will set you two straight next time! Never laugh at a make up artist! We work hard! Understand! Understand. What? Latrice asked. Oh! Just telling these two that I can't wait to do your make-up. Oh. Okay Latrice said. What happen Mia all the red roses couldn't fit in my bedroom. No mom. It was to many. I was going to ask about all the beautiful red roses you have in here. I thought I walked into the Garden of Eden. Twinkle said. No my date sent them. There's more in my bedroom. Wow! The roses are red so it must be real serious Twinkle said. Now let's get started. By the way I love your dress Latrice. After I get done with your make up you are going to knock him dead! Shit! Twinkle I don't want to do that! Ha! Ha! Ha! Latrice. Dear your funny. Twinkle said. Now close those big eyes so I can get started. Big eyes mom! Marcus laughed. Boy be quiet! Okay. Oh! Mom we have a basketball game early in the morning tomorrow. Will you be able to take me? Hell yeah! Latrice said. Be still Latrice! While I'm putting these eye lashes on you! Okay. Twinkle. Now I don't have to lie to Tim about a game. It's the truth! I said to myself. While getting my face made. I can get use to this. When I'm rich. I will wake up and just sit in a chair and get my face made every single day! Just glamorous! Costly but just beautiful. Well Latrice I'm just about done. Twinkle said. Let me get the right color for you. Out of my lip stick bag. I'm going to put something soft and natural on you. Okay. Twinkle said. Your already on fire in that bright red dress! Girl. Okay. The natural look will be just fine. I said. Okay now hold your head up and pucker your lips together. Like this. Oh! Shit! Wait did I just see that big red vase move. Twinkle said. What? My big red vase. Yes. On that glass shelf over there. I said. Yes! Yes! That big one over there. Latrice opened her eyes and looked at the vase that the coco was in. And quickly said No! That vase didn't move! You must be seeing things! Maybe you been on your feet to long making your clients faces. I laughed. No! No! No! I haven't I know what I seen! Latrice And that was that vase moving! Twinkle yelled! Whatever. I said Are you done yet? Just about. Close your mouth. So I can do the finishing touches. And get the hell out of your house! What! Look now I really don't have! Mom! Me and Marcus will be in the bedroom. Just holla if you need something. Mia said laughing as her and Marcus walked to their bedrooms. Okay. I said. I am all done. Ms. Latrice! Twinkle said. Good right on time! I said. As I thought to myself. It's about that time to pray to the coco. Would you like to see my work? Twinkle asked. You damn right! I do! Okay Ms. Lady let me grab my mirror out of my make up bag for you Twinkle said. Okay. Twinkle reached down into his make up bag and Ouch! Ouch! Ouch! He cut his finger on a pair of tweezer's while taking the mirror out and dropped the mirror on the floor and broke it. Now breaking a mirror we all know the saying to that shit right. Yeah. So. Are you alright Twinkle? Hell no! I'm not he said as he put his finger that he cut up to his mouth and begin to suck the blood from it. As the blood continued to run down the side of his finger and drip on my floor. I told him I will go get my first aid kit from my bathroom for him. As I begin to walk to my bathroom I was starting to get mad. Mumbling this mutha fucking asshole just had to cut his-self. So I grabbed the first aid kit out of my medicine cabinet and begin to walk back to the front room. Oh! Shit let me check the time. I step back and glanced at my clock in my bedroom on my night stand. Damn! The time is flying I have to hurry up and pray the coco. Tim's driver will be here in about 20 minutes! Let me help Twinkle with this first aid shit and he better not get blood on me or my dress! Twinkle come on I said. Let's get that finger wrapped up now! Shit my date's driver will be here to pick me up. In less than 20 minutes now. So give me your finger. So I grabbed his hand quickly. Ouch! Twinkle screamed. What? Why do you have to be so rough? Look here Mr. T. I have a hot date with an ex that is financially stable! Handsome and the best in bed! Wow! That sounds like my type of man! Twinkle said while softly holding his wrapped up cut finger. Well not this one! He's mine! Where done right? I said. Well. Yes. I do have something to say Twinkle said. While putting all his make up and lip sticks up. Here is your money. Thank you. Ms Latrice Twinkle said. But I also want an apology. What? I said. From who? Twinkle take your money and go please. Okay I will. But I came here to do your make up to make you feel sexy and glamorous Which I did. Yes. You did I agree. Latrice said. So what's the problem? Well those two that left out of here. Who my kids? Yes! Your children! Twinkle shouted. Were laughing at the hair on my big toes. When I took my shoes off. I don't have time to keep up with myself to much anymore do to my magic fingers making miracles with my make up as well as just glamouring most of my clients. Twinkle said. As he grabbed his make up bag and headed for the front door. I will have the both of them call you at work and apologize to you. Thank you so much.I would appreciate that. And next time you want your make up done honey! You come to the shop. If you want me to do it. Okay. Because you have some kind of evil spirit in your home! I can feel it! And I seen it move that big red vase over there! And when I tried to let you know about it. I cut myself and dropped my mirror and broke it.That's bad luck! Is what I'm leaving here with. Twinkle said. But you are living here with it in your home! And at the end of the day honey! Your going to need more than just a priest with an open Bible and a swinging cross with sprinkles of holy water walking through your house praying to get it out of here! You watch and see blam! What was that noise in your kitchen? Twinkle asked. Shit! I don't know maybe a dish just settling in the sink. Well whatever it was I'm out of here! Oh! Twinkle stop being so scary before you tinkle on yourself. Really! Anyway! Ms. Latrice. I am leaving! Okay. Thanks again. Your welcome. Enjoy your date. Oh! Don't worry I will. Okay save some of him for me! Twinkle said. As he walked down the stairs of my apartment. I love me some chocolate! Twinkle said. Melt in your mouth not in your hands! Oh! Wow! Now that I can't do! And plus he's caramel! Um! Sweet and sticky! Love it! Bye Twinkle! Bye Bye. Girl. So I finally closed my front door. Now I must pray to the coco. Let me get in position and begin to pray. I prayed. Okay. Now let me get up. Don't want to mess my dress up. Ding Dong! Ding Dong! I got it! I already know who it is. Just a minute Mr V. Okay Madam! I remember he was always on time even back then. I said to myself as I open the front door. Good evening Madam Latrice. You look very beautiful! Thank you. Mr V. I know Mr. Rose will love to see you in a little bit. Here's the food you asked for from Big Burgers for the children. Okay thank you so much. My pleasure. I will be waiting for you by the car ready to open your door. Tell the children I said enjoy. Okay. I will be out in 6 minutes Mr V. Okay I would say take your time Madam Latrice. But I cant because Mr. Rose is on his yacht waiting for you. Okay. Mia! Marcus! Yes mom! Mia said. Where is that crazy make up artist? Marcus asked. Gone! Thank God. He started tripping saying some crazy shit! Like what? Mom. Mia asked. Saying there is something evil in this house. It's so evil a church priest can't have it removed! Or an open bible. Oh. Mom don't believe that crap. Marcus said. Plus I smell food! Oh. Yeah. Here's your food. From Tim. That Mr V. his driver brought and said enjoy. Pass me my food! Marcus said. Here boy. Mmm! It smells good! Yeah it does smell good! I said.

Mom you want a couple of french fries Mia asked. French fries! I said as I handed Mia her bag of food. No! No! No! Girl. Mom have a big buttery lobster waiting for me tonight by candle light on Tim's yacht. I said. Oh. Okay. Mia said. I will be eating so much of that good sea food. Tonight! And when the coco make me rich! Ha! Ha! Ha! Oh. Mom not that again. Marcus said. With shredded lettuce falling from his mouth. While eating and talking at the same time. Boy. Shut up! I said. And both of you listen up. I shouted. As the music for the coco played very low. In between the sheets by the Isley Brothers. Which I begin to snap my fingers! And sing. Hey! Making love between the sheets. I got to go now kids! Okay. Mom. So I walked into the bathroom and unwrapped my hair. It was so straight and silky! My make up. Was Excellent! And my dress on fire! Hey you two! How do I look? I asked. Pretty! I said. While snapping my fingers and turning all the way around. No mom you look. Hot! Why. Thank you, Thank you son. Your Welcome! Now go have fun Ms. Lady! Marcus said.

Okay boy pass me my handbag off my bed. Okay mom. Oh. And Yell out my window to Mr V. and tell him I'm coming down now. I got you mom Mia said. Marcus you just get her handbag off her bed. Mia opened my bedroom window. Excuse me! Mr V. Yes. Little Lady. My mom is on her way down to the car now! Okay Mr V. said. Here's your handbag mom. Thank you son. Mia get my perfume! Okay. Mom. Which one? Um my red hot! Your red hot! Mia said. Yes! Hurry Mia! I have to go. Okay! Okay! Mom I have to blow all this dust off the perfume bottle. What? I said. Yes mom! Mia said. Shit! It's been that long! I yelled. Yes mom aren't you glad I ran into Tim. Mia said. Well. Um.Yes. Mia. I whispered. But in my mind I was yelling so loud hell mutha fucking yeah! You hooked yo momma back up! What you say mom? Huh. Oh. Nothing. But thanks Mia. I thought she could read my mind. I was so loud in it. Anyway. Now you two listen up. No staying up late. Turn the tv off before falling to sleep. No company! Oh! Man I was thinking about having a candle light dinner myself with the finest rapper! On earth. Girl! I yelled. Just kidding. Mom. Mia said laughing. Stop playing. Now don't touch the radio. Do not turn the music station at all. Don't go near the vase. Don't bring none of those balloons or the red roses out of the bedrooms. Understand! Yes. Mom They both said. Now be good. No arguing. Okay mom. Go! Tim is waiting for you I know! I know! I feel like a teenager going to my prom. Where's the gum and condom's! I said. WHAT!! Mia & Marcus said! Oops! Just kidding. Okay see you two tomorrow morning you have my number and get Tim's phone number from the caller ID. Okay mom give me a kiss and don't mess up my make up. Muah! Okay remember stay away from the coco and the radio. Got it! We got it! Okay come and lock the front door please. So I begin to walk down the stairs and walk down the drive way to the car Mr V. Opened the door for me. As I got closer to the car. While walking to the car. I looked to my left and Miguel and his brother Jose was cleaning up the trash from the party they had earlier. Miguel stopped cleaning and grabbed his beer and passed his brother Jose one. They both sat down on Miguel's patio chairs and started talking. What? I can't believe it. Miguel is actually chilling out tonight with his lil bro with no invention on the table. Wow. I said to myself. Hey Latrice looking good Miguel said. Si mucho caliente! His little brother Jose said. Muy Bonita Miguel said. Aw. Thanks guys. Have fun! Miguel said. I will! Thanks Miguel! Anytime

Latrice! Si Si. Anytime Jose said. Mmm. Latrice one day I'm going to smack it, flip it, rub it down! Miguel whispered. What did you say? Jose asked. You heard me homes. Latrice's ass! I'm going to hit that watch. In your dreams Jose said. Laughing. They both stood up and Jose was still laughing at Miguel so he started chasing Jose. Jose ran on his lawn. Hey! Not my lawn asshole! A fuck your lawn! No fuck you Miguel shouted at Jose.They both ran to Miguel's backyard. Okay. Well here I am ready to go. I said to Mr V. as I approached the passenger side of the limo Mr V. opened the door to the back sit of the limp for me and asked may I take your hand Madam Latrice. Sure Mr V. so he gently grabbed my right hand and led me into the limo. Thank you sir. I said. You are very welcome Madam Latrice. Mr V. said. As he closed the door. Wow! I said to myself this is finally happening! Me and Tim, Tim and me. Shit! I can't wait to get butt naked with him. Wait! Wait! Latrice. Slow down just enjoy the night with him first. You know that Tim's sex will always have you leaving with a great big smile on your face. And the thoughts of I will come again! and again! Definitely the best service! Ha! Ha! Ha! I laughed out loud! Is everything okay back there Madam Latrice Mr V. asked. Oh yes. I said. I took my mirror out of my handbag and begin to fix my hair. And freshen up my lip stick. And blew a kiss muah! to myself in the mirror and said girl you hot! Inside and out! I whispered laughing to myself. Were getting close Madam Latrice two more blocks you will see Mr. Rose's yacht. Really I said. Yes. Madam. Oh Shit! Let me do the smell check on myself. I whispered. Okay. So I lift my dress a little bit put my right hand between my legs then rubbed it upward and down ward on my panties. And smelled my hand. Yes! Fresh as a summer breeze. My under arms smell sweet like candy. Thanks to Pete's peppermint deodorant. And last but not least my got damn breath! I put my left hand in front of my mouth and blew in my hand. Um! Let me pop two mint's in my mouth. Now let me take a deep breath and blow it out. Now that's fresh! Madam Latrice we have arrived. Let me phone Mr. Rose. Okay. I said. While Mr V. begin to call Tim I got a little nervous. I started thinking as I begin to adjust my titties in my bra so they can greet him before I do. Now. Am I nervous because I haven't seen him in a long time or because I haven't touched a man in over 50,000 years. I mean shit that's what it feels like. I said to myself. My pussy better not be closed shut like it's really been 50,000 years! That will be very paiful! Shit! He won't be able to open it! Like they couldn't open King Tut's Tume! Ha! Ha! Ha! I said to myself laughing. Mr V. parked the limo and hung up with Tim and got out and opened my door. And reached for my right hand and grabbed it tight as I stepped out the limo. Thank you sir. Your welcome Madam Latrice. Now walk down to aisle #3 and it will be the big golden yacht with the big red rose on the side with black writing saying rose's are red. Mr V. said. Okay. Got cha! So I begin to walk towards Tim's yacht. Oh and Madam Latrice. Yes. Mr V. If you don't mind me asking what fragrance is that called you rubbed in your hands? What? Oh ah summer breeze lotion! Oh wow madam. It smell's delightful! Ha. Ha. Ha. I laughed. And said. Why thank you Mr V. I'm sure Mr. Rose will love that fragrance! Oh my god thank you very much. I said. Oh and Madam Latrice. Enjoy yourself tonight with Mr Rose. I will sir I said. I begin to walk down aisle #3 and laughed quietly to myself and said Mr V. was talking about that fresh pussy smell on my hand from the smell check I did in the limo. Ha! Ha! Ha! I couldn't stop laughing! Oh God! Let me stop laughing before my make up start running this make up cost me a fortune I can't let a tear drop from my eye's behind laughing. Mr V. is right Mr Rose will love my fragrance all over his face mouth and fingers and his! Hey baby over here Tim said. I looked up and there his fine ass was standing at the top of the steps of his yacht. Dressed to empress like always. The million dollar man! Come on! Get up here baby! I have been waiting on you for hours! Coming! Shit he ain't said nothing but a word I said to myself, I begin to walk up the steps holding on to the rail with my left hand as I got closer to him I begin to step faster up the steps making my titties bounce at him! Oh yeah. I said. Just look at him. He can't take his eye's off these titties just a bouncing! And a bouncing until I reached the top step. Tim reached out and grabbed my right hand. Pulled me up and opened my right hand and put it up to his nose and took a deep breath in my palm and begin to look me in my eyes and say Mmm! And kissed my lips and kissed my cleavage. I noticed he had a long stem fully bloomed red rose in his left hand. Here. Baby. He said. As he snapped the rose off the top of the long stem leaving enough stem on the red rose to stick in the left side of my hair. And said. A beautiful rose for a beautiful woman. Now follow me. So we begin to walk down the side of his yacht. It was so long. And so nice. Red carpet. So we walked to the back of the yacht and he asked me to close my eyes.

So I did. He held my hand and led me downstairs. When walking down the stairs I could hear some music playing some of that good R&B music! Shit! I love this! I said. As I walk down the last step. Tim said. Open your eyes baby. So I did. Wow! It was breath taking the whole set up. Was absolutely beautiful. The red roses. The candle light dinner the bottle's of PI. Were on the bar like 50 bottles. 1 bottle of P.I is 1,000$^{00.}$ So we will be drinking that good shit all night! No dreaming this time. I said to myself. You want a drink baby. Yes! Yes! Yes! I do. Okay baby I got you. Tim said. So he walk me over to the table and pulled my chair out for me so I sat down and crossed my legs. Okay. Two drinks coming up. He said. As he walked over to the bar and grabbed a bottle of PI. and two glasses and begin to walk back to the table. When walking back he aimed the PI bottle towards the ceiling and POPPED! It opened. Tim set the glasses down on the table and begin pouring PI. into our glasses. Shit before he could stop I picked up my glass and started drinking it. And so did he. Are you hungry he asked. Yes I am. I said. Okay. So he picked up a bell on the table and begin to ring it! And his cook came out. Maria! Maria! Look who's here with me tonight. Oh! My God! Ms. Latrice! How have you been? Maria said as she gave me a hug. Mr Rose had missed you so much! Maria! Shhh! Tim said. Really! I said. Yes he was looking for you lady! No way! I said. Si Si! Maria said. No! Tim said. Maria go bring in our food. Salad's first! Okay! Okay! Mr. Rose Maria begin to walk back to the kitchen and yelled it's the truth Ms. Latrice it's the truth! So you been looking for me? Huh? I asked. Well something like that. Tim said. Why? Because you miss me! I said. As I got out of my chair and walked up to Tim and politely pushed him down into his chair and sat on his lap straddling him holding both of his hands up and started kissing him all over his face and then start tongue kissing him. And then got up, and sat back in my chair and begin to drink some more PI. I see you still know how to take control baby. Always I said. Always! Mr Rose Here are you salads Maria said. Ms Latrice would you like a side of fresh fruit? Sure Maria thank you. No problem. I bring. Maria said. Hey! Maria! Yes Mr Rose. Bring the sweet apple dressing out. Okay! Damn baby. I see you emptied that glass of PI. Yes did. I said. This time just give me my own bottle. And I will turn it up like it's my last! I swear. I swear. I will! Well let me grab two more bottles. Shit! This is a celebration! Tim said. So Tim walked over to the bar again and brought back two bottles of PI. And aimed both bottles to the ceiling and POP! POP! Those bottles like shooting a pistol in the air making me scream! As he laughed and blew me a kiss. Then gave me a bottle and he took the other one and begin to drink it out the bottle. I set my bottle on the table. And sat down in my chair. I begin to take my high heels off leaving them under the dinner table. This is going to be along night. I said to myself as I grabbed the bottle of PI. and started drinking it from the bottle. Here's your fresh fruit Ms. Latrice. Maria said with my famous apple dressing enjoy I will be back with your dinner plates. Lobster and hot butter sauce on the way! Maria said. Thanks. Maria. I can't wait I said. I am so hungry. I'm going to eat some of this salad. Pass me that apple salad dressing Tim. Here you go baby. Thank you sexy! I poured the dressing on my salad and grab my fork. I'm feeling a little tipsy and hungry. I begin to eat my salad. Mmm! This is delicious I said. Is this made from scratch? Yep! Tim said. It's Maria's mom's old pico green apple mexican dressing recipe. Really. She ought to bottle this. I told her that many of times Tim said. But Maria made a promise to her mom before she passed away that she will never sell or market her recipe. Aw! Well we are the lucky one's we get to taste it. I said. Yeah we are Tim said. How about this fresh fruit. I said as I grabbed a piece of watermelon and poured some PI on it and ate it. Then started drinking out the PI. bottle like it was a bottle of cold water after running a couple of laps. Mmm! I picked up my fork and started to pick up more fruit from the shiny glass bowl and eat watermelon, melon, cantaloupe, Mmm! Pineapple! Yeah! We all know what's been said about pineapples right? We'll see if it's true later on tonight. Mmm! Mmm! Sweet! Oh. Here's a strawberry Tim. Want this in your mouth? Hell yeah! Put it all in my mouth Tim said. Okay! Oh! Wait pour some of that platinum ice drink all over it first and let it drip from the strawberry then come put it in my mouth! Well alright I said. So I picked up the biggest strawberry out of the shiny bowl pulled the leaves off and stuck my fork in the top of the strawberry and held it over my salad plate and started pouring the P.I. all over the strawberry and said open wide as I begin to lean towards him on the dinner table and stuck the big juicy wet strawberry in Tim's mouth now bite down on it I said. As I pulled the fork out of the top of the strawberry. I set the fork on the table. And begin to lean and put my left knee on the table and scooted closer to him. I then put my mouth on the top of the strawberry and bit down on it and started to chew and suck on the strawberry slowly until I reached Tim's lips. Mmm! Tasty. I whispered as I left Tim only one small piece of strawberry in his mouth to chew. I then begin to stick my tongue in his mouth and kiss him making him swallow that piece of strawberry whole. He begin to cough while swallowing the piece of strawberry. Are you okay I asked. I stop kissing him and looked him in his eyes. And wiped some of the PI and strawberry liquid from his mouth. Yeah baby I'm fine he said. You sure? Yes! Baby! Yes! Now give me some mo suga! Tim said. Mmm! Okay. So I started kissing him again grabbing his right hand placing it on my left breast. Caress it baby, rub it! I whispered. Squeeze and pinch my nipple, then run your finger across my nipple get it hard so you can see it through my dress I demanded! As I continued to kiss Tim. Okay baby! He said. Damn you still feel so soft he said. Oh really I said. Yes baby he said as he begin to stand up from his chair and took his left hand and grabbed me by my right hand. He started to slowly pull me across the dinner table knocking the salad plates to the floor! Kissing me as I got closer, Tim's kiss became more passionate! Causing my body to tingle all over. He then started to kiss and lick my lips, chin and neck. And down my chest between my cleavage. Taking his right hand from my breast. Pulling my dress and bra strap off of my shoulder! He gently grabbed my left breast out of my bra and starred at my erected nipple. He licked his lips as he starred.

Damn Girl! Tim said. As he begin to lick and kiss and softly suck my nipple! Shit! That feel good I whispered to him thinking in my mind I just want to scream so loud right now I needed this Tim! Thank you! Thank you! You like that he asked. Hell yes! I said in my mind. To him I said oh yes real camly. I want both titties baby. So he took his right hand and pulled my right breast out of my bra and dress. Oh! Yeah! Those big pretty titties belong to me he said as he laughed. Kissing each one of my nipples muah! Muah making my right nipple hard. Aw! Shit! I can't wait! I said to myself. So as he put both of my breast together and rubbed his face all over and between them. He grabbed his bottle of platinum ice and turned it up over my breast and. Hey! You two dinner is served! Maria said as she walked in on us. I quickly put my breast back in my bra and dress fix my hair and scooted off the table with my head down. As Tim sat down and looked at me he whispered Latrice. I looked at him as he winked his eye and blew me a kiss and said I am going to beat that pussy up! You hear me girl? I didn't say anything because I knew what he was saying was true! He was going to beat this pussy up up up! With that million dollar pipe he's packing! Ms. Latrice here's your lobster plate! And yours Mr Rose when I come in I see you two were having dessert already Maria said. Tim laughed and said Damn Maria your right we were about to have dessert! Tim said I was about to have the hottest cherry pie with the cream all over my face and my fingers. Oh my god Mr Rose I don't want to hear this Maria shouted. Okay Maria but wait! Tim said Latrice was about to have the biggest banana split with cream all over her face then put her cherry on top! Tim! I said. Oh my! Mr Rose your loco! Maria said as she begin to walk back to the kitchen fanning her face with her hands. Enjoy your lobster plates! If you need anything else I will be in the kitchen sir! Just ring your bell. Maria said. Ring! Ring! Ring! Tim rung the bell before Maria could enter the kitchen door. Yes Mr Rose Maria can you grab me two bottles of PI from the bar before you go back to the kitchen! Yes Mr Rose. Maria walked over to the bar sweating and blushing she grabbed the two bottles of platinum ice. Tim got up and took the two bottles of PI. from Maria's hands and shook them and aimed them up to the ceiling and POP! POP! POPPED! Them! Bottles! Sending Maria running into the kitchen screaming saying! I yei yei! Holding her right hand over her heart running quickly into the kitchen talking in Spanish. Puto! Coolo! Negro! I love you to Maria. Tim said laughing. Whatever Maria just said it didn't sound nice. I said. Who care's what she said. Baby she's just the help! Tim said. Tonight is about me and you baby! Now let's eat some of this good lobster with this butter sauce and drink, drink, drink some more! Here you go dinner is served he said as he pass me my plate and a napkin for my lap he then sat down to his plate. Wow! This Looks delicious! I said. I begin to break me a piece of the lobster meat and dipped it in the butter sauce then ate it. Wait! Wait! Latrice. Tim said. Let's make a toast. To my new job position! And making my bank account's even fatter! He said as we both raised our opened bottle's of platinum ice up high to the sky! Oh! And don't forget to us! And that good tight pussy of yours I will be eaten and beaten til morning! Tim shouted as we tapped our bottles together and begin drinking! Tim slammed his bottle on the dinner table he was becoming very tipsy. Now let's eat! He said. I begin to grab another piece of my lobster meat and dipped it in the butter sauce. Give me that piece girl! Tim said you come get it! I said so he got up and stood in front of me then leaned down and I placed the buttery lobster meat in his mouth. As he licked my fingers. Stop it Tim! I said let me eat. I said. Okay baby. I took another piece and started to eat it. Tim got up and sat down by his plate and started to eat his own lobster. This is good! I said. Ring! Ring! Ring! Ring! My phone is ringing! I reached over the table and opened my handbag and looked at my caller ID on my cellphone. Oh It's the kids. So I answered it. Hello Mom yes hi Mia. What's up? Well me and Marcus are to scared to go to sleep. What do you mean? I said. Mom we keep hearing weird noises. Weird noises? Yes mom! Like what Mia? Well we are in the living room and Hey baby is everything okay with the kids Tim asked in the background. Yes Tim their fine. Oh okay. Now what were you saying Mia? Mom it sounds like someone is in the freezer beating on some African drums. What girl? I started to laugh. Stop playing Mia! I'm not playing mom. I'm serious. The sound keeps getting louder and louder than it stops! Mom it's true Marcus said in the background. What! I don't believe you guys. It's late. Now try and get some sleep! You two we have to leave early for the basketball game in Oakwood tomorrow. Okay I said. Yes mom. If you need to call me back you can okay. Okay mom. Goodnight you two. Bye. So the basketball game is really early..... Tim said. Yes it is I said. And I have to pray to the coco as well. You what? Tim said. Oh. Ah! Nothing. Oops! Shit! I almost said something it must be this liquor talking. I got to be more careful! Let me finish this lobster. I see your done with your lobster. Hell! Yeah! babe and ready to get up and dance. Tim said. How about you? Hell yeah! I said. Let me dip this last piece of lobster meat in the butter sauce. No! Baby allow me. Okay I said. Tim took the lobster meat from my hand and dipped it in my butter sauce. About two to three times and said open your mouth baby. And I did. He put that tender buttery piece of lobster in my mouth as the butter sauce dripped onto my chest. Tim began to lick it off! And started kissing my neck and chest. Damn! He is so sexy! I just want to Ring! Ring! Ring! Ring! Wait Tim. It's the kids again. Yes! Hello mom! Yes Marcus. Mom your radio you left on is going crazy! What do you mean? Marcus. Mom the radio is turning the channels from the oldies station to the mexican station playing it loud. Then hip hop! The mexican station, R&B station then back to the oldies you hear it? Mom. Um! A little bit. Hey baby I'll be on the dance floor waiting for you Tim said. Okay. I Whispered. Hey Maria! Ring! Ring! Ring! Tim rang that bell again like he was crazy. Come remove our dinner plates Tim yelled he was still ringing the bell loudly. Okay! Okay! Coming Mr Rose. Take two more bottles of platinum ice to the bar by the dance floor and put them on ice. Clean up everything and your free to go. Okay. Mr Rose. Gracias. Maria said. We will be porting out in about 20 minutes. I know you don't like the ride. The water makes you nauseous. Si! Maria said. Mr Rose. Enjoy your night. With Ms Latrice. I know you missed her very much Maria said. Tim gave her a thumbs up. I still was on the phone with Marcus. Okay Marcus. If the radio keep changing stations just unplug it! Okay. Mom I will. Okay. I'll see you in the morning. Okay mom. Marcus said. Sorry to bother you. That's okay son. Bye mom. Bye, Bye. After hanging up the phone. I started to think about what Kwana said. About the coco only workers to oldies music. And I just told Marcus to unplug the radio. Well shit the radio wasn't even staying on the oldie station. Oh well I'll deal with that shit in the morning! Let me get my ass up here to the top deck with this fine ass young man! So I grabbed my handbag and turned my cellphone off and put it inside my handbag took the bottle of PI and turned it up and killed it! Mmm! Mmm! I started to walk and stumble up the steps to the top deck. I could hear the music playing loud. I walked to the back of the yacht and there were two doors made of glass with golden knobs. Damn! This shit is nice I said to myself. I opened the doors. And there was a big dance floor in there with Tim standing in the middle of it with his shirt off telling me to come in. As I begin to walk towards him the driver of the yacht got on the loud speaker letting us know that we are about to leave the dock now. And head out on the water. There was no sign of Maria she finished up and got the hell out of here. I went to set my handbag down at the wet bar. She did leave the two bottle's of P.I. on ice like he requested. Shit! I can't wait to get rich with the help of the coco and the voodoo to live like this. Wow! Hey baby! Get over here Tim said. While clapping his hands twice. Diming the lights and the song changed to R. Kelly's Bump and Grind. O my God! This was our song. Here I come! I said I quickly walked up to him and begin to rub and touch his chest and he grabbed both of my hands and begin to kiss my fore head and turned me around and bent me over "doggy style" and palmed both titties from under my arms and started grinding my ass like he did back then. And I loved it. Pulling him closer. Just to feel this man up on me like this was amazing! I wanted him so fucking bad! This dancing shit was teasing me! I swear! As the song played Tim took his hands from my titties and started to raise up my dress from the back! Do it! Do it! Is what I was saying in my mind. As he continued to lift my dress up he whispered to me I know what you want and I know what you need. And I got it right here baby. Okay! Then give it to me please! I said to myself. He finally got my dress up my back and almost over my head then the music was interrupted. Mr. Rose you have a important call on line one. What! Are you kidding me who could that be? He said. Baby let me take this call don't move I will be right back. Oh Sure. I said. As I stood straight up and put my dress back down. Well the song went off. And oh. Here he comes. Hey babe the phone is for you. Me? Yes it's Mia. Mia! Again. There's a phone over by the wet bar. Okay. Press line one. And when you get off the phone bring those two bottles of PI. to me. Okay. Now what do these kids want now! I picked up the phone and pressed line one. Yes Mia! Hello mom! Yes. Mom your not going to believe this. What now? Mom the smoke detector keep going off! What? Why? I can hear it. Mom it smells like someone is in here smoking cigars and no one is smoking. What! I know you two aren't smoking. What mom! Hell no! What? I said. Oops. I mean no mom I don't like cigars or cigarettes! Mom something aint right! What? I can't hear you Mia that smoke alarm is very loud! I know mom! Go take the batteries out of all of the smoke detector until I get home in the morning. Okay hold on mom. Let me do it now. Where's Marcus he's on the couch with a pillow over his head and ears. Oh! Okay I'll hold on! Okay Mia said. While being on hold with Mia. I turned around to see what Tim was doing he was sitting down waiting on me. Blowing kisses and put up two fingers at me and put his tongue between his two fingers pointing at me with another finger, I just smiled and put up the okay sign with my fingers. Hello mom you there. Yeah. Okay I took all the batteries out. I know I don't hear anything buzzing. Now what about the smoke smell? Just open a couple of window's. Okay mom see you in the morning. Is that it. I said. Yes mom! You sure. Oh! Mom what if what that make up artist Twinkie! Not Twinkie, Twinkle. Well whatever. His name is, was right! About what? Something evil in our house. No Mia. Okay mom just saying. We'll talk about it in the morning okay. Yes mom. Okay. Goodnight and don't let the evil spirit's bite. Mom! Just kidding. Goodnight. I hung up. Tim! Yes baby tell them to take message's on anymore calls. You sure? Yes but the kids Tim said. They'll be fine. I'm sure they got your number from my caller ID. But I told them if it's an emergency. That's okay babe. No what's okay is finishing what we started on the dance floor. I said as I grabbed the two bottles of PI and walked back over to the dance floor. Hey Capitan can you hold all calls and take a message. Okay thank you. Sure Mr. Rose. Okay baby no more interruptions. He said as he walked back to the dance floor. Now! Where were we he said as he clapped his hands twice dimming the lights again and another song begin to play. Adore by Prince. As the music played Tim begin to walk up to me and touch my face with both hands kissing my lips and all over my face. Then pulling me close when he took his hands from my face then putting them around my waist. Whispering in my right ear. I don't think your ready for this! Now are you? He asked. Yes! I said in a cracky light scared voice. All I being to think about after he asked. That was what my co worker "Debbie" was saying girl he is going to knock the dust out that pussy Ha Ha Ha! I can hear her laughing so loud in my head! As if she was here dancing too. That's crazy! So we danced the whole rest of the song. Then Tim walked over and grabbed that famous bottle of platinum ice that we have been drinking all night! Shit! I am faded! And ready to get naked with this sexy million dollar man! I said while watching Tim pop that bottle of PI and took it to the head! Dam I said to myself. Then he came out of his pants! Yes! Dropped them right down to the floor and stepped out of them. Then turned around and smiled. I stood on the dance floor and laughed. And said Tim you crazy! Just when I said that. The song Downtown begin to play by SWV. Perfect I said to myself. So as the song played I pointed my finger at Tim and said get over here as I moved my hips to the music. Tim begin pointing to his chest and moving his lips saying who me? And I knotted my head up and down. He then picked his pants up and placed them on the chair. And started walking towards me with the bottle of open platinum ice in his right hand. The closer he got to me I begin to get butterflies! He wouldn't stop looking me in my eyes. It kind of creeped me out so as he stood there in my face. I begin to dance a little bit on his drunk ass and took two steps back and turn around and kept dancing. He then took two steps towards me and grabbed me and pulled me to his chest then took one step back and just starred into my eyes again for a good minute. I said to myself Latrice you better keep looking into his eyes. Don't show no fear or submission. If you do. He is going to take yo ass down! Physically, mentally and emotionally! I can't handle it! Was the last words I said the last time we hooked-up. Never let a man hear you say that! You will be setting yourself up! Did you say something baby? Huh? Oh ah no! I said. Good! Now raise both your arms up for me. Okay. So I raised my arms up and he set the bottle of PI. on the floor and begin to slowly pull my dress up and off of me. Leaving me standing there in front of him in my panties and bra. As the song Downtown by SWV continued to play. He picked up the bottle of platinum ice with his right hand and held the open bottle over my head telling me to close my eyes and open my mouth! And take your bra off! Tim whispered. Shit! Think I didn't. Un-hook my bra and threw it on the floor. Now close those big pretty brown eyes baby. And open those big powdy lips for me. Tim said. What are you going to do? Shh! He said as he put his finger to my lips. Just do it. He said okay. Tim begin to pour the bottle of platinum ice on top of my head it ran down my face into my mouth. As he poured the entire bottle on me it ran down all over my body.

That drink ran down every crack, scratch, lump and bump on my body! Leaving me freezing standing in a liquor potal. Tim! I yelled. Shh! Baby don't worry he said calmly I got you. Muah! Muah! He begin to kiss and lick my face & my chin. Keep your eyes closed he said. I got this! As he continued to kiss, lick and suck the liquor off my body! All I could hear is the words to that song playing by SWV. As I kept my eyes closed the hole time feeling good! "Keep on doing, doing what your doing til you feel the passion burning up inside of me." Is all I heard. As he licked and kissed my chest and sucked the wetness from my nipples. Oh Tim! What baby? That feels so good! I said. Yeah baby then I must be doing something right he whispered. When he begin to lick my stomach. Then stick his tongue in my belly button! Oh God! Now he's going below the belt! 1 2 3 kisses as he pulled my wet panties down under my panty line with his teeth! Muah! Muah! Muah! Tim I said. Don't stop. I begin to get very hot! And wet! As his soft lips continued to kiss my hairless pussy. He wouldn't stop pulling my panties down using both hands to pull my wet panties down off my ass. While pulling my panties down Tim begin to rub and caress my ass. Got damn this man is the bomb! I said to myself. Now he finally got my panties rolled down to my ankles. As he stayed on his knees. Telling me to step back as he took his hands off my ass. All I could think to myself is whatever he tell me to do. I am so ready to do it! Now step out your panties! Tim said. And I did. He aint said nothing but a word! Panties are off. He still stayed on his knee's in front of me just looking at this fat wet pussy! So you like what you see? I asked. Hell yeah. Now bring that pussy to me! Okay. I said as I walked up two steps closer. Putting my pussy lips right on his lips. Damn girl. Just the smell of it! Tim said. Aw. And the taste of it He said. He started to kiss my pussy lips and stuck his tongue in between my pussy lips. Just Licking and Kissing and gently pull sucking my clit! Oh my goodness! I whispered an moaned I just stood there like a block of ice starting to melt! All I could do is stand there! It felt so so good! I couldn't move! I listen to Tim. Damn! Baby! Mmm! Smacking! Kissing muah! And softly sucking my clit! Oh! Shit! Wait a minute! No! No! No! He said. Shhh! He whispered as he begin to stick his middle finger up inside of me.

Now I'm shaking! feeling so good! I swear it has been so so long. Just that one finger felt like his whole hand and arm was inside of me with that one finger tickling my uterus! I couldn't take it! My knee's begin to buckle! Got damn you Latrice! You can't let him take you down like a wounded horse! Come on Latrice! I said to myself. As I begin to slowly lose my grip with my feet on the floor as he continued to eat my pussy and put his middle finger in me! Okay! Okay! Tim! I said as I slid down to the floor in a open split position! Damn! He got me! As I sat on the floor. His mouth stayed locked in my pussy and his finger going in and out of me! Oh! my god this man is the best! I begin to take my legs and wrap them around his neck tightly! To slow him down on all that pleasure he was giving me. I just couldn't handle it! Shit! Aw! Wow! Tim! Stop it! I said as he pushed my body all the way down on the floor with his left hand. Holding me down! Watching me as I squirmed and made faces leaving me speechless once again! Bringing tears to my eyes as I bit my bottom lip! He continued. I could feel the biggest orgasm inside of me laying in wait! To just explode! Oh my god I uttered. It's coming! Tim! I am trying to hold it back! I said. You better give it to me! Tim said. No! Yes he said. Right in my mouth!

Come on Latrice Baldwin! Tim said. As he sucked and licked and kissed and even spanked my pussy non stop! You ready? I said. Hell yeah! Give it to me! Tim yelled. Oh! Here you go! Aw Aw! Tim! Here you go! Damn! Baby! Mmm! Mmm! He said. As he took his face out my pussy with my juices all over his young handsome million dollar making face! And he pulled his finger out of me. It was so wet! Look girl! He said. To me as I layed on the floor dazed. Look at what. I said. This! He took the finger he pulled out my pussy and begin to lick my juices off of his finger! I love to taste you that pussy still good! Tim said. As he started to pull me up and take my legs from around his shoulders. And put them around his waist. And putting my arms around his neck lifting my drunk big orgasm having ass up! As I layed my face in his chest. Kissing it! Muah! Telling him thank you I really needed that. I know baby I know. Tim said. As he held on to me. He carried me into this beautiful bedroom with windows from the ceiling to the floor. Wow! I said to myself. While opening and closing my eyes. I am so ready for this life. Tim gently layed me down on this giant round bed full of big fluffy pillows. I just layed my naked ass back on the soft fluffy pillows and felt like a queen. The red rose fell from my hair onto the pillow. I picked it up and held it in my hand. Tim walked over to the double doors to the bedroom and closed the doors and turn the lights down low. I begin to think as I held the short stem red rose in my hand about what Kwana said about the roses. And the coco. Could that shit be true. Maybe. The kids were calling saying some crazy shit! Or maybe not. This is my first time out leaving them by themselves overnight. Hum! I'll see when I get home in the morning. I said as I leaned over and set the rose on Tim's night stand. And layed my head back down on the fluffy pillows on his bed. Shit. I begin to get tired. All that drinking and the big orgasm. I thought to myself I started to dose off as Tim started to walk back over to the bed. He got in the bed from the foot of it I continued to dose off. I can hear the music still playing as the song changed to Janet Jackson's anytime. Now that's my song. Now when Timothy Rose rich handsome young ass is making love to you while listing to those lyrics to that song. You will be hooked and put to sleep. Hey! Hey! Hey! Baby. Hey. I said. As I looked up at Tim on top of me in a push up position. You ready Latrice baby. He whispered. Um! I ah. You um. What? Tim said. As he kiss my lips and said put your legs on my shoulders baby. So I can give you what your came here for. Okay I whispered. And put my legs up on his shoulders locking them tightly. Knowing that this plumber is about to lay some pipe! I said As he processed to go to work! All I can do is fall deeper into those fluffy pillows and close my eyes and enjoy the ride with the music playing. Straight indulging into ecstasy!

The next morning. Waking up to kisses on my back and whispered in my ear. As I layed in the bed with Tim in a spoon position. You up baby he said. Um. Yes. How you feeling? He asked. Happy. Hurting with a hang over! O yeah! He laughed as he continued to kiss my back and neck. What time is it? I asked. I'm Thinking about the prayer to the coco. Well it's a about. Ah about what? I said. I sat up fast. Hold on baby I didn't forget about you getting home early this morning for Marcus basketball game in Oakwood. Tim said as he grabbed my right arm. Oh okay. Damn. Baby calm down. I got you. Shit you got me thinking you got a husband at home that I don't know about. He just don't know the coco is like my husband I have to be in before sunrise and before sunset I said to myself. Well do you? Do I what? Have a husband I don't know about. No! If I had a husband do you think I would be here with you? We both looked at each other and said hell yes! And started laughing. You sure you don't want to stay for breakfast Latrice? I can have Maria whip up something real quick. Like some Belgin waffles a side of fruit with some freshly squeezed orange juice. Wow that sounds good. But I can't stay. Okay baby I tried he said as he pulled the covers back all I seen was his early morning big hard dick standing straight up as he grabbed his robe from off the floor then got his sexy naked ass out the bed and put the robe on and tied the belt to where the head of his dick look like it was peeking out of his robe.I laid in the bed just looking at that dick sticking out his robe as he walked around the bedroom looking for nothing. Shit I can't lie I would love another round but the thought of the coco was going through my mind. Tim where's my dress, my bra and my panties? Oh don't worry baby I'll go get your things. He said. As he opened the double doors to the bedroom. And walked out and I will call my driver Mr V. he yelled so he can be outside waiting for you. I don't want you to be late for Marcus' basketball game. He yelled. Yeah! I said you know how Marcus is about basketball. Yes I do. Tim said. Hello hey V. Can you be outside in about 15 minutes for Latrice. Sure Mr. Rose. Thank you Tim said. Then hung the phone up. He grabbed my things and brought them in the bedroom to me okay here's your dress he layed on his bed. Your bra. And your panties. Oh Wait! Wait! Wait! The panties stay with me he said he put his head through them and wore them around his neck. Oh and here's your handbag. Oh shit can't forget that. Come on give me my panties! I said. No baby I got up out the bed and stood in front of Tim naked bending over reaching for my bra he just stood there and watched then I heard here baby let me help you so he grabbed my bra and put my dress over his shoulder and took my hand and walked my naked ass over to this full length mirror. And stood behind telling me to put my arms out so he can put my arms through my bra straps well at least that's what I thought he was about to do. Instead he put my bra over his shoulder on top of my dress. And started pulling my hair back behind my ears and my neck and started kissing my neck and shoulders. Watching me in the mirror he started caressing my breast and rubbing my nipples As I stood there looking in the mirror at him. Saying to myself. Got damn you! Mr. Timothy Rose! He continued to kiss my neck and my shoulders and my back. I just stood there still looking at him in the mirror I watched him take both of his hands on my pussy lips using his left hand and fingers to hold my pussy lips open he used his right hand and fingers to gently rub and wiggle his fingers all over my clit. Oh god! Causing my clit to start pulsating and get enlarged from his fucking touch! Aw Shit! I can't do this I said. No Tim I whispered I have to go he stopped kissing me and begin to whisper in my ear. Just a little bit baby Damn! I said. No. Why baby look at you I can see it in your eyes you want more he said and you know what he wasn't lying I did want more I could see his big hard dick starting to peek out the opening of his robe again he seen me looking at his dick in the mirror so he begin to poke and rub his big hard dick all over and between my naked ass he continued to play with my clit and all in my pussy while standing behind me Why! This mutha fucka here! Got this pussy feeling great! I said to myself as I couldn't be still! And I couldn't take my eyes off him in that mirror even if I couldn't stand still that shit he was doing was looking so good to me in that mirror I mean finger licking good! Mmm! Mmm! Shit Tim ah ah what time is it now? I asked. You know I have to go. Yes I know baby it's still early he said I can't be late I said. I know baby. I know. Just let me show you something real quick. Aw! What? I said. Look at this baby in the mirror what I'm about to do he said. You hear me. Yes! I hear you okay now watch me this will only take a minute Tim whispered as he took his fingers out my pussy his fingers were dripping wet my clit enlarged Shit! I was so ready to get fucked! So you teasing me this morning! Tim shh! He said just keep looking in the mirror at me. So I did. But I start feeling a little frustrated, because he had stopped playing with my pussy something that makes me go crazy! Play in my pussy I said to myself. You watching baby he whispered to me again while blowing a kiss at me in the mirror muah! he turn me to my right side in front of the mirror. And slightly bent me over with his right hand and stood behind me with the head of his hard dick still peeking out that robe it was standing right at my pussy hole as he stood behind me wait a minute Tim started taking his belt a loose with his left hand letting that robe drop to the floor. Giving me a full right side view of that big delicious dick! I couldn't stop looking at it. I got to have some of that! I said to myself I don't care right now. If I make it home late to pray to the coco but I do care about Marcus basketball game. Shit I swear this man got me feeling like Ms. Gi Gi with her light color candles on her altar! Mr. Timothy Rose with that big hard dick standing behind me is definitely a got damn NEED!! You want this dick baby? I see you looking at it he said. As he turned his body to the mirror and shook that big pretty hard dick at me in the mirror in a side to side and circular motion. Blowing multiple kisses at me as he grabbed his dick and started to stroke it with his right hand from the shaft to the head at me!

And I watched as the pre-cum dripped to the floor like honey! Straight! Out that fat mushroom shaped head Damn! You so nasty! I shouted! You want this dick baby? Tim whispered. Hell yeah! I said. Give it to me! He turned back to the right and walked up behind me and said I don't think your ready for this dick. Oh no. I said. No. He whispered. Stop talking and stick that big steel bat inside of me and beat this pussy up! I said. Well okay. Tim said. Then give me that pussy! You aint said nothing but a word! I said and bent my ass over and backed my pussy up to the head of his dick bumping my pussy hole on the head of his dick with all that pre cum on it looking sticky like syrup and sweet like it to wait a minute baby he said. Let me open that pussy. Tim took both hands and spread my pussy open and looked at my pussy hole as it stayed puckered and ready for Tim to slide that big hard mushroom head dick inside me. Ready! Latrice

Baldwin for all this dick? Tim asked. I been ready I said. Really. Tim said. Oh God! I said to myself. I'm up this morning with a little hangover. He stuck that dick in me fast and gently and started stroking take that dick Latrice! You can do it!Is what my mind kept playing over and over and over in my head while he was fucking me I begin to moan and say his name ah Tim! I watched in the mirror from my right side as he gently pushed and pulled deep into my pussy on his tippy toes gripping my ass tightly making sure that dick stay deep inside and secured in this pussy in and out,out and in is all I felt. Got damn! This feels so AMAZING! I said to Tim. As I continued to moan uncontrollably he continued to fuck me! Just working this pussy yes he still is the best I ever had I couldn't take my eyes off the mirror still I had one eye open and the other eye shut. I could see my juices just shining that big hard dick up! Mmm. what a sight to see. Ah Yes Latrice! He yelled. You still got that BOOM, BAM, BOMB, POW, PUSSY! What? I begin to roll my pussy and shake it on his dick! Leaving his rich ass speechless! Ha! Now shut your mouth and take that! I said. Aww! He moaned my pussy started to get real wet. We both listen to my pussy smacking on that dick. Smack! Smack! It sounded so good and it felt good we both moaned and groaned until Tim shouted. Ah! Baby! You hear that? That is the sweet sound of success! You like that sound! I asked. Ah! Hell! Yes! He yelled. As he slapped my ass! And asked me are you hot! Baby you hot! Are you hot? Aw yes! I said. he continued to stroke this pussy faster and faster I got something to cool you down is what he said just before he came and Aw! Ou! Ouch! What the fuck! He stuck three of his fingers in my ass!! Just taking your temperature he said as he came inside of me. He started laughing! Aw! That was the shit!! He said did you see your face in the mirror when I stuck my fingers in your ass that was a mugshot picture you look like you just got caught stealing something he said as he pulled out and went to wash his hands still laughing As he walked into the bathroom. I stood there in front of the mirror and said to myself. That finger shit through me off! Now I'm mad!

Marcus has a basketball game. I have to pray to the coco. Now I'm running late. I have to go Tim! I yelled. Okay! Okay! Here I come. I stayed longer to get some fingers up my ass! And not get my rocks off this morning! Wow! Smart move Latrice. I said to myself as I grabbed my bra and dress mad as hell. You need some help baby? Tim said. Oh! No! I said.

I got this! Okay. Well here take this he threw me a hot wet wash rag to clean myself up. No shower action. Tim said. I can wash your body from head to toe for you. I can wash your hair too. He said as he winked his eye at me. No! No! No! Tim. This wash rag is just fine until I get home plus I have to go! I said while cleaning myself up. Then putting my bra and dress on. Where's my panties? I asked. Your panties? Yeah! Where did you put them? Baby those panties are mine I am keeping them. What! Stop playing I said I'm not playing baby Wait! I got something for you Tim said. Here take this he said as he reached into the top drawer of his dresser. He took my right hand and put a 100^{00} bill in it and closed my hand and kissed my lips. Then whispered. Go buy you four or five pair of panties. Okay. Baby well okay. I said as I smiled at Tim. I'm sure my driver is outside waiting for you. Are you ready to go? Tim asked. Yes I'm ready I said. Oh! And here I have something for you too. Oh! Yeah. What is it? Close your eyes and open your hands Okay Tim said. I drop the wash rag in his hands that I just cleaned my ass up with. What! He said as he opened his eyes. Why thank you I'll keep this with your panties. And everytime I think of you I will rub my face with the wash rag and smell your panties. Ha! Ha! Ha! Your crazy Tim. No! I'm serious Latrice. Oh! Really. I said. Yes! Really baby. m Wow! I said to myself. I'm ready to go Okay. I will walk you out why thank you sir I said. As I grabbed my handbag off the night stand opened it and put that 100^{00} bill in there that Tim gave me and I closed and zipped my handbag up put it on my shoulder I looked on the nightstand at the red rose I took out of my hair and set on that nightstand. I picked the red rose up and held it in my hand I reached down to pick up my shoes. Don't worry baby I'll pick up your shoes so Tim grabbed my shoes Oh! Wait baby let me get you one of my suit jackets out the closet for you to put on it's cold out this morning he said so he reached into his closet and pulled a silvertone suit jacket around me here you go this should keep you warm he said as he looked down at my hands and seen the red rose in my hand he took it from my hand and put it in my hair on the left side and said for a beautiful woman we begin to walk from the bedroom through to the dance floor room his assistant was waiting for him at the bar good morning Mr Rose, Mr Rose! You have two meetings today. I booked your flight you have one hour to get ready to go she said as she look down at the opening of his robe he quickly closed it and said okay. Mr Rose your car is ready to take you home you must get ready sir! Okay! Okay! Tim shouted while holding his robe closed let me walk my girlfriend out he said to his staff while looking me in my eyes. Did he just say his girlfriend I shouted in my mind! Yes! But wait remember he was and still is a very busy man look he's flighting out of town in a hour I don't know where he will be Okay Latrice this looks like this is the end of the line until we meet again my girlfriend I see Mr V. got the door open waiting on you. Mr V. you make sure you have that heat on in the car for Latrice. Don't worry I do sir I do and drive her home safely Mr V. I will sir I will okay baby like I said this looks like this is the end of the line yes I know I said Well baby here's your shoes I wish I could carry you down these stairs and to the car but I got to get ready to catch this flight plus you know I'm naked under this robe we wouldn't want my pipe to peak out at Mr V. while carrying you don't these stairs cause I know before I get you down all these stairs my dick will get hard! Before we get to the bottom step oh no we don't want that I said I can walk down by myself okay So I'll call you in a couple of days Tim said okay I said we started kissing mmm! Girl if I could wake up to this with you everyday. Muah! Muah! Muah! kisses I would really love it really I said yes really Latrice Tim said well until next time we meet chow baby yeah bye Tim Mr Rose! Mr Rose! Come on your going to miss your flight! His assistant yelled behind us okay Rita! Okay! Now Mr Rose! She yelled. Okay baby got to go, their calling me I know I said so I walked down the stairs and Tim went back into his yacht I then walked down the #3 aisle and to the parking lot. Where Mr V. was waiting for me by the car with the door open. Good morning Madam Latrice. Good morning Mr V. he grabbed my hand and I got into the back seat of the limo Mr V. closed the door. I put my seat belt on opened my handbag and took my cellphone out and turned it on Mr V. started the car and begin to drive off I couldn't stop thinking about Mr. Timothy Rose damn! I said to myself as I turned my head and looked out the back window of the limo at Tim's yacht as Mr V. drove further and further away from the dock I begin to sigh as I turned my head back around okay Latrice! Don't start that catching feelings shit again I said to myself you do remember what happen before right hell yeah that fucking job of his had him just up and leave me like he had another woman on the side and that really fucked me up I couldn't eat and I couldn't sleep and I really couldn't stop crying behind that man I was like a dope phein and Mr. Timothy Rose was my fix I swear I promised myself that I wouldn't let this happen to me again with him or any other man I guess I must of been telling one of my fantastic lies to myself. Because I feel myself once again feeling the same way I did before about him. Ring! Ring! Ring! Ring! Good morning Mia. Morning mom! Finally you turned your cellphone on did you get me and Marcus messages? Well um no mom we left you messages all night really yes mom we sure did! Marcus yelled in the background let me talk to mom! Hold on mom Marcus wants to talk to you hello mom yes Marcus are we going to make it on time to my basketball game this morning in Oakwood? Yes son I will be home in fifteen minutes Okay Thank you! Marcus said. Oh! Mom. I wanted to tell you that I was just playing that day when I said bring back a evil spirit. I didn't think you really was going to do it! Do what? What are you talking about? Marcus. Um. Oh. Nothing. Just forget it. Marcus said. I'll tell you later. Yeah. Okay. I said. Anything else. Yes! Mom ask that driver to stop at the donut shop for us. Okay. I will see. Tell Mia I will be there soon. Okay. Bye mom. Bye Bye. After hanging up with the kids. I asked Mr. V. If he could stop at the donut shop. So he did. As we pulled up to the donut shop. I told Mr V. can he go get a dozen glazed donuts with two small carton's of milk. I reached into my handbag to give Mr V. the money Tim gave me. And Mr V. said don't worry I will pay for the milk and donuts. Thank you Mr V. I said. As I put the money back in my handbag and waited in the car. While waiting I begin to check my messages, twenty five messages! What the fuck! I started to check a couple of the messages. Beep! Mom pick up your phone! Me and Marcus can't sleep we keep hearing beating noises coming from the kitchen. Beep! Next message. Mom! This is Marcus I'm scared to go in the kitchen and I'm hungry! Beep! Okay. I have heard enough! I said as I hung up my cellphone. They heard some beating noises in the kitchen? Oh god. My kids are crazy! I said. Mr V. walked back to the car with the box of donuts. I opened the door. Here you go Madam Latrice. Mr V. said as he gave me the box of donuts. Thank you Mr V. Your welcome. He said. As he closed the car door. After Mr V. closed the car door. I set the box of donut down next to me on the seat. As we began to leave the parking lot of the donut shop. I started thinking about last night with Tim. Shit! I truly needed that! Plus that early morning too! Damn! I just couldn't stop thinking about it! But wait! Thought of what my co worker "Debbie" said. About her sisters boyfriend keeping her panties and doing voodoo on her to wear she lost her mind. And Debbie saying you don't know! Who do voodoo! That's why I don't have a man. I rather be by myself. Debbie said. Shit! I don't know how she do it I said to myself as I laughed thinking about all those different vibrator's she told me she had. Wait! A minute. I did let Tim keep my panties! I whispered to myself. Damn! Latrice! Really I don't think Tim has time to do voodoo on me. He's always working. So I'm not going to worry about that. Shit! I wonder what time it is. I said. As Mr V. pulled up in front of my apartment. Mr V. double parked put his hazards on and got out to open my door. He opened my door and reached for my right hand. So I grabbed the box of donuts with my left hand and Mr V. helped me out. Well Madam Latrice this looks like this is the end of the line. I hope you enjoyed yourself. I did Mr V. I said as I stepped out the car. Laughing to myself saying yeah. I had a good time up into Tim stuck his fingers in my ass! I still don't know what that was all about. Anyway I told Mr V. thank you. And drive safely as he got in the car and begin to drive off. I stepped onto the side walk and started to walk down the driveway to my apartment with my shoes and handbag on top off the box of donuts. So as I continued to walk down the driveway. I noticed that my neighbor Miguel didn't have his garage up. That's odd. I said. Usually he's up and out at this time of morning. Maybe he still sleeping. So I begin to walk up the stairs to my apartment and got to the door and was to tired to get my keys out of my handbag. So I rung the doorbell. Ding! Dong! Ding! Dong! Who is it? Mia said. It's me mom! Okay. Mia said. She opened the door. Hey mom! Hey Mia. Mom is that you? Marcus said. Yes! Son. Come get this box of donuts Marcus! Donuts! Marcus yelled. As he jogged into the living room. Dressed to go play his first basketball game in Oakwood City. I see you ready to go. Yes! Mom. He said as he grabbed the box of donuts from me and set my shoes on the floor and my handbag on the coffee table. Mia had closed and locked the front door. I see she was dressed also. They both were ready to go to the basketball game. What time is it I asked. I knew it was getting late because it was well passed sunrise when I got out of the car. Okay kids your going to have to step out I have to pray to the coco. I'm late on praying. Okay. Mom. Mia said. And mom hurry up we have to go. I'm starting in the game. Okay. Okay. Just go! So they both walked out. So I walked to the hallway opened the closet door and grabbed the pillow I use for my knee's when I pray to the coco. So I placed the pillow on the floor. Before I got ready to pray I looked around and some of the red roses and balloons were still in the living room. Shit! We have to get that stuff out of here. So I got on my knee's to pray. I put my head down and begin the prayer and then the chanting. As soon as I completed the chant. Ou! Ou! Ou! I screamed. Something hot! And blood red dropped on my back! Ou! I quickly got up! I seen that red rose that Tim stuck back in my hair fall on that pillow I put my knee's on. As I ran into the bathroom. I quickly turned on the shower and took my dress and bra off and jumped into the shower! Mom! Are you okay! Mia said. No! I don't know! What happen! Mia said. I don't know Mia! Get me my towel! Okay. Mia walked into the bathroom and brought me my towel. I grabbed it and wrapped it around me. Help me out the shower Mia. I said. Okay mom. So I got out the shower. Mia turned the shower off. Mia is there something on my back? Let me see mom. I moved my towel down to my butt! Mom! What happen! Mia said. You got burnt! I got burnt? Yes! It's blistered let me get some cream from the medicine cabinet to put on it. I turned my back to the mirror to look at my back but I couldn't see the burn. Here mom. Mia gave me a small mirror from the bathroom drawer. As she grabbed the cream for burns for my back. I took the small mirror and looked through it and I could see that my back was really burnt! Mia started putting the cream on my back. How in the hell did I just get burnt like that. Now this is crazy. I said. What? Mom. Mia I don't know what just burnt me. So you don't know what could of burnt your back in there like that. Wait a minute mom! Me either! Mia said. While putting a big bandage on my back. Okay mom I'm done. Do you want me to go get you some clothes to put on mom? Mia said. Yes. Please. Okay. So Mia walked out. Oh my god! My back is burning. Here you go mom. Thanks. Mia I have a question were you and Marcus just playing around on my phone leaving those messages. No! Mom. It was really some creepy things happening here when you went on your date with Tim. You can ask Marcus. Really. I said. Yes mom. Watch. Marcus! Mia yelled. Wait let's talk about it in the car on the way to his basketball game. Oh okay. What do you want Mia? Marcus said. Are you ready to go? Yes! I been ready! Okay let's go. I said. As I slowly put my shirt on over my blistered back.

In the bathroom. Now I'm ready to go. But first I need to go see what could of burnt me. So I stepped out the bathroom and walked into the living room and started looking around to see if something was leaking from the ceiling or just from anywhere. After looking around I didn't find a leak anywhere in my living room. So I picked up that red rose and my pillow from the floor. The rose was dead. And the pillow didn't have anything on it at all. That was blood red. I knew it was blood red because it splashed in my hair when it burnt my back. I even looked at the vase the coconut is in and didn't see any signs of a leak from the vase. I know I'm not crazy. I said to myself. Shit! Something burnt me! I have a blistered back. Shit! Let's go! Mia and Marcus. I yelled. Okay! Mom were coming let me grab my basketball out of my room. Marcus said. I'm ready mom. Mia said. Okay. Let's take all these roses and balloon's out to the trash can out back. On our way out. Okay I'll start taking some down now. Mia said. Okay I'm right behind you. Come on Marcus! Come grab the last two set of roses. I got it. So we took that stuff and threw it out. And got in the car and left. I got on the Freeway. Into the carpool lane. To make sure we make it to Marcus game on time. Okay you two. What really happen when I went out with Tim. Well. Mom it was like a horror movie Marcus said. I was to scared to go in the kitchen! It sound like there was a African drummer in our freezer. Sending signals to his african friends in africa. What! Really. Mom the drumming got louder and louder to where I had to cover my ears with my pillow. Am I lying Mia? Marcus said. No! Your not. It was stuff falling on the floor. The radio was changing stations and it smelled like someone was smoking a cigar and no one was there but us. Mia said. Mom. We are not lying it was some scary stuff going on in the house. And it seem like it was taking so long for daylight you know sunrise! Marcus said.

I know Mia said. Mom next time can you please just send us to your brother's house. I rather stay there and eat nuts and berries then stay home with no one here with us. Okay I said. As I got out the carpool lane to get off the freeway. Hey mom I was just playing when I said bring back a evil spirit. Marcus said. Ha Ha! Boy your funny. No mom. I'm serious. Marcus said. I'm not laughing at all. Okay. I wont leave you home alone again. Thank you! They both said. So we made it to the Oakwood gym. I let Marcus out right in front. While I parked the car. Mia grabbed his water bottle and ran into the gym after I parked. So I locked the car and started walking to the gym. My back wouldn't stop burning. I still didn't know what burnt me. There was no signs of anything dripping. That's crazy! I said to myself as I entered the basketball gym. Hey mom! Mia yelled from the other side of the gym. Over here mom I saved you a seat! She said. Come on! Okay coming! So I walked around the basketball court as the game started. I quickly went to my seat and before I sat down. I looked at Marcus and he look at me and he smiled as I gave him the two thumbs up. The whistle blew! And the game started. So I sat down next to Mia and we both clapped and cheered for Marcus and his team. The game went on to the second quarter. Marcus team was leading by two points. I begin to go into a daze. I started thinking about the shit with the coco. I haven't seen any results yet! I said to myself. It's just been weird things happening. That shit with Kwana and that fucking coco just might not be real. Cause I have been praying and chanting my ass off! Day and night and night and day! So what, if I prayed to the coco a couple of minutes after sunrise. That aint shit! Bonk!! The bell rung! Oh! Shit! I yelled. Are you alright mom? Mia said. No! That bell scared me. Well it isn't halftime. Weren't you watching the game. No I dazed off. I said. Oh mom. What's the score I asked. Marcus team fell back six points. Oh! No! I said. Mom I'll be right back Mia said. I'm going to take Marcus his water bottle and go get me a soda and some popcorn. Do you want anything? Mia asked. No. I'm fine. Okay. Mom. I'll be right back. Okay. I said. Hurry back! I will. Mia said. So I watched Mia take Marcus his water bottle as he sat on the bench and waved. At me. Then I waved back. Bonk!! There's the bell for the third quarter to start. I see Marcus sitting down for this half. And Mia haven't made it back yet. Damn. I wonder what Tim is doing. He's probably on the plane. On his way to close a deal. Like always. It don't even seem like I just was with him a couple of hours ago. Hey! Mom. Huh? I'm back Mia said. As she sat down in her seat. You sure you didn't want anything mom. From the snack area. Mia asked. No. Mia I'm okay. Okay. Oh? Look mom! Marcus team scored two points their catching up! Mia said while stuffing buttered popcorn all in her mouth. Look! It's the forth quarter and the coach is putting Marcus back in. Yes! I said. Go Marcus! Score to win! Mia said. So their in the last quarter and both teams are going hard in the paint! It's back and forth. The other team has the ball he shoot's! And misses it! Now Marcus team has the ball the guy shoot's and it goes in! Yeah! Now it's down to the wire! The game is down to under 45 seconds on the clock! The other team has the ball! Number 11 has the ball dribbling and moving across the court! Oh! Shit! I said. Marcus grab the ball from him. I yelled. Mom! Look Marcus stole the ball and dribbled and moved quickly down the right side of the court and dribbled as the time was going fast on the clock 15 seconds. The crowd was screaming shoot it! Some were screaming miss it! I was just screaming! Because I knew my son was going to.... He shot the ball and ladies and gentlemen he made it! Yah! Mia yelled. That's my boy! I yelled. Marcus turned around and gave us a thumbs up! Just before his teammates grabbed him and picked him up and chanted Marcus Marcus! Then they all went into the locker room. Mia and I waited for Marcus to come out. We stood next to the bleachers by the boys locker room. While everyone else started to leave the bleachers. Finally the crowed was leaving the gym. Do you see Marcus yet? Mia. Let me see. Yes! Is that him? He's coming out the locker room. Good! Game! My man! Someone said to Marcus and padded him on his back. Thanks. Marcus said. Hey Marcus! We went from standing next to the bleachers onto the basketball court meeting up with Marcus in the middle of the basketball court. Good job! Son. I said. While giving Marcus a big hug. Thanks mom. You did that my brother! Mia yelled. Giving Marcus a high five. Then hugging him. This cause for a celebration! I said. Let's go eat. Marcus said. Okay! I say we go to Paul's Pizza! Yes! The one by our house. I said. Yes! Marcus said. Let's go! So we walked out the gym and headed to the car. I got on the freeway. And we made it to Paul's Pizza in ten minutes. Come on Let's fine a good table. I said. And order! Marcus said. Okay. Hi and welcome to Paul's Pizza may I take your order. Yes! Marcus said. We want a extra large thick crust assorted meaty pizza. Okay. Oh! And three large drinks. Does that complete your order the lady said. Yes. I said. Your total is 25.10 okay. Here's 30$^{\underline{00}}$ I said. Here's your change and your number is 47. Okay thank you. Sure she said. Enjoy your meal. Thanks. I said. Now let's find a seat. So we walked over to a round table and sat down. Mom. I'll be right back Marcus said. I have to use the restroom. Okay. I said. Well Mia my back stop burning. Thank God. Aw. Mom. That was weird what happen to you. Yeah. I know. I'm back. Marcus said. Where's the pizza! It's coming Marcus. Yeah boy! We know your hungry! Mia said. Sit down. I said. Okay. Okay. But they better hurry up with that pizza cause I am hungry!

Number 47. That's us! I said. I'll go get it. Okay. Mom. Number 47. Here you go ma'am. How many plates do you need? Ah just three. Here's your plates. Enjoy. Thank you. I said. So I walk back to the table. Marcus! Grab these plates! I said. Okay mom. Marcus grabbed the plates and I set the big hot pizza down on the table. Let's dig in! Marcus said. As he reached for a piece of pizza. And started eating it before he could put it on his plate. Ou! It's hot! Marcus said. Boy slow down! I said while smacking his hand. Ouch! He said. Marcus go get our drinks please. Okay mom. Well Mia I guess we can go pick up a Christmas tree tomorrow morning. Okay mom. Here's your drinks. Marcus said. Now let me eat! I'm so hungry! Marcus shouted. As he grabbed another piece of pizza. Well you two you know I have to get back to the house and pray to the coco. Oh. Yeah. Mom I'll go get a to go tray for the pizza Mia said. Okay. It is getting late. I said. So Mia brought the tray and a bag and packed the rest of the pizza up. Marcus! Mia yelled. What? Just one more slice. Okay get it Mia said. Thank you girl. So you two ready to go. Yes. Mom. Okay. So we left. Got to the house I drove down the driveway. There's Miguel. Mom. He's waving at you. Mia said. Oh! Hey I said waving my hand at him as he kept waving. As he stood out in his front yard talking to a well dressed man with a briefcase. Hey mom. I wonder who's that man Miguel is talking too. Mia said. Shit. Probably somebody looking at something he made. Huh. Yeah. Marcus said. He stay making something in that garage everyday. I know. I said. We all laughed. Then I turned my engine off. And got out the car. Don't forget that pizza! Mia. Marcus said. Boy! I got it! So we walked upstairs and I unlocked the front door and we walked into the house and the music was on playing the oldies station. Did you leave the music on Mia no! You Marcus? No! I didn't turn it on. Maybe your coco thing did it! Marcus said. That coco like oldies right. Oh! Shut up Marcus. Mia yelled. Yeah! Your right Marcus. I said. Maybe I left it on. I said. As I looked up at the big red vase on my glass shelf. Thinking to myself. I still don't know what burnt me this morning. Anyway let me lock this front door. Maybe the radio just came back on after having a little electrical problem. Well both of you clear the room so I can pray to the coco. Okay mom they both said. So I walked to my bedroom and set my handbag on my dresser and took my shoes off and went to the hallway closet and got my pillow I tossed the pillow on the floor in front of the glass shelf. Shit! I'm kinda scared to bow my head down after getting burnt by what? I don't know. Well I have to pray if I want to be rich right. So I go on my knee's and bowed my head and being to chant and pray. While praying I couldn't concentrate. The radio was on and it begin to play loud. So I said the chant and the prayer really fast. So I could go turn the radio down. But when I finished the radio was no longer loud. It turned down. Hmm. That's strange. I said as I picked up the pillow from the floor and walked to the hallway closet and threw the pillow into the closet. Okay! Mia, Marcus I'm done! I yelled. Okay mom! I'm about to take a shower Marcus said. And get some sleep. So I'll be ready to go get a Christmas tree in the morning. Okay son. Well you better hurry up boy! Mia said. I need to take a shower too. You sure do Marcus said. Boy you need a shower! More than I do. Yeah right! You do! Hey you two! Stop it! I said. Marcus go take your shower and Mia go get your things ready for the shower. Okay mom. Mia said. So we all took a shower and called it a night. The next day I'm up early I prayed to the coco and made me a cup of coffee. I sat down in the living room waiting on Mia and Marcus to get dressed so we can go get a Christmas tree. While waiting I started thinking to myself. Shit! I have been praying for awhile now and I haven't found a lucky penny on the ground yet! I said. As I looked up at that bright red vase. I'm going to give it alittle more time. Kwana did say up to 90 days. Mom! Were ready to go get our Christmas tree. Okay. Let's go. I said. So I grabbed my keys and handbag and headed out the door. Marcus closed and locked the front door. So he did, we got in the car and left. Mom. There's a place about eight blocks down that are selling Christmas tree's. Mia said. Okay well let's go there. I said. Let's sing a Christmas song. Marcus said. Okay. What song I said. Um! Jingle Bells' Marcus said. Okay. So we all begin to sing. Jingle bells jingle bells, jingle all the way. O! What fun it is to ride in a one horse open slay. Hey! Here's the place mom. Over here to the right. I see it. I said. So I made a right turn in the christmas trees parking lot. We stop singing and got out and walked over to the tree's. I see one mom! Mia said. Do you? Where? Right over here! And it's already flocked. And its about 6 feet tall. I don't see it! Marcus said. Right over here boy! Mia said. Okay. Let's walk over to it. I said. See look mom it's beautiful Mia said. Oh yeah. That one is nice. I said. Excuse me lady are you interested in that tree your looking at? Well. Um. Yes I am. Okay let me grab the tag off it for you. By the way my name is Edward. But everyone calls me Eddie And your name is? Latrice. Okay Latrice this tree is eighty five dollars. Oh okay. Does that fit your budget? Eddie asked. Yes! That's no problem. I'll take it. Alright. I just wanted to make sure your getting the tree for christmas you all want Eddie said. This is the tree my kids want. Right. Kids. Yes! Mom we want this tree. Mia and Marcus said. Eddie we will take it. Okay, Latrice will you like it delivered? How much more will it be? I said. Well. Um. How far do you live from here? We stay eight blocks from here. Oh! Oh! Okay. Well I'll tell you what I will throw in a free delivery for christmas okay. Why thank you Eddie. My pleasure Merry Christmas. Eddie said. Now come over to my desk to paid for your tree and write down your phone number and address so we can get this tree delivered to you tonight! Okay. Ms. Latrice. Yes! So I paid for the tree and wrote my phone number and address down and took my receipt. Then we left. We drove back to the house. I told Marcus to get the Christmas ordiments out the closet for the tree. When we get upstairs. Okay mom. So we got out the car. And walked upstairs excited about trimming the tree tonight. I hope the tree comes before I have to pray to the coco. Pass me the keys mom. Marcus said. I tossed him the keys and he opened the front door. Now go get the christmas decorations Marcus. Mia said. I am! Marcus said. Be careful don't break nothing Marcus! I said. Alright mom I won't. So Marcus took out all of our christmas decorations and we went through all the boxes taking everything out for the tree. All the christmas lights. Marcus plugged them in to make sure they were still good to use. And they were. So we put all the decorations together for two hours. Then the phone rung. I got it. I said. Hello. Yes. This is she. Okay. Thanks Eddie. Bye, Bye. Okay the tree will be delivered in twenty five minutes. Yay! Mia said. Now hold on you two I have to pray to the coco before they get here. Okay mom. Marcus said. Mom. I will be so glad when your done with that coco thing. Mia said. I don't really think that was a good idea mom. What girl! The coco just chose to work slow on my wish! I guess. Now get out of here so I can pray! Then we can decorate the christmas tree. When it get's here. Okay. Mom. Mia said. As she walked to her bedroom. Now let me get my pillow out the closet real quick. Set it down and I prayed. I got up and put the pillow back in the closet. And thought to myself. I hope what Mia said is just how she feel about this today. Cause at the end of the day I really do want to be rich! Ding! Dong!

Get the door Mia. Okay. Mom. So Mia answered the door. It's the tree mom! Okay. Coming. I'm not going to worry about this shit with the coco. Right now. I'm just going to enjoy the holidays. Where do you want them to put the tree. Mom! Oh, oh right next to the living room window. Okay. Marcus! Yeah mom! The christmas tree is here. Okay. Here I come. I gave the tree guy a tip. Thank you miss. Can you sign right here. Sure. I said Okay. Merry Christmas. And Merry Christmas to you to sir I said. As I closed the front door behind him. Are you ready to decorate the tree! I shouted Yes! Let's do it. So Marcus grabbed the christmas lights and got a chair to stand on to put the lights around the tree. It took us three hours to decorate the tree. I am so tired. But the christmas tree is beautiful. I want you to turn the christmas lights on that christmas tree Marcus! Let's see. Marcus said. When Marcus went to plug the christmas lights and all the electric went out in our apartment. Mia screamed! O Shit! What the fuck just happen I said as I walk to the kitchen to grab a flash light. When I got to the kitchen door. The electric came back on. What the hell! I said as I walked back into the living room. Marcus just leave the lights on don't turn them off. Okay. Mom. Should I unplug the radio. No! No! Remember I have to keep that on for the coco. Never unplug that! Okay. Okay. Mom. Are you okay Mia? No mom. I really want you to get rid of that vase. It gives me the creeps. I can't do that Mia. I paid a lot of money for that coconut in that vase. Okay mom. Just forget it! I'm going to bed. Mia said. Me too. I said. Not me. Marcus said. I'm hungry! Got to go find me something to eat. Okay now son, make sure you clean up your mess. And turn all the lights off. Except the christmas tree lights. Okay mom. Marcus said. I'm going to lay down. So I walked to my bedroom and laid across my bed and dosed off. I slept for about two hours. I was startled out of my sleep by the radio playing loud. What the fuck! I said. So I got up. Marcus! Is that you turning that music up like that I said. I walked down the hallway and entered the living room. Marcus! Is that you, are you still up? Marcus never answered. The music turned down. Mia? Are you up? Still no answer from neither one of them. So I turned around and started to walk back to my bedroom. Soon as I begin to walk down the hallway I heard something fall and break in the living room. I quickly turned and looked and it was a glass christmas ball that fell off the tree. Shit! It scared me! It sound like someone grabbed it off the christmas tree and threw it to the floor. Let me clean it up. So I walked to the kitchen and got the broom and grabbed the dust pan and walked back into the living room turned the lamp on and started to clean up the broken christmas ball up off the floor. That's strange when I picked up the dust pan and looked at the christmas ball the broken christmas ball still had the hook on it so how did it fall off the tree? I said to myself. It begin to get cold in the house. I grab the broom and the dust panand took them back into the kitchen. I dumped the dust pan in the trash can and set both the broom and dust pan back on the service porch. Then walk back to my bedroom. Oh god why is it so cold in here. I stopped in the hallway and turned the heater on. Then changed my clothes, putting on my gown and getting in my bed under the covers. Thinking to myself. How did that Christmas ball fall off the tree. And it still had the hook on it.

So the next day I'm up I prayed to the coco and I'm ready to go shopping for christmas. We have a couple of days until christmas anyway. Mia! Marcus! I'm leaving I'll be back in a couple of hours okay! Okay mom! Marcus come lock the door! Here I come. So I'll see you two in a couple of hours. Okay mom! Marcus said. Oh. Marcus last night I heard some noise in the living room so I got up to see what it was a christmas ball was on the floor broken. Did you hear anything? No. I made me something to eat and went to sleep. Oh okay well lock the door. Oh! Mom don't forget to tell Santa I want a new basketball for christmas. Okay Marcus I will. See you later son. So I walk down to the car got in and backed out the apartment driveway. While backing out I see Miguel putting his Christmas lights up. He waved at me as he stood on his roof with the Christmas lights in his hands. I waved back and continued to back out the driveway. Slowly. Okay all clear for me to back out onto the street. So I'm on my way to the Milleniium Mall to shop! Let me take the freeway. I get on the Freeway it is bumper to bumper! Let me just take the streets then. So I got off the freeway at the next off ramp. Okay the mall is about ten blocks away. It is so much traffic on the streets to. Everybody is Christmas shopping today I said as I waited in the right turning lane to get to the mall parking lot. Shit. Let me park in valet. That way when I get rich with the voodoo they will already know who I am I said as I laughed. So I pulled up in valet. And the parking attendant quickly opened my door. Why thank you! I said. Now that's what I'm talking about. Here's your flat rate ticket. I took the ticket and looked at the price. Damn! Shit! 25^{00}. Did you say something miss? The parking attendant asked. Oh! Oh! No! Okay enjoy your shopping. Shit! I mumbled. I better hurry up and get rich! I said while pushing the elevator button. The elevator opened and I got in thinking and saying to myself. Shit Latrice your on a budget. So shop lightly, now that I can do I only brought two credit cards. Second floor the elevator voice said. That's me! I said as I made my way out of the crowded elevator. Okay. Let me go pick Mia up a couple of outfit's. The cherry phone 7 with a couple of these pretty phone cases. And a gift card to Glit Glam beauty bar. For 150^{00}. Okay now let me shop for Marcus. Let me go to Sport Spirit! Shit these bag are heavy! I know when I get rich I will have my help with me. Anyway let me see I walk into Sport Spirit and I'm looking for the basketball area. Hello did you need some help? Miss. Ah yes. I'm looking for the basketballs. Oh. Okay. You go straight down this aisle and make a right and you will find all our basketball items. Oh alright thank you. No problem. So I begin to walk down the aisle and turned right. Wow! Let me grab a couple of arm sleeves, head band and six pair of basketball socks. And two knee pads and what else oh! Some basketball shorts. Okay this should be it! So I begin to take everything to the check out counter. Did you find everything okay miss? Um. Yes. I think. Well I see you have all this basketball gear. Did you need any basketballs as well. The cashier said. Oh! My God! Yes. I do need a basketball! Can I run and get it? I said. Sure miss. Okay. So I went back to the basketball area and looked for the ball size for Marcus and grabbed it and went back to the counter and paid for everything and told the cashier thank you very much! Sure miss no problem. Merry Christmas. Merry Christmas I said. While grabbing all my shopping bags. Now I have to get some wrapping paper. So I walk back into the mall so I can get some wrapping paper. Let me see. Okay I see Rita's Wrapping Paper five shops down in the mall. That would be my last stop. So I started walking in the crowd on the second floor it was really crowded people were shopping. Wow! This shit got me sweating! Okay here it is Rita's Wrapping Paper Shop. I stepped in. And seen so much beautiful wrapping paper. It was very hard to pick. Oh. Here's some solid colors. Red and gold. So I grabbed four rolls of that wrapping paper. Buy three get one more free is what the sign said. So I did good. By buying those. Merry Christmas come again. Now let me head to my car. I begin to walk over to the elevator and press the down button with ten other people waiting on the elevator too. Oh! God! I said to myself. I'm just going to have to be squished. Cause I'm not waiting for the other elevator to come. Ding! The doors opened going down is what it said. I quickly pushed my way in and two or three other people did too. So I asked some one close to the door to push B1 the valet level. And they did as I stood towards the back of the elevator. Next to this handsome nice dressed guy with a small bag with two handles. The elevator door open and said first floor no one got off. But about four more people squeezed in. Pushing me in that handsome nice dressed man's face. As if we were about to slow dance. Shit! I was fine with that. Until he said. Merry Christmas! And I smelled his breath! O Hell No! I said to myself. I have to get the fuck off this elevator now! I just smiled as I held my breath! The elevator door opened. And said B1. Yes! That's my floor I said as I blew air from my mouth. Excuse me! I need to get out. Thank you. So I got out of the elevator and started coughing. Looking at that handsome bad breath guy as he smiled until the elevator doors closed. I then turned around and being to walk to my car. Saying that is one thing I can't stand is a bad breath man! I set my bags down by the car and reached into my handbag and took my car keys out and open the door put my bags in then jumped in the car started it up and drove off. Damn! Christmas is in three days. I will be so glad when it's here and gone! I said while pulling into the driveway of my apartment building. Wow! Look at Miguel's Christmas lights! They are beautiful! And he's having another party! It was more people in his garage this time then at his last party! Damn! And their are people standing outside on his lawn! Oh wow I don't believe it! I said. As I drove slowly down my driveway looking. Finally I parked. Now let me put these bags in my trunk until tomorrow morning after I pray to the coco. Oh! Shit! It's time for me to pray to the coco. Now So I put the bags in the trunk. Grabbed my handbag and locked my car up. And started to quickly walk to the stairs. Until I heard pss! Hey Latrice! Who's that? I said. Ah. Ah. It's me Miguel. Oh. Hey Miguel. What are you doing in your back yard? I asked. Oh. Nothing just drinking a little beer. I'm having a get together did you want to come over? Latrice. Miguel asked. You know maybe have a beer and a couple of tacos. Oh. No thank you Miguel. I'm tired. I've been in the mall all day shopping for christmas, my feet hurt. Aw. Do you need me to rub your feet for you or maybe a booty massage oops! I mean a body massage with a margarita please Latrice. Excuse me. Hell no! I said. Miguel laughed. You sure Latrice? Am I what? No! Miguel! Okay. Okay. Well how about alittle eggnog and a kiss under the mistle toe. That would make you feel better. What! Did this mutha fucka just say to me! I said to myself. As I just stood there looking at his stupid ass. He must be drunk. Now I'm mad. What the fuck did you just ask me Miguel! I yelled. I know you don't want me to go into my handbag and grab my pepper spray, shake it! And spray your freak nasty ass like a cock roach on the wall! Right? I said while digging in my handbag. Oh! Ah! Oh! No! Latrice. No! Please I'm sorry you have a goodnight and merry christmas. Yeah! And the same to you Miguel. You freak! What kind of shit was that! I mumbled as I walked upstairs to my apartment. I took my keys out when I got to the door. Shit! I have to pray. I opened the door quickly! Hey Mom! Hey kids! I got to pray to the coco. Okay we'll be in the bedroom Mia said. Come on Marcus. Coming big sis! So I threw my handbag on the couch locked the front door and headed straight to the hallway closet to grab my pillow. Got it and got down on the floor and prayed. Okay now let me take a shower and relax. So I go grab some clothes out of my dresser drawer. And went straight to the bathroom and turned the shower on. I got in and soap myself up rinsed off and jump out. Man! What a day at that crowded ass mall. I said. I picked my clothes up off the bathroom floor and took them to the washer machine and dropped them in. Went to the kitchen and grabbed a cup of noodle out of the kitchen cabinet reached in the refrigerator and took the ranch dressing and shredded cheese out. And begin making my favor dish. Wow! I am so tired. I made my noodle and put the stuff I used in my noodle back in the refrigerator grabbed a fork from the kitchen drawer closed it and picked up my cup of noodle and went into my bedroom and sat down on my recliner on the right side of my bed grabbed the remote off my bed and layed back and put my feet up. Then turned the tv on. Mom! You done? Mia asked. Oh yes I'm in my bedroom! Okay. I'll be in there. Do you want me to turn the christmas lights on mom. Oh yeah! Girl go ahead. Okay. So Mia turned the christmas lights on. Mom it smells like cigar smoke in the living room. What? Yeah. Did you go somewhere? Where people were smoking? Mia said. No! Maybe you might smell Miguel's christmas party next door. Oh! Maybe Mia said. But why would the cigar smoke smell like it's coming from that big red vase of yours in the livingroom. Mia your tripping. I said. Come in my bedroom So I can tell you what Miguel said to me downstairs. What? Here I come mom. Mia entered my bedroom.What did Miguel say to you? Wait. Where's Marcus? I said. Oh playing a video game in his bedroom. Oh okay. So what did he say? Mia asked. Well. I was coming from parking the car. And I heard someone say pss. It was Miguel in his backyard. Mia said. What was he doing back there? Shit! I don't know. But what I do know. Is his ass was drunk! Asking me to come over and have some egg nog and a kiss under a mistle toe. And get a booty, body massage and some more bullshit. What! Oh No he didn't Mia said. Laughing loudly. Ha!Ha!Ha! Shh! Mia. That's not funny I got really mad at him. I threaten to pepper spray his ass. I really don't want to speak to him anymore. Oh mom he probably didn't mean any harm he is just enjoying the holiday. Mia said. Oh Really. Well he better enjoy it with one of those chica's he have at his party I said. Mia laughed. Mom your crazy. I'm going to bed. Mia said. Okay. Shit Miguel's music is so loud, how can you go to sleep. I'll use my ear plugs. Mia said. Oh Okay. Well goodnight. Goodnight mom. So I stayed up and watched some tv. And ate my noodle. While sitting in my recliner. Two hours went by and finally Miguel's music had stopped the christmas party was over, but you could here the people leaving laughing, singing, christmas carol's and honking their horns and burning rubber in the street in their cars on their motorcycles for about 30 minutes. Then all the noise stopped it got quiet out there and real cold in my apartment it felt like a freezer so I pulled the handle up on my recliner and got up to throw my cup of noodle away and turn the heater on I walked to the living room. I could hear the tv on in Marcus room it was really loud. So I went into his bedroom. And there he was knocked out with the game controller still in his hands. And the game was on loud. I took the controller from his hands and turned the game off and the tv off and covered him up as he layed sleep on his bed with two of his blankets. I checked on Mia and she was sleep with her headphones on instead of her ear plugs. So I turned her cd player off and took her ear phones off of her ears and set them on her night stand and turned her lamp off. Damn! It is so cold in this apartment! I whispered to myself. As I walked back into the kitchen. Oh let me throw this cup of noodle in the trash. And let me turn the heater on before I could turn the heater on there was a CRASH! sound Oh! Shit! What was that I heard coming from the living room. I looked from the kitchen and thought I seen something small and black jump from my big red vase and ran under my christmas tree! Hell no! I must be seeing things. I said. Let me turn the living room light on. Okay now let me look under the christmas tree. Before I could get on my knee's. There was another broken christmas ball on the floor. With the hook on it. What the fuck! I said. I got on my knee's and checked under the christmas tree and there was nothing under there. I said. It started to get colder I got up off the floor and went and turn the heater on and grabbed the broom and dust pan. And went and cleaned up the broken christmas ball off the floor. As I walked to the kitchen and walk by the big red vase it sound like the plant was shaking! But when I looked at it. The noise stopped. So I walked into the kitchen scared a little bit. I must be really tired and I'm hearing things. And seeing things. But what about the christmas ball falling from the tree. For the second time. Shit! One fell yesterday. Maybe the tree branches are still fresh and weak. I don't know. Let me go get back in the bed. So I did. I left my lamp on and the tv. My eyes started to get heavy. As I layed on my back. I begin to dose off. And then I realized that my body was completely paralyzed! I couldn't move a muscle! Something was in my bedroom it even felt like it walked across my bed slowly I tried to scream. But I couldn't. Only a slight noise came from my throat! I could feel something grabbing my throat and started to strangle me! My chest felt like something or someone sat on my chest crushing it and putting pressure on my chest. And in a instances. I was being smothered! Ah, Ah Oh! God! I said in my mind! As I layed there in my bed trying to move but I couldn't! Don't panic. Latrice is what I thought in my mind! I couldn't see! What the fuck is happening to me! I didn't understand. You must call on God! Latrice. Dear Lord! Save me! I said as I could feel my body move just a little bit. I know the Lords prayer. Say it Latrice! So I did. Our father, toward heaven, hollow be thy name. As I continued to pray I could open my eyes full of tears. My chest wasn't heavy anymore I could breath again! And I could finally move my limps. So I sat up in my bed holding my pillow scared as fuck and in disbelief. Looking around and didn't see anyone or anything in my bedroom I took a deep breath and started wiping my tears from my eyes. Still sitting up in my bed. Scared to go back to sleep. Shit! I Didn't want to dose off again.

So I just at there quietly waiting for the sun to rise. This was one time I didn't need my morning coffee. I was up! And staying up! So I grabbed my remote and turned the volume up some on the tv and stayed up watching it. Three hours went by and I was still up watching tv. I heard some noise in the hallway. Like a bag being balled up. I turned the tv volume down. Then I heard foot steps. I am not getting up to see what that is. The hallway was to dark. I looked from my bedroom while still sitting up in my bed. Then I looked away and started to watch tv. And suddenly! I see a person in my doorway. I scream! Hey! Mom! It's me! Mia. Oh God! Mia you scared me. Sorry mom. Are you okay? You look like you just seen a ghost. No. No. I'm fine Mia. Little did she know I was straight spooked from that shit that just happen to me. I didn't want to say anything about it. It would probably scare her. Mom. Do you know what time it is? No not really. I said. It's sunrise don't you have to pray to that coco thing! In that vase. Oh Yeah! I said. I finally got up out of my bed and walked over to the tv and turned it off. Okay mom. If you need anything I will be in my bedroom. Oh! And good morning mom. Good morning Mia. I said as I walked into the hallway and grabbed my pillow out of the hallway closet slamming the closet door. Mad! I just didn't understand what had just happen to me! I couldn't stop thinking about it. I thought while getting on my knee's to pray to the coco. Oh Latrice pray and concentrate. So I prayed. I'm done. I got up and grab my pillow the phone Rung! Ring! Ring! Ring! I went to answer the phone. I mumble, who could that be this time of morning. Hello! No one said anything. Hello! They were just holding the phone. Hello! Oh! Go fuck yourself! And have a great day! I said. Click! They hung up. So I hung up and walked to the hallway and threw my pillow in the closet. And went back into my bedroom. And sat down on the edge of my bed. Trying not to think about what happen to me. I think I can go down to the car tonight and get the christmas gifts out and wrap them up and put them in my closet until tomorrow night. Sounds like a plan. If those two don't stay up late tonight.

So the day went by. Mia was in the kitchen making christmas cookies. With Marcus in the kitchen talking to her. Boy! Get your hands off the cookies! Mia yelled. Okay. Just one sis. Marcus said. I swear those two. Ring! Ring! Ring! Ring! I got it mom! Marcus said. Hello! Hey! Hello! Marcus said. Click! And F you too! Marcus yelled. Who was on the phone

Marcus? I asked. Nobody! What do you mean nobody. They didn't say nothing. What! Again someone called earlier and didn't say anything. That's crazy. I wonder who that could be? Mom! The cookies are done! Come in the kitchen mom! Mia said. I made different kinds of cookies. Here I come! I said. Grab a glass of milk. Cause you will be the taste tester! The taste tester? I said to myself. Don't worry mom. I'm a taste tester too! Marcus said. I know you are boy! So I got up from my bed and walked to the kitchen. Mmm! Smells good. I said. Okay you and Marcus have a seat in the dining room at the table. And I will bring the plates out to you with the different cookies on it. So grab your glass of milk now before you sit down. Okay. Don't worry mom. I'll get us some milk. Marcus said. You want ice? Yes son! Okay. So I went into the dining room and sat down at the table. Then Marcus brought our glasses of milk out and set them on the table. I grabbed mine. Thank you Marcus. Your welcome mom. He said. While rubbing his hands together. Ready! For Mia's cookies. Come on girl! We want cookies! Boy! Be quiet! Here I come! Mia yelled. As she walked out the kitchen with two large plates full of cookies. All kind of cookies. Different shapes and colors. Oh! God! Stomach get ready. I said laughing to myself. Here you go mom. Why thank you Mia. And Marcus here's yours. She said as Marcus grabbed two cookies off the plate before she could set his plate down. And started dipping the cookies in his glass of milk. Mmm! You did good sis. Marcus said with a mouth full of cookies. Try one mom. Marcus said. So I looked down on my plate and picked up a nicely decorated christmas tree cookie. Well it looks good. I said to Mia. I dipped it into my glass of milk. I bit the cookie. And it was delicious! Mmm! Mia you did do good! Thanks Mom. Mia said. Try some more. So I did. I was eating cookies and drinking milk for almost two hours with them. Laughing and talking with Mia and Marcus. I felt alot better. Well tomorrow is christmas eve. Marcus said. Yeah. I know. I said then christmas. And then the following week a new year's and should that be my year I yelled. Girl I can't eat no more cookies. Aw. Okay mom. But I can say that they are good. Shit! Save some for santa I said we all laughed. Sure mom I will Mia said. As she picked up my plate. What about you Marcus you done. Oh! No! But you can take my glass and pour me some more milk. He said as he burped! Your nasty Mia yelled. Give me your glass. Mia grabbed his glass and walked back into the kitchen. I got up to get ready to take a shower. So I walked in my bedroom grabbed my things for the shower and headed to the bathroom, walked in turned the shower on and closed the bathroom door. Dropped my clothes to the floor and got in the shower wow this water feels good let me wash my hair so I grab the shampoo and started pouring it into my hands then putting it all over my hair. Thinking to myself. Will I be rich next year. Which is in a week. We'll see. I said. I held my head back to let the water from the shower wash the shampoo out of my hair. As I continued to hold my head back. I thought I heard someone call my name in the shower. Latrice! Latrice! I quickly turned the shower off! And got the fuck out of the shower grabbed my robe from the hook on the bathroom door. Then grabbed a towel and wrapped my hair up in it. I looked in the mirror at myself and said Latrice you must still be tired from not getting any sleep last night. Shit! Got you hearing voices! So I put my gown on and took the towel from my head and let my hair air dry. And left out the bathroom. Hey! You two! I'll be in my bedroom watching a couple of christmas movies. Okay. I'm putting these cookies up I made. And I'm finishing up these cookies Mia made. Mmm. Chocolate chip. Marcus said. Well if you need me just come to my bedroom. Okay mom. So I turned my lamp on and got in the bed and turned the channel's until I came across a good christmas movie. I turned the channel for about fifteen minutes. Before I could find one to watch. Oh Here we go. The snowflakes are falling for christmas. Okay I'll watch this christmas movie. Hopefully by the time it's over. Mia and Marcus will be sleep. And I can go down to the car and get those christmas gifts from my trunk.

So a couple of hours went by and those two were still up. I went to check and Mia was on the computer and Marcus was on the video game. Oh. Well I guess I'll watch another christmas movie. I said to myself on my way back to my bedroom. So I sat back down on my bed and watched another christmas movie it had just came on. So I begin to watch it. One hour went by and I had to get up and go pray to the coco. So I did. The same routine. Grabbed the pillow from the closet got on my knee's head down and prayed. I'm done. Get up put the pillow back in the hallway closet. And went back in my bedroom. And sat on my bed. Looked over at the tv and the christmas movie had went off. So I reach over into my bottom drawer of my night stand. And grabbed a word search book and a pencil. Sat with my back against the pillows and started to circle words and think. Thinking to myself. I really need to wrap those gifts tonight. And I really don't want to fall asleep I'm to scared. After what happen to me. Let me check again on them two. They should be sleep by now. So I checked their bedrooms. And yes they both were knocked out. So I went back to my bedroom and grabbed my robe put it on and picked up my keys from the dresser and put on my house shoes. And walked out the house down the stairs to the car. Popped the trunk open and took all the bags out. Closed the trunk and begin to walk back up the stairs and got to my front door I set the bags down and quietly opened the front door. I reached down and picked up all the bags while holding the front door with my foot. Then pulling my foot from the door slowly. While holding the bags. I set some of the bags down on the floor to lock the front door. Then I picked up the bags again and headed to my bedroom. I walked into my bedroom and set all the bags down on the side of my bed. And went to the kitchen to get some tap and a pair of scissors from the kitchen drawer. So I can get started with wrapping up the gifts and putting them in my closet. Okay. I got what I need. Now let me go get started. I took the wrapping paper out the bag opened it and spreaded it across my bed and begin to take everything out of the bags to wrap. I set everything on my bed. Okay. I started wrapping up all the gift fast. After the fifth gift I could feel myself getting tired. I just couldn't keep my eyes open. I still had more gifts to wrap. Shit! I need to stay up to finish these gifts. And plus I'm still spooked from what happened to me. I don't want that to happen to me again. It felt like someone was trying to kill me. Oh God. I don't want to think about it. So I continued to wrap up the gifts. I begin to nod out. So I stop wrapping the gift got up off my bed and went to the kitchen to make a cup of coffee. I stood in the kitchen waiting on my coffee to get done in the coffee machine. It's done. So I put my sugar and creamers in my cup. Grab the cup of coffee and went back into my bedroom. But before I walked out the kitchen the lights in the kitchen started blinking on and off. Damn! I guess I need to change the light bulbs in the kitchen I mumbled on my way out the kitchen as turned the lights off. And went back to my bedroom. I set my coffee on the nightstand and sat back down on my bed. Let me drink some of my coffee. So I grabbed my coffee cup and blew it and drunk some. Okay! Now I should be up to finish wrapping up these christmas gifts. So I put my coffee cup back down on the night stand. Feeling alot more energized!

So I finished wrapping those gifts. Let me move something's around in my closet on the floor so I can put all the christmas gifts in my closet on the floor. So I did. Good now every gift fit in my closet on the floor perfectly! So I closed my closet door. And got back on my bed. Drunk the rest of my coffee up, got under my blankets and sat up against my pillow's again. And grabbed the remote control to the tv. And started watching tv again. I couldn't stop thinking about this voodoo shit! Thinking What am I doing and How long it's taking for that got damn coco to make me rich. I wonder if I miss a day or two of not praying to the coco. Will the coco speed up the work for me. Yeah! That's what I'm going to do. Not pray on christmas eve tomorrow and don't pray on christmas day either. Sense I haven't seen any results. Just strange things been happening lately. Fuck the coco! I said and laughed. As I started to get really sleepy. I don't know why I'm so tired. I said. I watched alittle more tv. Then I begin to get so sleepy I couldn't keep my eye's open and I couldn't fight it. Here I go yawning and scooting down from my pillows. My eyes start getting very, very heavy then everything went blank. I begin to dream. I thought? This dream felt so real! But my dream was so foggy. There was this man that came into my bedroom. I couldn't see his face it was so dark in my bedroom it felt like I was blind folded. He never spoke. He just went under my covers and lifted my gown up and opened my legs and stuck his big hard dick in me and started fucking me! This dream felt so real and so good! Ah. Ah. Ah! I was speechless as I started to climax. I then had the biggest squirting orgasm ever. It left me weak! I opened my eyes from the dream. My gown had been lifted up to my neck. And I was soak and wet! Like I really just had sex with someone. And no-one was there. Oh my. Let me get in the shower. I said after I pulled my gown back down. I got up out the bed and grabbed some clothes from my dresser drawer and went into the bathroom. Saying to myself. What kind of dream was that! It felt so real and so, so good I said. While turning the shower on. I guess that's what happen's when you don't sleep in panties. Let me make sure I have a pair to put on. So I went and grabbed a pair of granny panties from my top drawer. Maybe these panties will scare whoever and whatever that was off I said. And went back into the bathroom to get in the shower. So I took my gown off got in the shower and washed up real quick then got out. I dried off with my towel and begin to get dressed. I brushed my teeth comb my hair and picked up my gown after hanging my towel on the towel rack. opened the bathroom door and walked out to put my gown in the washer and I went to take my sheets off my bed. So I went back to my bedroom to take my sheets off the bed to put them in the washer, I pulled the sheets off. And took them and put the sheets in the washer. Turned the washer on and put the soap in. Closed the top. And went back into my bedroom. The sun is up now. So I grabbed another set of sheets from the hallway closet and started making up my bed. Mumbling to myself. That shit that happen to me. Made me feel good, but weird. How did that shit feel so real? I said to myself looking puzzled. So I continued to finish making up my bed. Hey good morning mom. Oh hey. Good morning Mia. You up bright and early Mia said. Yes I am. I said. Did you do your prayer already? Hell no! I said. And I'm not going to today or tomorrow. Oh. Wait a minute mom. What's wrong? Nothing. You sure. Well. Um. Damn should I tell her what happen to me. That shit is embarrassing. I said to myself. Are you okay mom? No. I'm not. What's wrong? Well I had two things happen to me while I was half asleep and asleep. Like what mom! Well the other night it felt like someone was trying to smother me! What! Mia yelled. And last night it felt like I was having sex with someone. Really! Did you like it? Um yes, I mean no! I said. That is crazy mom. You are not alone Mia said. Mia! Don't make a joke right now! I'm not. Mia said. Now. I didn't see this guys face in my dream. That grabbed my throat. And smother me! And who was I having sex with? Mom! Maybe you were having sex with the headless horse man! Mia said. As she laughed. Ha! Ha! Ha! Mia. Stop playing! This is serious! Okay. Mom I know. I'm sorry. Let me see. I'm going to look it up on the computer and see what I can find out about what happen to you in your sleep. Now let's see. Being smothered in your sleep. And I couldn't see, speak or move! Add what I just said. What mom! Okay I'll add that in while typing on the computer. Here we go! Being smothered, couldn't see, speak or move while sleeping. Mom! I found it! What! What does it say? I asked Wait a minute mom it's loading. Okay. Now listen to this! An evil sinister spirit may grab a sleeping human by the throat and sit on their chest and in an instances begin to smother them! Wow! That is some killer type shit! I shouted. Right. Okay! Mom that is crazy! Mia said. Now let's look up the next thing that happened! Wait! Wait! Mia let me sit down on my bed. Okay Mia said. Now falling asleep feeling like your having sex. Oh! Shit! Mom! What Mia! Listen to this. What is it? I said. Now this is some crazy shit! Oh! God! What is it girl. Mom you had sex in your sleep with a incubus! A incu what! I yelled. Incubus! A male demon form who lies upon sleeping women in order to engage in sexual activity with them! Oh! My God! Mom you had sex with a Incubus! That wasn't a dream! Mom. That was a freaky spirit! Oh! Mia! Stop! Your scaring me! Oh! Wait!Wait! One minute. And listen to this. There is also a female demon that does the same thing to men called the succubus! Mia! I don't want to hear anymore! How can you get rid of those evil, freaky, killer, spirits? I asked.Now I'm having second thoughts about this getting rich shit with the coco. Well mom I don't know about the coco. But I know about these freaky deaky spirit's we just looked up. Let me see how to get rid of the kind of spirits that pray on you in your house while sleeping. Please find it Mia. I'm scared to go back to sleep in our apartment. Really scared about that smothering spirit. But the incu whatever spirit. I'm so scared that I might start taking sleeping pills and sleeping naked every night so it can come fuck me! I screamed inside my head! Mom. Okay. I found it! How to rid evil spirits from your home with a bundle of sage! Sage! I said. Yes mom sage! Burn a bundle of sage all through your home. While reading the Holy Bibles 91st Psalm's over and over until the sage burns out. What! I said. Well let's go get some sage and a Holy Bible Mia. Hold on mom we have to find a place that sale's sage and pick up a Bible from the nearest church. Okay well keep on searching online Mia. So we can go get it before tonight. I don't want that shit to happen to me again. At least not get smothered. But the sex demon Mmm. Never mind. Okay mom. Let's not tell Marcus about this. You hear me Mia? Yes mom. Oh! Look I found a place that has the sage! It's called the smoke out we rid all unwanted EVIL SPIRITS, FRIENDLY, AND NOT SO FRIENDLY GHOST, GOULS AND GOBBLING AND WE SPECIALIZE IN GETTING RID OF THE DEMON THAT WANTS TO FREAK YOUR WIFE AND TAKE YOUR LIFE and all other unwanted spiritual things, No PROBLEM! The smoke out will make you shout! Thank you! Smoke out! Do they have a phone number Mia? Yes! They do. Call and see what time they close today on christmas eve. Okay. Mom. So I passed Mia my cellphone. And she called. Hello. Yes. I was calling to see if you have any sage? Of course we do. What time do you close today? We close at 7:00 pm. Oh good! And your address is 5530 S. Breeze Street. Okay. Thank you. Your welcome. Okay mom let me put some clothes on. Okay. Tell Marcus we are going to the market real quick and he can stay here. I said. Okay. So I grabbed my jacket, keys and handbag. And headed out the door. Come on Mia! I yelled. Coming mom. Mia said as she grabbed her jacket. Marcus we'll be right back. Okay mom! So we both walked out Mia closed the front door behind us. We got in the car and drove down the driveway. Look mom Miguel's garage is halfway open. Good he need to keep it all the way closed now. After what he said to me the other night. Anyway, fuck him. I said. And I drove out the driveway made a right turn and got into traffic. How far is it Mia? About fifteen blocks from us. Oh okay. So were on our way. Mom so when we get the sage and burn it in the house what are you going to do with the coco? Shit! Nothing. That so called spirit haven't did nothing for me yet! I'm starting to think it's not real. Mom! Your not supposed to say that. Mia said. Well shit! I'm still broke and got burnt and got! I know I know mom. Oh Here's the place to your right make a right after the light. Okay. So I turned into this small shopping center parking lot and parked. Here Mia. Here's fifty dollars it shouldn't be no more than that. Right? Yeah. It shouldn't be that much. You coming in mom. Hell! No! I see that gargoyle at the front door of that shop. Okay mom I will be right back. Okay I'lll be right here waiting. So Mia went in. I sat in the car. I really hope that sage work. Cause I am not trying to get smothered again but the sex Hmm? Maybe one more night sleeping on my stomach and it can come and get it "doggy style" it was pretty good to be a demon oh shit what am I saying. I want that shit out of my house! Here comes Mia that was fast. I said. Okay mom I got some sage. Thank God! I said. And the person at the register told me it's a church open for holiday prayers two blocks up the street it's on the corner to the right we can't miss it. Okay! Let's go! So I started up the car and headed over to the church. There it is mom turn right here. So I turned in the church parking lot it was very crowed people were standing in a long line to get into the church to pray on christmas eve. Mom I will go in and ask for a bible I'll be right back. Hey Mia. Yes mom. Get two Bibles. Okay. Sure mom. So she went inside the church I sat in the car waiting, and watching all kind of people in line waiting to go into the church there were Homeless people, Families and more some stood there looking around at other's as tho they had deep dark secrets! They needed prayer for, shit it made me think I needed to stand in line myself from messing around with the voodoo, maybe I should go stand in line I said to myself I opened my car door and got out, oh man. Here comes Mia and plus the line was to long. So I got back in the car and closed my car door and said to myself maybe some other time.I got the bibles mom. Okay. Let's go I said. Okay Mom. As I started up the car I held my head down on the steering wheel. Are you okay mom? Mia asked. I sat with my head down in silence thinking to myself I know that I'm wrong putting this voodoo before my god. But I was in to deep to stop. I really want to be rich and ask for forgiveness later. Oh! Um! Yeah. I'm okay. I said. As I started up the car and left. Do you know how to light the sage? Mia. Yeah. Mom. They showed me how at that shop. Oh okay. So we made it home. I begin to drive down the apartment driveway. I looked over at Miguel's garage and it was still halfway down. Shit. He probably have a hangover from drinking to much. And I bet he haven't built anything in a couple of days. Anyway I pulled all the way down the driveway and parked. Okay! Mia. Let's get started. I said as we got out of the car. Mia grabbed the bag with the sage and got out the car and then I got out the car and locked it. Then we both walked towards the steps. So mom what are you going to tell Marcus when we start burning the sage. Because they said at the shop if there's a evil spirit in your house that the smoke from the sage will get real thick in the air. What? I know damn well Mia the smoke aint going to be like fog! I said. Cough! Cough! What the fuck! I was wrong! When Mia lit the sage and started to read the bible. It was so smokey in the apartment. I could barely see my hands in front of my face When I followed Mia through the whole apartment. She prayed with the bible in her left hand and she held the sage like a torch in her right hand. She entered Marcus bedroom. And he started coughing and screaming! Saying. What is that! I can't breath! I can't see! Cough! Cough! Mia continued to pray holding in her laugh. Then walked out of Marcus bedroom. Mom! Marcus yelled. What is that! Oh! Boy. It's just a new incense I picked up called walking in the fog smoking a pipe! I said. As I held my laugh in. And walked out of his bedroom. I caught up to Mia as she entered my bedroom. As she walked by the left side of my bed I could see the sage crackling! Popping and sparks jumping to the floor as my bedroom got real smokey! Damn! Mia. What the demon's were in there having a meeting about running a train on me tonight! Mom! Shh! I'm praying! Oh Sorry. AMEN. Mia said. While coughing! Look mom your bedroom is the smokey place in here. Right now. So do you want me to smoke out the living room too? Hell yeah! You sure. Mia said. Yes! Yes! Yes! Do it Mia! I said. But what about the coco! Girl please you better smoke out the mutha fucking livingroom Mia! Now! I yelled. Okay. Whatever you say mom. So Mia lit a fresh sage and walked into the livingroom and started praying. As she prayed the smoke alarm went off. Beep! Beep! It was so loud she had to stop and open the front door and open the window's. Then the music from the radio begin to play loud. Ready or not here I come. By the Delfonic's. It scared me so bad I ran into my smokey ass hallway. Mia ran to but as she ran towards my bedroom holding the sage and the Holy Bible. The plant from the big red vase with the coco in it died! And fell to the floor. And Mia tripped and fell on it. Dropping the burning sage on top of the Holy Bible! Causing it to catch a fire. Mom! The Bible is on fire! I quickly ran into the kitchen went to the kitchen cabinet and grabbed my bag of flour tore it open and poured it all over Mia the bible and the burning sage to put the fire out! Are you okay Mia! I yelled. Yes! Mom! She yelled. Spitting flour out of her mouth. She got up from the floor. Are you okay mom? Yes! I said. With flour all over my face and in my hair. Mom. I'm done. I hope that sage works. She said. While wiping her face on her shirt. I know I hope it works too. I said. I'm going to take a shower Mia said. As she started limping to her bedroom. Okay I'm going to sweep up this mess. I said as I wiped my face on my shirt too. So the radio finally turned down. I think I should get the radio checked out. I said. So the smoke begin to clear from the livingroom quickly through the front door and the open window's. The smoke alarm finally stopped going off. Thank God. Hey mom! Is everything okay in there? Marcus asked. Yes! Son. Don't worry I got it. Okay I'm going to close my door and open my window. Okay. I said. So I walked into the kitchen and grabbed the broom and dust pan. And a kitchen towel and wet it. I went back into the livingroom and the smoke was all the way cleared out. So I closed the front door and the window's and walked back over to clean up the mess on the floor. So while walking back. I notice the plant laying on the floor. Oh! Shit! What the Fuck! Do I do now! I yelled. I scooped it up with the dust pan and took it to the kitchen. Grabbed a plate and shook the plant from the dust pan onto the plate. Then went back into the livingroom and started sweeping up the flour and ashes on the floor. After sweeping everything into a pile. I picked up the burnt bible and looked at it and shook my head. Then took it to the kitchen. And threw it in the trash can. Then went back into the livingroom to finish sweeping everything into the dust pan. I picked up the dust pan and grab the broom and dumped the dust pan in the trash can and set the broom and dust pan back into the kitchen.Then I walked back into my bedroom. Where it was still kind of smokey. I sat down on my bed with alittle flour still on my face and in my hair. Saying to myself. What just happened here today. Now I don't know if I am suppose to replant that plant or if the plant did that because I didn't pray today or if the sage just killed it. Well I guess I'll call Kwana. Let me see. Hey mom! Yeah. Come here. Okay. I will call Kwana later. So I got up and went to the bathroom where Mia was. Look mom! What? I got burnt! Mia said. Where? On my left hand. So I looked. Oh! My God! Mia. That looks bad! I said. I know mom. You want to go to Emergency? No! No! mom! I will be okay. I'll just use the cream I gave you for your burn on your back and some gauze and the first aid tape. Okay now you sure Mia. Yes mom I'll be fine. Okay. I said. I'm going to get ready for a shower myself. Okay. I'm going to go wrap my hand up and get on the internet. Okay. So I walked back to my bedroom. Saying to myself we sure keep getting burnt around here. Oh the smoke finally cleared up. Leaving just alittle haze in the room. Let me grab a full body suit to sleep in tonight. No gowns for me. So I took out my things from my drawer and went to the shower. Got in and got out. After coming out the bathroom I took my flour covered clothes to the service porch. Then walked to the livingroom. Sat down on the couch and turned the tv on. And sat there watching some cartoons. Then all of a sudden I hear a BIG POP NOISE! What was that. I said as I turned my head to the left and looked. I see some dirt coming out of the right side of the big red vase. I got up to see. And when I got close to it, it was a big crack in the vase with the dirt slowly falling out. Oh! Wow! Now how did this happen? Now I really don't know what to do. I'm going to have to call Kwana now. It's probably to late to call tonight plus it's christmas eve. Her shop is closed I'm sure. I'll call her after Christmas Day.

Well it started to get really late. So I walked back over to the couch grabbed the remote and turned the tv off. And walked to my bedroom to get the gifts for christmas from my closet. As soon as I walked by the big red vase it made another loud pop sound. POP! And more dirt started to fall to the floor from the crack on the right side of the vase. Shit! I said. It scared me so I begin to walk faster to my bedroom. I Got to the door of my bedroom and stopped right at the door. And said to myself. Do I really want to go in here. I stood in the doorway starring at my bed. Feeling so tired. Fuck it! I said. I'm going in! My bedroom was sage-d and I'm going to bed in a body suit tonight I said. Laughing and still feeling scared. I walked in my bedroom and went to my closet and grabbed some of the christmas gifts out of there. Then walked back into the living room and put the gifts under the christmas tree. I walked back to my bedroom to grab the last of the christmas gifts. Then walked out and placed the gifts under the christmas tree. Went back to my bedroom and sat on my bed. I started to get sleepy. So I laid down and covered up. I tried to keep one eye open but I couldn't I was to sleepy. I fell asleep.

Merry Christmas! Mom! You sleep? Mia said. Well. Um. I was. I said. Come on mom get up it's Christmas! Did you sleep good? Mia asked. Actually I did. I didn't get assaulted or raped. Last night. Good. See mom that sage worked. With that prayer. I know, thank you Mia. Your welcome mom. Even tho I got burnt. Mia said Oh. I know how is it healing? I said. It's healing pretty fast. I just took the bandage off this morning. What time is it? I asked. Time for you to get up and come watch me and Marcus open our Christmas gifts. Okay. Okay. Let me go wash my face and brush my teeth. Okay mom. We'll be in the livingroom waiting for you. Okay. I said so I got up and headed to the bathroom to wash my face and brush my teeth. So I washed my face and begin to brush my teeth thinking about the crack in that vase and not praying to the coco the plant dying and falling from the vase. Shit! I must call Kwana! Mom you done? Marcus said. Oh. Yeah! Well come on! Marcus said. Here I come! I'll call Kwana in a couple of days. So I walked out the bathroom. And headed to the livingroom. Sat down on the couch. Okay. Let's get these christmas gifts open. Mia said. So they both opened all their christmas gifts and loved every gift, gave me a kiss on my cheek and a hug. Okay! Now let's get this mess cleaned up. Aw! mom. Come on now I said. Come on Marcus. Alright Marcus said. Thank you. I said Oh Mom I have a surprise for you. Mia said. And what would that be? I asked. I am cooking us christmas dinner tonight. What! Marcus said. I thought we were going out to eat like we do every christmas! Not this christmas boy. I am cooking! Mia said. Well okay. I said. Do you need some help with anything? I asked. Nope I got it mom. Okay. I said. But Marcus you can set the table. Do I have to mom? Yes son, let your sister make us dinner. Okay. You don't have to set the table yet. In three more hours. See Marcus. You have a couple of hours. I said. Okay. Marcus said. As he started picking up all the wrapping paper from the livingroom floor. I started to help him pick up the wrapping paper too. Go head and cook Mia. Me and Marcus can clean up all this wrapping paper and throw it out. Okay. Mom. I'll be in the kitchen cooking. Marcus started laughing. Stop that. I said to Marcus. Okay mom. Let's get all this wrapping paper up. I said. So we grabbed all the wrapping paper up and Marcus went to the kitchen and grabbed a big black trash bag. So we put all the wrapping paper in the bag. Then Marcus took it out to the trash can Downstairs in the back of the apartment building. Marcus then came back in and said he'll be in the bedroom checking out some of his christmas gifts. Okay. And I'll be in my bedroom looking for something to wear. Okay. Mom. Marcus said. So I walk to my bedroom I looked at the big red vase and I could see more cracks in the vase. I stopped and said you punk ass spirit you better give me what I wished for! Before you fall out of that vase! After saying that the vase cracked and popped again. Scarring me. I begin to walk away. Fuck! I said to myself as I entered my bedroom. I went to my closet to look for something to wear. Mia! Yes! Mom. Are we having a formal dinner or what? I said. Oh! Mom. You don't have to dress up. Mia said. As she laughed. Just dress comfortable. Okay. I said. So I grabbed one of my velour sweat suits. From the closet and put it on with a spaghetti strap t-shirt. And went to the bathroom and brushed my hair into a high ponytail and put on some make up. And a pair of bamboo earrings. And dance-d in the mirror to the music that was playing in the livingroom for the coco. I left the bathroom and went to put my tennis shoes on. In my bedroom. Sat down in my chair and turned the tv on. And started watching the christmas parade. One hour went by. I could smell Mia's christmas dinner cooking. Wow! It really smelled good. Mia! Yes mom. Smell's good! Thanks mom! So I continued to watch tv until Mia get done cooking. I begin Dazing off thinking about Tim I haven't heard from him sense that date we had. I guess he'll call me when he get time. I said to myself as I smiled then turned the tv off and went to the dining room and sat at the table. Marcus! Mia yelled. You can start setting the table! Okay! Marcus said. So Marcus went into the kitchen and grabbed everything he needed to set the table. You need some help Marcus. I said No. Mom. I got it. Just relax. Oh Okay. I'll just sit here and watch you make the table look nice. Okay. So I sat there listening to the oldies station play. Mom the food is just about done. Mia said. Okay. Take your time. The phone rings. Ring! Ring! I'll get it! I said. Hello! Merry Christmas. And Merry Christmas to you Big Sis. Hey Jimmy How are you? I said. I'm good and Yolanda and the kids. They're fine. And how's Mia and Marcus? Jimmy asked. They're good. So what are you doing today for Christmas? Jimmy said. Oh. Just staying home waiting on Mia to finish cooking christmas dinner. Oh! Really. What are you doing today? I asked. Well we are going to go eat at Veggie-O. Oh. Okay. Well tell Yolanda and the kids I said Merry Christmas. Okay I will. Talk to you later. I said. Okay sis. Bye, Bye Bye. Man. Mom. Your brother is! Don't say it boy! Finish setting the table. Okay. Mom. Mom who was that on the phone. It was Jimmy. Marcus said. Saying Merry Christmas. Oh. Mia said. Anyway Marcus are you almost done? Mia asked. Yep! Okay. Give me about twenty more minutes. And I will be bringing the food out. Mmm! We can't wait! No mom you can't wait Marcus whispered as Mia walked back into the kitchen. I'm scared! Marcus said. What? Scared of what. I said laughing. Of Mia's cooking! You never even tasted her cooking. I know that's what I'm scared of! Boy! Stop it! I said. You eat everything Marcus! I know mom. Marcus said. Well you will be okay. I said. I don't smell anything burning. Do you? I asked. Well no. Marcus said. Okay. So let's get ready to eat. Okay mom. I'm done setting this table. It's nice. Thanks mom. Marcus said. Okay mom and Marcus christmas dinner is served! Mia yelled. As she brought some of the food out and set it on the table. Wow! Look at the yams and those greens and that macaroni and cheese. Let me go get the rest. Mia said. Now do this look scary! Marcus. I said. I know it don't look or smell scary to me! I said. You right mom. It do look good! Marcus said. Look she's bringing out mashed potatoes with some dinner rolls. Wow! Mia! I said. Wait! Let me go get the ham! Ham! Marcus said. Mia brought that ham out and it was beautiful! With the pineapples, cloves and cherries. Now I'm ready to eat. I said. Hold on mom. Let me go get the ice bucket and the fruit punch I made. Hurry up Mia! Me and Marcus said. Okay! Okay! Mia said.

As she quickly went back into the kitchen. Here it is! Mia said. While walking from the kitchen to the dining room. Okay. Let's eat! I said. Mom aren't you forgetting something. Mia said. Oh. Yeah. My plate. No mom! Mia said. Let us pray over this food. Mom. Um. I just sat there. I couldn't remember really how to pray to god. From praying to the coco for so long. That's okay mom. I'll pray Marcus said. Thanks son I said as I put my head down in shame. It's okay mom. It's okay. Mia said. So as Marcus began to pray. I started to think to myself is the voodoo really worth it.

AMEN! Mom. Mom! Oh. Huh! Did you hear Marcus prayer. Oh. Um Yeah! Mom. Mia said. Okay let's eat! I said. Yeah! Let's eat Marcus said. Pass me those yams! I said. Here you go Mom. Mia said. So we piled food on our plates and filled up our glasses. And ate and ate and laughed and drank and got full. And wished each other a Very Merry Christmas.

Four weeks later. I'm sick! I can't stand the smell of my own skin! I'm sleeping and I've been throwing up. And my period is late. I'm suppose to go back to work tomorrow. I'm going to call in sick. Hello. Yes this is Latrice Baldwin I am calling in sick. Okay for how many days. I need a week. Okay I'll put it in for you. Thank you. Your welcome hope you feel better. Yeah. Me too. I said while hanging up the phone. Mia and Marcus are still out of school until next week. So. Now I think I better go get a pregnancy test today. Oh. God. Let me tell Mia. That I need to go get a pregnancy test. Maybe she can drive me to pick one up. Mia! Yes mom! Come here! Okay! Coming! Yes. Mia come in and close my door. Oh. Okay. What's wrong. I don't know. I'm sick and I have been real tired. Really mom! What if your pregnant! Mia shouted. Shh! Not so loud. Mia. I don't want Marcus to know. Yet. Mom. He needs to know too. Girl. I don't even know if I am. I need you to take me to the store to pick up a pregnancy test. No. You don't mom. I'll be right back. What! Mia. Hold on mom. So Mia opened my door and walked out of my bedroom. So I stayed in my bed. Okay. Mom. Here you go. What is it? I said. She put a pregnancy test in my hand. Mia! Where did you get this from? Oh! Mom.

Just use it. You just never know when you need those kind of things. Not a pregnancy test! I said. I heard of condom's. Mia. Okay. Okay. Mom. I got some of those too. Mia! I yelled. Please mom just take the test. Let me get you a glass of water. Okay. I said. So I sat up in my bed and begin to open the pregnancy test box. And took the pregnancy stick out. Here you go mom. Your glass of it's positive or negative answer. I really don't want to know. I said. As I started to drink the glass of water. Okay. Mom. Me and Marcus will be sitting in the livingroom waiting. Oh. And mom. I think the only thing that will bother Marcus about you being pregnant is that you will be eating more than him! What! Mia! Your so funny. I said. As I got up from my bed. I'll see you and Marcus in two minutes. I said then I set the glass of water down on my night stand and took the pregnancy test to the bathroom. Okay Latrice Baldwin let's wet this stick. So I peed on the stick and waited. I swear this is the longest two minutes ever. I looked at myself in the mirror. I washed my face. Then I brushed my teeth while waiting on the answer on the pregnancy test. I took my ponytail down and brushed my hair. Oh god my nerves. I said as I put my hair back up in a ponytail. Then walked over to the pregnancy test on the edge of the bathtub. Bend down and closed my eyes. Then opened my eyes and the test is positive! Oh! Shit! I screamed! As all kind of shit started to go through my mind! Mom are you alright in there! Mia yelled. Yes! Here I come. Oh my god. This is crazy! I said to myself. So I grabbed the pregnancy test and opened the bathroom door with it in my left hand. Walk into the living room and stop right where the vase with the coco in it. And screamed! I'm having a baby! Mia and Marcus screamed and ran over to me and hugged me tight! As we begin laughing and talking about it. Mia started screaming in horror and pointing at the big red vase. Mom! What is that! Mia screamed! I turned around and moved away from the vase. And something fell out of the vase hitting the floor. What is that mom! Marcus yelled. I don't know it looks like a giant mushroom! Mom it looks nasty! It's wet and it's moving. Mia screams again! I'm sorry mom but I'm not picking that up! Marcus said. Okay! Okay! Calm down. I said as I tried to get a closer look at it. Watch out mom! Mia screamed as she pulled me back. Look mom another one fell to the floor. Mia start screaming louder!! Okay now what the fuck is this? I said. Mom I don't know! Mia yelled. But I think you should forget this whole getting rich thing with the voodoo and throw that vase out! Mia shouted. You got burnt by something when you were kneeling down praying to it! You haven't seen a change yet! What are these things laying on the floor! Moving around. I don't think that you should go on with this! Mia said. We are fine mom. How we are. We don't need to be rich! As long as we have each other and our trust in God we will be just fine. No Mia! I'm not fine living like this. Come on mom you just found out your pregnant by a millionaire what more do you need! Mia said. My own! Mia my own! I said. Mom I'm done. Please get that vase out of here before things get worse! Mia yelled as she ran to her bedroom and slammed the door. Mom. Mia is right Marcus said. Now it's getting scary. Okay. Okay. I'll call Kwana in the morning. Who? Marcus said. The psychic reader I went too. Oh! Even her name sounds creepy! Marcus said. Yeah. I know. I said. Come on letting pick this shit up. Do I have too? Yes boy! Okay mom. So Marcus went into the kitchen and grabbed a big black bag and the dust pan. Go get us some gloves too. Please son! Okay mom. So Marcus got some gloves from the hallway closet. Marcus gave me a pair. I put them on and he put his gloves on and opened the big black bag up. Okay hold the bag open Marcus and I will scoop them from the floor. So I squatted down and begin to scoop up whatever that was on the floor. I screamed! When I pick that shit up. Oh! My God! I said. What are those things! Marcus said. I don't know and don't care just pick them up fast mom! Okay Marcus just open the bag! I said. I dumped them in the bag. Now take this bag out to the trash can! Please! Okay. Mom. Can you go open the front door for me. Marcus said. Yes! Yes! Just go! I yelled. I quickly walked over to the front door and held it open for Marcus. He ran out with the bag. It gave me chills! When he ran pass me. After throwing the bag out Marcus ran back up the steps and in the front door. I then closed and locked the door. Mom. I'm going to go wash my hands. Marcus said. Okay. Thanks for being brave taking that bag out. I couldn't of did it. I said. I'm going to go grab the mop and the bleach. So I can clean the floor. Okay. Mom. Marcus said. I'll be in my bedroom if you need me. Marcus said. Okay. So I walked to the service porch. Got the mop and grabbed the bleach and walked back into the livingroom. I stood near the spot where those things fell on the floor. Opened the bleach and poured alittle bit on the floor. Then I set the open bleach down on the floor. And started mopping. While mopping. It felt like I was being watched. So I stop mopping and looked around. It was just me still feeling weird from that shit falling from the vase. I guess. So I continued to mop. And started coughing from the smell of the bleach start making me feel sick. Pregnancy right I said to myself. So I grabbed the open bleach and held my breath and put the top on it then took the mop and put them both back on the service porch. Now I've had enough of this creepy shit! Let me call Kwana. I said. As I walked into my bedroom. I grabbed my cellphone off my dresser and called Kwana. Ring! Ring! Hello! Yes. Kwana! Yes. Latrice Baldwin. How are you? Not good! Aw. That's to bad. Kwana said. What seems to be the problem? Kwana asked. Well there has been strange noises in my apartment. And things falling and dropping I said. What? Things that you dropped Latrice Baldwin. What! I didn't drop anything. I yelled. You don't have to yell at me. Kwana said. Now what else you claim happened. Latrice Baldwin. The vase cracked! You cracked it! Kwana said. No! I didn't! I said. I don't believe you Latrice Baldwin. What! Your crazy! I said. No your crazy or should I say your going crazy! Because the coco didn't make those noises or drop anything. Oh. Really. I said. Okay. Well tell me why a couple of weeks ago. I was falling asleep and I begin to get smothered! And the following night I was having sex with a demon! Ha! Ha! Ha! Kwana laughed. Then asked. Was it good? Well. Um. Yes! I mean. No! I believe that the coco called upon a couple of spirit friends to ashalt me and rape me! No! Kwana yelled. You watch what you say about the coco! No! I said. Because it's true! I shouted. And then earlier today the vase had some kind of mushroom looking thingies fall out of the vase on my floor! They were stinking, wet and moving around! I said. What! Kwana yelled. The coco never dropped anything from the vase! You plante-d those mushroom thingies! With the coconut! What? I yelled. Why? Did you do that Latrice Baldwin. I didn't! I yelled. Why must you tell so many lies on the coco! What lies? I said. Your a liar Latrice Baldwin! What! Now! For being such a liar! I feel you deserved to be smothered! And you wanted to get raped! Being that your so lonely! Ms. Baldwin! Lonely! I shouted. Now that is a lie! Your the lonely one! I said. As a matter of fact why don't you take one of those big dick candles you have in your shop and stick it in your mouth and suck it! I yelled. Enough! You Bitch! Kwana shouted. I will not take such disrespect from you! Your the bitch! I shouted. Uh! No! Latrice Baldwin! I will say as of today! To take away!

What you pray. To the coco! Fuck your wish! I curse you bitch! Whatever! I said. As I begin to walk back and fourth in my bedroom! Then I sat down on the edge of my bed. I want my money back! You ugly lady! I yelled. Ha! Ha! Ha! Kwana laughed. There is no refund! Oh! Really! I yelled. Well I guess I'll be calling the fire department on your ass and your black ass statue! I said. I am going to tell them about you burning candles in your little creepy shop. That has no smoke detector's and no fire extinguisher's Bitch! I am going to shut you down! You hear me Kwana! Shut you down! Curse you! Latrice Baldwin! I curse you! Click! I thought so! The bitch hung up on me! Now let me call the fire department! So I did. I called the fire department for three days straight! What's the address. The dispatcher asked. Okay. Thanks for your call. We will take care of it. After hanging up my cellphone. My house phone started to ring. Ring! Ring! Ring! Ring! I got it! I yelled. Hello. Hey baby. How are you. Tim asked. Oh! I'm fine. I have some good news baby. First off. I miss you. I'm out of the country. And I won't be coming back to the states. What! I yelled. Why Tim? Well I just came from this meeting and this company NCB International want me baby. They are going to pay me five times more than what my job in the states is paying me. Isn't that great! Baby. Yeah. Great. I said. What's wrong baby? You don't sound to happy for me. Well because I'm going to miss you. Aw. Baby don't worry I can send for you. How about that. Tim said. Plus I haven't forgot about that breakfast in bed you owe me. Tim said. Speaking of breakfast. He said. I ate something this morning that didn't agree with my stomach. I threw up. And I've been real tired. Oh! My God! I said to myself. Should I tell him? Latrice! Huh. Did you hear me baby Tim said. Oh. Yeah. Maybe it's because your in another country. Yeah maybe your right baby. The change of climate maybe and the food. I said. Well get better. Shit! Baby you know I will. I have one of the biggest offer's waiting for me to sign and accept tomorrow morning. And after I sign on the dotted line. I will be featured on the front of Money Line Magazine as one of the youngest, wealthiest men in the world! Tim shouted. So what do you think about that baby! Wow! Tim that's great. I said. As tears begin to fall from my eyes. And I started to sniff. What's wrong? Tim asked. Oh. Nothing just alittle cold coming on. Oh. Baby you better take care of yourself out there. Don't worry I will. I know you will Latrice. Well I got to go. I have to pick up something from the drug store for my stomach. Can't go into that meeting tomorrow sick. Okay Tim. I'll talk to you soon. And congratulations on your new job. Thank you baby. Tim said. Your Welcome. Well I'm a let you go. I said. Okay. Latrice, I miss you girl. Tim said. I miss you too. I said. Until we speak again, Chow baby. Tim said. Bye. Tim

After hanging up the phone with Mr. Timothy Rose. I begin to cry. I just couldn't bring myself to telling this man I was pregnant with his baby! He was just to happy about that new job offer. He'll be signing tomorrow morning. Hey mom! Who was that on the phone. Tim. I said. Did you tell him your pregnant? Mia asked. No. I said as I begin to cry even more. Aw. Why? Mom. Because he was to excited about his new job position out the country. He will be signing on with this big company out of the country first thing tomorrow morning. I got scared. Mia. And get this the name of the company is NCB International. Yeah. Mia said. Never Coming Back! International. I said. Aw mom. He said he's been getting sick. Really. Mia said. Yes. He thinks it's something he ate. Oh. God mom your gonna have to tell him. I know Mia. I know, I will, I will, tell Tim. I said. While crying and walking into the kitchen. Don't cry mom. Mia said as she went into the bathroom and brought me some tissue and wiped my eyes. Your going to be fine mom. Mia said.

Four days later. After talking shit to Kwana and not telling Tim I'm pregnant with his baby. I decided to go to the doctor to start my prenatal care. Mia drove me. And it was official I was definitely pregnant. The doctor said. What a blessing I said. As I walked out the doctor's office. And got into the car. Okay. Mia you have to stop and get me some cottage cheese and black olives! I said. What! Yuck. Mia said. Yes girl. Okay. Mom. So we stopped at the Super A Market. And Mia got out and went in the store and got the cottage cheese and black olives. For me. I sat in the car. While sitting in the car. I put my seat back and laid back. When laying back in the seat before closing my eyes. I notice a couple of crow's flying in a circle above the car. They were harking so loud. I covered my ears. Shit! I can still hear the crow's with my hands covering my ears. So I sat up. O Here come's Mia! Thank God! I said. That shit was creepy. Here you go mom. Mia did you see those crow's. Huh? Oh! Wait. Mom. I forgot to get you a fork. I got your black olives from the salad bar in the market. Mia yelled as she walked back into the store. That's fine! I yelled. I looked up at the sky again. And the crow's were gone. What the? I said. Okay. I know I'm not crazy. Where did those crow's just go? I said to myself. Hey! Here you go mom. Mia said. As she passed me a fork. Thanks. So Mia got in the car and started up the car and we headed home. We started laughing and talking on the way home. I couldn't stop laughing off of something Mia said. Girl shut up! I said while putting my spoon to my mouth to eat my cottage cheese and black olives. When I put the spoon in my mouth I notice two crow's fly from the left side in front of our car. So I slowly chewed my food then swallowed it and continued to look out the front window of the car while Mia was still talking. I got quiet. And watched another crow fly in front of the car from the right side. Mom! Did you hear me? Oh! Ah. Yeah. Yeah. Isn't that funny. Mom. Oh. Yeah. Mia. Mom are you listening? Mia said. Oh. Yeah. Yeah. I'm listening. I said. Okay. Then what was I talking about. Um. I'm sorry Mia. I didn't heard you. I'm just alittle tired. I said. While closing up my cottage cheese container putting it back in the bag with my spoon sitting here wondering to myself why do I keep seeing crow's today. We were a couple of blocks away from my apartment. And Mia was still driving and talking, and talking, and talking. Until a crow flew from the left side so low in front of the car with something dead in it's mouth! We both screamed! Mia closed her eye's and begin to swerve into the oncoming traffic! I quickly reached over and grabbed the steering wheel with both my hands turning the car back into our lane! Open your eye's Mia! I screamed. And calm down. Get over to the right and pull over. I said. I let go of the steering wheel. Letting her take control as she calmed down. Pull over! I said again. Let me drive. Okay. Okay. Mom. So Mia got over to the right lane and pulled over. We both got out and asked if each other was alright. I am so sorry mom. That scared me! I never seen a crow fly so low and that close carrying something dead in it's mouth! Yeah I know me either. I said. So we both got back in the car. And I begin to drive. Put your seatbelt on Mia. I said. While buckling up myself. Mia you know what's crazy before this shit that just happened with those crow's. I was trying to tell you. When you came out of the store to look at the crow's circling in the sky above the car. But you went back in the store to get me a fork. What! Mia said. Mom that's creepy. Yeah. I know. And when you were driving and talking the crow's kept flying back and fourth in front of the car. Mom. I wasn't even paying attention. I know you weren't you were driving and talking. I finally pull up in the apartment driveway and drove down to my parking stall and parked. Wait mom. Before we get out. Let me go on my cellphone and look up what just happen to us with those crow's. Girl! No. I said. Mom. Really you never know. Okay. Let's see what it says. Okay. What does it mean when a crow flies in front of you when driving. Mia said. Listen mom. According to an evil voodoo ritual. Someone has put a curse on whomever is in the car. You hear that mom. I sat there in silence. And what does it mean to have a crow fly in front of you with something dead in it's mouth. A voodoo practitioner has put a CURSE OF DEATH ON YOU! And you will. Um. Shit! My phone died. Mia yelled. We both begin to get out of the car. After hearing that I couldn't stop thinking about the argument I had with Kwana. Mom! Huh! That's weird why would someone want to put a curse on us. And want us to die. Mia said. I didn't answer. I just lock the car and started walked towards the stairs to my apartment. Wait! Up mom. Mia said. Are you okay? Mia asked. Yeah. I'm fine. I said. So we both walked upstairs to my apartment. Marcus was already standing at the front door. How did everything go at the doctor's office. It went well. I said. I'm going to go lay down. I'm feeling alittle tired. I said. As I walked to my bedroom. Mia is everything okay? Marcus said. After closing and locking the front door. Well. Yeah. Except for a couple of crow's flying in front of the car trying to make us crash. What! Marcus said. I think mom might of gotten shooken up alittle bit from it. Yeah. That's crazy. Marcus said. I know Mia said as she walked to her bedroom and closed her door. So I slept for a couple of hours. Then got up. Thinking to myself. I have to get rid of that big red vase! I walked to the livingroom and looked at the vase then went to the kitchen and grabbed some big black bags out. The kitchen drawer. I walked down the hallway to Mia and Marcus bedroom's and knocked on their doors. What's wrong mom. Marcus said. Is everything okay Mia said. As she opened her door. No! I want that vase out of here now! I yelled. Okay. Come on Marcus. Alright let me put my shoes on real quick. Marcus said. Okay. Hurry up! Mia said. So me and Mia walked to the livingroom. Let me take it out. I can do it by myself Mia said. She started reaching up grabbing the vase. Dirt fell in her eyes. Oh! Shit! Mia! Sorry mom. It's to heavy and some of the dirt got in my eyes. Okay ladies I'm ready. Let me get the ladder from the service porch. Marcus said. So he went and got it.

Opened it and stepped up on it. And begin pulling and tugging, moving the vase around trying to get it to down. Man! This vase is heavy! It feel like someone is holding it down. It is that evil spirit! Mia yelled. Mom it wont move. Shit! Mia go run next door and ask Miguel can he come help take this vase out of here. Okay. Mom. Marcus get off the ladder and go with her please. Sure mom. So they both went next door. I went and sat down on the couch and waited for them to come back. Here they come. Wow! That was fast. Yeah! That's because Miguel's garage was closed with a big lock on it. Mia said. And there's a For Sale sign on his lawn. Marcus said. Are you serious! I said. Yes. We even rung his door bell and no one answered. And Marcus went to the side of his house and knocked on the window There were no curtains. He even looked in the window and guess what. What? The house was empty. Really! I said. Good I'm glad his nasty ass is gone. What do you mean mom? Marcus asked.Uh boy it's a long story I'll tell you later. Now what are we going to do Mia said. We have to get this vase out of here! She yelled. Shu! I know. We might have to pay somebody to help us get it out of here Marcus said as he grabbed the ladder and closed it up and took it back to the service porch. He's right mom. Bad as we want it out of here. Mia said. We will have to find someone to help us tomorrow. In the meantime let's get some rest so we can deal with this vase in the morning. I said. Okay. Mom. Marcus put those bags on the table so we can use them tomorrow to get that vase out of here. Alright mom. Marcus said. Tomorrow let's just clean the whole apartment. And call somebody to help us get the vase out. Okay. You know me and Marcus go back to school in two days. Yes. I know. I said. So tomorrow we need to get up and clean the apartment. And after cleaning. Maybe I can call your uncle my brother to come help get the vase out of here. What do you two think? Does that sound like a plan? I said. Yes! They both said. Okay. Now let's get some sleep.

The next day. I'm up before sunrise. Thinking about that Kwana and her fucking voodoo shop. I'm going to go drive pass her shop this morning. I said. While grabbing my keys and my jacket and slipping on my house shoes. So I leave. I get in my car and drive down my apartments driveway. When I get to the end of the driveway to make a right turn. I stop and look to my left at Miguel's house. And Mia and Marcus was right! There's the For Sale sign on his lawn. And a big lock on his garage. Wow. The kids were telling the truth. I said. Then I made a right turn. So I drove down a couple of blocks to go checkout the psychic reader Kwana's shop. So I drove by it. And no one is there all of the lights are off. But I do see a big red tag on her door. So I make a U turn and parked my car right in front of the shop. It's still kind of dark out. So I grabbed my flashlight out of my glove compartment unlocked my car door grab my keys and walked up to the front door of Kwana's psychic reading shop. As I got closer to the red tag taped to the door. I turned my flashlight on so I could read what it said on the red tag. Closed to the public until further notice. No trespassing. Yes! I shouted. I shut her fucking shop down! I walked over to the shops window and looked in. Oh! Shit! What was that! I just saw run by on the floor in there. It was black! And it ran by real fast! My heart started beating real fast! Let me stop looking in this window. So I hurried back to my car. Got in and drove off! Scared! I made it back to my apartment. The sun was coming up. So I parked my car. Got out the car and locked it. And went upstairs. I put my key in the front door quietly. Then I walked in and headed to my bedroom still feeling scared. Before I could walk in my bedroom. Hey! Mom! Mia said. I screamed. Mia! Don't do that! I yelled. Do what? Mia said. Scare me! I wasn't trying to scare you. Even tho you do look like you just seen a ghost! Mia said. Where did you go this morning. Mia asked. Um. Out to get some fresh air. I said. Oh.Well I'm already cleaning the bathroom. Good. I'm going to go lay down for about one hour. I said. When I get up I will help you clean. Okay mom when you get up I'll still be cleaning. I'll get Marcus up in about thirty minutes to help me throw out some old clothes and all the trash. Mom try to figure out what time to call your brother to come throw that vase out. When you get up. Or Maybe I can just break it open with a hammer.

Oh. Yeah. We do need to get that vase out of here. Today. We can call my brother. When I get up. I said. So I went to lay down and fell asleep. Two hours went by and the phone rung. Ring! Ring! Ring! Ring! Ring! Ring! Mia! Get the phone! Marcus answer that phone. Ring! Ring! Shit! I said. I got up to answer the phone. I walked to the livingroom and picked up the phone. Hello. Hello! They laughed. Ha! Ha! Ha! And then hung the phone up in my face. So I hung up. I seen the front door was open with a couple of boxes and a trash bag in the doorway. The kids must be throwing out something. I said I begin to walk back to my bedroom. As I started to walk pass the big red vase. It made a big loud pop noise! Then it felt like someone was watching me. So I turned and looked at the big red vase. Then I looked behind me at the front door. Then turned back around and started to walk to my bedroom, the music turned up loud. And it played louder and louder. No-one touched it. I covered my ears and continued to walk to my bedroom and then POW! OUCH! I felt something hot as hell hit my left calf! Like someone just shot me with a bowen arrow! The music stopped! I fell to the floor on my stomach! And I couldn't get up! I could feel my stomach cramping. I just laid there. I couldn't move. Then my left leg started to swell up so big that it look like it was going to bust. I was in pain! I begin to cry and pull myself across the floor in the hallway and to the bathroom floor. As soon as I pulled myself into the bathroom. I just laid there on the side of the toilet. Then all of a sudden! Blood begin to pour out of my vagina like a broken water faucet. I was in so much pain! I couldn't do anything. But just lay still with tears falling from my eyes. All I though was. Now! Why? Am I laying here in a pool of my own blood? I am in disbelief saying, what in the hell did I get myself into?

Help! Help! Somebody help me please! Mia! Marcus! I'm bleeding help me! Call 911! Mom! Mia yelled! Yes! Mia. I'm in the bathroom! Hurry! Here Marcus you take the rest of these boxes down. I'll go see what's wrong with mom. Okay. Marcus said. Coming mom! Before Mia could make it to the bathroom. I begin to feel cold I was loosing so much blood. While feeling multiple large blood clots coming out of me. Oh! God! I'm going to lose my baby. Oh! No! I screamed. Mia finally made it to the bathroom door. And screamed! Mom! What happen! I don't know Mia! I don't know! I said crying. I can't move. Okay mom. Let me call 911. So she grabbed her cellphone from her back pocket and called. 911 What's your emergency? Um! It's my mom! What happen to your mom? I don't know she's laying here on the bathroom floor in a pool of her own blood and she can't move! Okay is she conscious? Yes! Yes! She is! Mia said. Okay don't move her. Okay I won't! Oh! And she's pregnant! Okay. I'm dispatching a unit out now. What is your address. Mia gave the address. And hung up. Their coming mom.Mia said as she squatted down beside me and put a blanket over me. Your going to be fine. Mom you hear me. No! I'm not Mia. I cried. I could hear the siren's. Hey Mia! Did you call 911? Marcus yelled. Yes! Were in here! In the bathroom! Mia yelled. Sir their in the bathroom down this hall. Marcus said. As he led the way to the bathroom. Thank God Marcus didn't walk into the bathroom and see mom like that. He stood in the hallway. Oh! Wow! What happen ma'am the fireman ask. I fell. I said. Did you trip on something? No. I didn't. Well how did you fall? I don't know. You don't know the fireman looked at his partner then looked back at me. I see your left leg is really swollen. Yeah I know. Did you bump it. No! No! No! I said. At that time the paramedics walked in. And said wow was this a crime scene! Hey. Miss what happen. I didn't say anything. This is what happen so the fireman walked out with one of the paramedic to the hallway. She fell but she don't know how she fell. The fireman said. Oh. Okay. So they brought in a gurney. Picked me up and laid me down on it dropping the bloody blanket on the bathroom floor. They started to push me out to my hallway While pushing me out I looked down on the bathroom floor at all that blood I lost. And said to myself Latrice I know you just lost your baby. Mom. Don't worry I will clean up the bathroom. Mia said. Oh! Wait! Sir let me grab her handbag and give it to her. Keep the keys Mia. You might have to pick me up. Okay. I love mom Marcus said as he kissed my forehead. I love you too. I said. The paramedics took me out and down the stairs and put me in the ambulance. Before closing the doors on the ambulance a small fire truck pulled up and parked. A fireman got out and walked up and tapped the paramedic on his back. He turned around and said. Hey Dave. How you been? Good Bob and you. Oh. I'm hanging in there. So how's the wife and kids. Bob asked. Everyone is doing great. Dave said. They begin to walk away from the ambulance over to the small fire truck. Hey! I yelled. Dave, Bob, Tom, Dick and Harry! Where are you going! I yelled. To the both of them. The paramedic quickly turned to me and put his hand up and said wait! What the fuck is he serious! I mumbled to myself. So they both stood by that fire truck laughing and talking. Until I just couldn't take it anymore! I was laying on that gurney fucked up in the ambulance. I wouldn't stop bleeding and my leg was hurting so bad! So I yelled. Hey! You stupid mutha fucka take me to the hospital now! I am going to bleed to death in here! You can ask about that asshole's wife and kids on your time! Your at work! So take me to the fucking hospital now! See I told you Dave I have a crazy one I have to transport. She claim she fell. But don't know how she fell. Bob said as he laughed and walked back over to the ambulance. She's a crazy one! Dave! No! Your the fucking crazy one! I yelled. Oh! Just stick a sock in it! Bob said while slamming the two doors closed on the ambulance. It was good to see you Dave! He shouted. You to Bob. Finally. He got in the ambulance and started to drive. Thank God! I was on my way to the hospital. So when we got there Bob opened the doors then pulled the gurney out and pushed me in. There was so much blood on the sheets and the gurney. I was feeling very weak and I was dizzy. The doctor ask did I get shot. So the ambulance driver started laughing and said no. He pulled the doctor to the side and said I was 51/50. She's a crazy one doc! Oh. Okay. We will take care of her. Nurse Linda please take this patient in Room #5 Okay doctor. So the nurse lifted my head and pushed me on the gurney into Room #5 she helped me off the gurney. I limped over to the hospital bed and laid down on it. The nurse passed me a urine cup and a gown and she grabbed two clean sheets. And put them on my lap. Thank you. I said. Your welcome. Do you need help walking to the restroom in here. No. I'm okay. I'll go by myself. Okay. I'm nurse Linda if you need anything else just press that button over there. Okay. Thank you. I said. So I got off the bed. Grabbing my handbag and the urine cup and started limping to the bathroom inside the hospital room. While in the bathroom I pee-d in the cup and placed it in that little window to the lab. Then I limped over to the sink and tried to clean myself up alittle bit. Then went back and sat down on the hospital bed. And waited for the doctor to come in. So in the meantime a lady from the front desk came in to get my information. Sign right here Ms. Baldwin. So I did. The doctor will be in here. In a few. Okay.

Thank you. After she walked out I said to myself. I'm not going to take my clothes off yet. Until I find out what happen to me. So I laid back on the hospital bed and covered up with the sheets nurse Linda gave me. It was so cold in there. So I just laid there for about twenty minutes. Then I could here the doctor talking outside my room. Then she walked into my room. Hi are you Latrice Baldwin. Yes. I said. Okay. I'm doctor Olsen. I was told that you told the paramedic that you were pregnant. I didn't tell him that. I told the firemen. I said. Okay. Well. Whoever you told. Your test came back negative! Your urine doesn't show any signs of a pregnancy at all. What! I said. That's not true! I went to the doctor and took a pregnncy test. Earlier today. I said. Oh. Really. Well they lied. No!

It's true I am pregnant or I was pregnant! Oh. Sure you were pregnant. I swear I'm not lying to you doctor! I yelled. Okay. Oh I believe you. You just need to calm down and lower your voice. Now also I was told you hurt your leg. Let me see it. So I pulled the sheet back and rolled up my pants leg. Wow! What happen! I don't know. I said. You don't know? No! I don't. So did you fall? Yes. I fell. I said. And the doctor looked at me and said I don't believe you. And started walking up closer to my face. Saying I don't think you fell. I think your trying to get over on the state. What! I said. Did you smash your leg in the door or hit it with a bat a couple of times for disability purposes! Huh? What are you talking about! I said to the doctor. Your the crazy one! I yelled. No I'm not. Honey doctor Olsen said. You know what.

You sit right here. I will go get you the proper help you need. Okay. It's about time. I said. Once the doctor stepped out and begin to use the phone. I could hear her saying. We got a crazy one down here! Send them down with the straight jacket! The straight jacket! I said. Oh! Hell no! I am not crazy! I quickly got up and put my shoes on and grabbed my handbag. And tiptoed to the door of the hospital room. I begin to peek out and I seen the doctor's back was turned while on the phone to my right. So I slowly started to walk out going the other way. As I walked down the hallway I begin to walk faster pushing through doors trying to find an exit. Ow! Ow! My leg is hurting so bad! I have to slow down. As I started to limp I still had blood coming down my legs. Leaving a small trail of blood drops. Fuck! I need to get to the restroom. So I kept limping to the end of the hallway. I could here the hospital staff looking for me. I limped to the left of the hallway then to the right and there was the restroom I limped into the restroom and locked the door. I put my handbag on the sink and started looking around the toilet for sanitary napkins, tampons, tissue or maybe some paper towels. Shit! Latrice think! While looking around. I can still hear the hospital staff yelling and running looking for me. Check the east wing one of the staff member's yelled. Then it got quiet. I guess all the staff went down the east wing. Now let me grab the toilet paper and knock! Knock! Knock! Hello! Is someone in there? This is nurse Tammy are you alright in there? I see drops of blood on the floor leading to the restroom. Do you need a doctor? Um! Shit! I mumbled. Let me change my voice. Like an older woman. Um! No nurse Tammy. I just had some blood taken and I'm a bleeder. Oh! I'm Sorry to hear that. Did you need some help in there. Oh! No! No! I got it plus I have to give a urine sample to the lab. Oh! Okay. Well I'm a go get something to clean this blood up out here for you. Okay. Nurse Tammy said. Damn bitch! I said under my breath. Oh! Okay. Thank you. So as nurse Tammy went to go get the mop and other things to clean the blood up. I grabbed the toilet paper and start unwrapping it rolling it around my arm. Until it was enough to put between my legs like a sanitary napkin. Then I turned the water on grabbed a couple of papertowels and wet them to clean the blood off of me. Then washed my hands and dried them. Grabbed my handbag and stepped out of the restroom leaving the water running in the sink and locked the restroom door. Then closed it And begin to walk down the hallway to the emergency exit stairway. I quickly opened the door and started walking down the stairs.

Fuck! I triggered the alarm off! I said as I limped down the stairs. I could hear the staff coming! Oh! God I have to get the hell out of here! I said as I look back up the stairs. The staff in the hospital sound like they were getting closer! Shit! I said. I then turned back around and Bam! Ouch! I bumped my face right into the hospital securities chest! Going somewhere miss. He said. Well. Um. I um! Come with me. He said. So he grabbed my arm and begin to walk me back up the stairs. As he held my arm I noticed that he had that red braided string around his wrist. I quickly thought about what Mia told me about Ms. Gigi. And asked the security. Excuse sir! I know what that red string around your wrist means. It's your protection to protect your soul. Right. I said. He stopped! And looked at me in my eyes and said. What did you say? Please I'm not crazy sir! I know you know about the voodoo! I do too. I said. Please listen to me. I did a voodoo job with the coco! After telling the security guard that he quickly let my arm go. My voodoo job went bad. I was cursed by a pyschic reader! Please let me go! Oh! Shit! He said. Come on follow me back down the stairs. Okay. I said. As he led the way. We both quickly went down the stairs to the ground floor. Here take this door. He said. It will lead you straight out into the parking lot. Okay. I said. I heard the door from the third floor open and you can hear the doctor yelling down the stairway. Hello down there! Then I heard more people starting to run down the stairs. Hurry go through that door. The security said. Okay. I opened the door then looked back at the security guard and whispered. Thank you. He bowed his head and shut the door behind me quickly. Hey! Is anyone down there on the ground floor? The doctor yelled. Um. Yes! It's just me the security! Did you see anyone come down there! It got quiet. No! He said. As he looked down at the red string tided on his left wrist. No! No! That was me that triggered the alarm. I'll call it in as a code 3. The security said. Okay. The doctor said. As she and the other hospital staff begin to walk back up the steps and back into the hospital. Well let's keep looking around she can't get to far! Doctor. Olsen said. So after I left out the emergency exit of the hospital it started to rain as I limped in pain crying my leg was still swollen! I could barely walk anymore. It started to rain harder! Come on Latrice just one more block! I can see up a head the Cho O Bowl Restaurant. I can sit in there and call me a cab to pick me up. So I kept walking. And crying I was in so much pain! Now before I got to the light to cross the street. I stopped walking and put my hands up in the air while the rain came down hard on me! I was soaked. I looked up to the sky and started yelling and crying asking God why me! The light turned green so I put my arms don't and looked straight ahead still crying as I limped across the street. Then I opened the door to the Cho O Bowl and sat down at a table wet as hell! With blood on my clothes. Everyone started starring at me. As if they knew I had a big voodoo curse on me. People were passing by me with their food on their trays looking at my leg. One lady covered her little girl's eyes and told her don't look at her. I just sat there. Then I grabbed a couple of napkins and wiped my face. I need to call a cab now! I mumbled. So I reached into my handbag and took my cellphone out the battery was very low. Just charged enough to make one phone call. I didn't know a number to a cab off hand. So I had to go to the counter. And ask them for a cab's phone number. So I got up and stood in line. I guess I'll order me a bowl of Cho O Chicken noodle soup. So I did and asked for a number for a cab. I grabbed my tray and the cashier handed me a card for a cab. Thank you. I said. As I still could barely walk back to my seat. I sat down. Then looked at the cab card and dialed the number. While waiting on the cab company to answer. I grabbed my spoon and begin to stir my soup and lift the spoon to my mouth and started blowing it. Then sipping the soup. While sipping my soup it felt like someone was watching me. So I turned around and looked behind me.

While waiting on hold with the cab company. They finally answered. 24 hour cab. How may I help you? I um a need a cab. Okay. What's your address? I couldn't really pay attention to what the cab company was saying. Because there was someone starring at me. Some woman shit some fat ass woman with dark long hair and she was wearing shades. Shades! This bitch must be crazy or she must be on drug's. I said to myself. What the fuck! I mumbled. Hello ma'am are you still there? Do you still need a cab? Oh! Yes! Yes! I said as I turned back around to my table. I taste my soup again. Okay ma'am what is your address? Um! I'm at the Cho O Bowl on a? Let me see. I turned back around and that fat lady with the long dark hair and the shades was gone. Ah. Hold on. I said. Excuse me sir I said to this guy sitting across from me. Do you know this address I asked. Ah! Yes. It's 1222 Long Creek Lane. Okay thank you. Hello! It's 1222 Long Creek Lane Okay ma'am your cab will be there in 5 minutes. What's your name? The dispatcher asked. My name is. Damn. The fat lady walked by quickly and dropped a business card on my table by my soup. Before I could give the cab people my name. Hey! Hey! I said she quickly walked out the side door of the restaurant Hello! What is your name ma'am! Um! Oh! It's Latrice. Latrice Baldwin! Okay thank you we will call your phone number back when your cab arrives. Ah. Okay Yeah. Yeah. So I hung my cellphone up and grabbed the business card got up and limped to the side door to see where the fat lady went. But by the time I got to that door her fat ass was gone! So I closed the door and started to limp back to my table and sat down. What the fuck kind of business card is this I said as I looked at the business card. The card read. Carmen's Spiritual Cleansings. We remove all curses. I stuck the card in my handbag. Then my cellphone rung. Ring! Ring. Hello. Latrice your cab is outside. Okay. Thank you. I said. My cellphone died. So I got up and limped out to the cab. The cab driver opened his umbrella and took my hand and walked me to the cab and opened the cab door for me. Thank you sir. Your welcome miss. He said and closed my door. And opened his door closed his umbrella and got in the car and ask me where am I going so I gave him my address. He started the meter and begin driving. So miss if you don't mind me asking. what happen to your leg? It's a long story. I said. Oh. Okay. Maybe it's better if I don't know. I didn't say anything. I just sat in the back seat looking out the window thinking about all that shit that just happen to me. Saying to myself as I laid my head on the door. Latrice Baldwin you fucked up! Hey. Miss. Yes. Were here. Oh. Okay that will be ten dollars. Oh. Okay. Let me get it. So I begin digging in my handbag for the ten dollars. The cab driver got out with his umbrella opened my door. And told me don't worry about the ten dollars it's on the house. He put his hand out to help me out the cab. And walked me to the stairway of my apartment. Thank you so much. Your welcome. God bless. He said as he walked back to the cab. I begin to limp up the stairs to get to my apartment. Then knocked on the door. Who is it? Marcus said. It's mom. He quickly opened the door. And helped me in. Walking me over to the couch. I sat down shaking. Let me go get you a blanket mom. Okay. Son. Mia! Mom is back. Oh! Mom! Mia said. Are you and the baby okay. No. I said. The doctor said I was crazy. And I was never pregnant then called for a straight jacket. What! Mia said as Marcus wrapped the blanket around me. Said you were crazy. Yes. I said as I started to cry. I snuck out the hospital. What! She said I needed a straight jacket! I yelled. The doctor really got on the phone and told them to come get me. Told Who? The crazy floor! Oh! My God. I am so sorry. You should of called me Mia said. No. I'm okay. I cleaned the bathroom up. Thank you. I said. Come on mom. Let's get you out of those wet clothes. Okay. So I got up and fell back down on the couch. Marcus help me up. Okay mom. He put my arm around his neck. And lifted me up. I limped to the bedroom. Wait! I turned around and looked the fucking big red vase was still in the livingroom. No! No! No! I yelled. What's wrong that vase get it out of here! Please! Get the hammer and bust it up in pieces and put it in a trash bag and throw it out! Now! Okay. Let me help you first. Marcus I got her go get mom a chair to sit on. So she won't mess up her bed with these wet clothes and all that blood still on her. He brought the chair. And I took the blanket from around me and then sat down on the chair. I'm a turn the shower on for you mom. Then grab a hammer. Marcus said. I'm going to help you break that vase Mia said. So wait for me. Okay Marcus said. As he walked into the kitchen. Okay mom let's get these pants off and get you in the! What happen to your leg! Mia screamed. Marcus come look at mom's leg. Marcus walked in holding the hammer. Oh! God! What happen mom! I don't know! You guys. Please let me get in the shower! I said. Just get that fucking vase out of here! Okay. Mom. You aint said nothing but a word. So Mia went in the kitchen to get her a hammer too. And two big trash bags. And some gloves. I got up and limped to the shower. I went into the bathroom and stood against the wall to take my clothes off. Finally I get in the shower. Mia came in and put some clothes on the sink for me to put on. So I washed up pretty fast. Oh! God my leg was still hurting and still swollen. I got out the shower and got dressed slowly. I could hear Mia and Marcus breaking the vase after turning the shower off. I opened the bathroom door and limped out holding on to the wall back to my bedroom were done mom. Thank God! I said. We just have to pick up the rest from the floor. Okay. I'm going to take a pain pill. I sat on my bed reached down in my night stand drawer. Got the bottle of pain relievers opened it and took two. And laid down. But didn't go to sleep. I could see from my bedroom that they got that vase out of there! Thank God! Now I can sleep better. Well at least I thought I would sleep better. But I didn't. I tossed and turned and cried all night. My leg! My leg! Was hurting! So bad. I didn't know what to do! I swear. I shouted. And started crying. What the fuck happen to me! I yelled. As I continued to cry. I grab two pillow's from the headboard of my bed and put them under my swollen leg. For elevation. Okay that feels a little better. I said. After elevating my left leg. Marcus came to my bedroom door. Are you okay? Mom. I don't know! I mean no! I start to crying. Marcus walked over to my bed and begin to hug me tight. I could feel his tears falling on my shoulder. Aw. Don't cry son. I did this to myself. I said. But I love you mom. I love you too. Your a female soldier. You here me mom! God got you! Thanks son. I said. As Marcus backed up from hugging me. Wiping his tears away. I'm a go shoot some hoop at the park for 45 minutes. I will be back to watch the basketball game. You want to watch the game with me mom? Sure son. Okay I'll be back. Oh! Marcus tell Mia to come here. Please. You two go back to school tomorrow. Yeah. I know. Marcus said. Okay I want Mia to drive me to go get me a cane. To help me walk around while you and Mia are at school. Okay mom. Do you want Mia to take you back to the doctor. Marcus said. Oh! Hell! No! I yelled. I mean no son. I'm scared to go back. They said I was crazy! And I'm not. Okay mom. Calm down. Let me go tell Mia to come in here right away. Okay can you help me down the stairs and into the car. Of course Mom. Marcus said Just before walking from my bedroom. Marcus! Yes. Mom. I haven't heard you talking about eating any food. I said. I know mom with all this stuff going on. Who could think about food. Aw. Baby don't starve yourself. I won't mom. When I come back from playing basketball I'm going to make me and you some fully loaded sandwiches! With chips and a soda. No noodles! Mom. Okay I said. Laughing. Ouch! Ouch! The pain in my leg! Mia! Mom needs you. Okay coming. Hey. Mom what's up? Aw. your leg. I know Mia. The swelling still wont go down. I said. I need you to take me to the drug store to pick me up a cane. A cane! Are you sure you want a cane mom. Yes Mia I can't walk to good on my left leg. Come on let's go. Marcus is going to help me down the stairs to the car. Okay. I'm ready to leave now Mia said. Is Marcus going with us? No Marcus wants to go play basketball. Okay. I'll go get my jacket Mia said. Hey! Mia. When we get there I'm going to just sit in the car, while you run inside the drug store and grab me a cane. Okay. Mom. Come on Marcus get me a jacket from my closet. So Marcus grabbed my jacket and helped me put it on. Then I put my right arm around his neck. And pulled myself up and stood up. You ready mom? Marcus asked. Yes. Let's go. Oh pass me my handbag. So I held my handbag and held on to Marcus and started limping from my bedroom through the livingroom out the house down the stairs and to the car. Marcus helped me get in the car. And Mia got in the car. Thank you. Marcus. Do you want a ride up to the park? Mia asked. No. I'll walk up there. Okay. Don't forget to have those sandwiches ready that you promise to make for us. When watching the basketball game today. Oh! I wont. I should be back before you and Mia. I will have the food ready. We'll watch the basketball game in your bedroom. Okay. I said. So Mia started up the car and started to drive down our apartment driveway. As we got to the end of the driveway. There was a big moving truck in front of Miguel's old house. Look mom it looks like we have some new neighbors. We could see the movers taking boxes into the house, a lady came out and waved at us. We waved back as Mia made a right turn to the street. So we drove to the drug store. Mia got out to go buy me a cane. I just sat in the car. While sitting in the car all I could think about was Kwana saying she cursed me. Did she? Or did I just fall. No! I didn't just fall on my leg. I fell on my stomach! Ou! Ouch! Now my leg is starting to hurt just thinking about the fall. Here come's Mia with a pink cane. Hey mom. How you like it! Mia said. I like it. I said. So Mia got in the car and passed me the pink cane. And said. Mom don't worry we are going to find out what really happen to you. I hope so. I said while gently rubbing my leg. So we headed back home. Oh! Mia before we go home can we stop at Cole's Coffee Shop, so I can grab a cup of coffee. Oh. Sure mom. Thank you I said while thinking in my mind about me getting that creepy bitch Kwana's psychic reading shop shut down laughing to myself. So we pulled up in front of Cole's Coffee Shop. And parked. I begin reaching inside my handbag for some change for a cup of coffee. Mia can you run inside of Cole's for me. I said. While looking down in my handbag for more change. Sure mom. Okay here you go Mia. She took the change. And got out of the car. Hey! Mia! Wait! I yelled. Huh? Mia said. Here. Here's some more change for a large cup of coffee. Okay mom. Your usual right? Yes. Okay. Mia walked back over to the car and stuck her hand in the window and took the rest of the change I had in my hand. Large black coffee with four packs of sugar and two creamers. Right? Mia said. Yep that's my usual. Alright. I'll be right back. Okay. I said. So I sat in the car I grabbed my handbag and zipped it up and set it on the seat next to me. I then looked across the street at the psychic readers shop. And what the fuck! The shop was back in business! With a even brighter blinking sign. That read. Come get your free card reading and make three wishes. I turned my face from that shit! And said What the fuck. I feel sorry for the next sucker that is about to get licked! Now after I said that. I could see Mia coming out the coffee shop with my cup of coffee in her hand. But as Mia got closer to the car she noticed a woman across the street inside the psychic reader's shop. Starring! Starring at me with her face and hands pressed against the big window. Ah mom, Here's your coffee. Oh. Thank you. I said. While grabbing my cup of coffee from her hand. Hey mom. Why? Is that lady in that window across the street starring at you like that. Huh? I said. What lady? Look across the street. Mia said. So I turned my head to my left and looked at the psychic reader shop's window. And Oh! My God! It was Kwana! I started to getting light headed and dizzy spilling my hot coffee all over my lap. OUCH! I quickly turned away and opened the car door and threw my coffee cup out the car on the sidewalk. And told Mia to get in the car let's go! What's wrong mom? Nothing! I said let's just go! Is everything okay? Stop asking me questions! Just get in the car Mia! My fucking leg started burning and swelling and everything I did with the voodoo at her shop begin to play in my mind. I felt sick to my stomach! Mia finally got her ass in the car. Now drive off! Please! Mia. So she started the car and drove off. I looked back through the back window of the car. And I seen Kwana walk out her psychic reading shop into the middle of the street and just stood there watching us then she started pointing her finger and stomping her feet and clapping her hands and shaking her ass and bouncing her titties at us while watching us drive away. Why the fuck was she doing that shit. I said to myself. If that was another curse she was trying to do on me. I sure in the hell didn't want it on me! Please drive faster Mia! And make a right turn at the next block. So she did. Damn! Mom! If looks could kill you would be slumped over and breathless right now! Yeah. I know. I said. While wiping the coffee off my lap with a napkins I took out of my handbag. Let's just go home. I said Okay. Mia said. So we headed home. Mia drove up into our driveway. Mom isn't it weird. How we're use to seeing that garage being up everyday when Miguel was there. The new neighbors have it closed. Oh! Yeah. Maybe they'll open it once they get settled in. Shit! I said to myself I don't give a fuck if they open it or not. I'm still thinking about what just happen? So Mia parked the car. Marcus came down to help me get out the car. Hey! Mom you ready to watch the game. Oh! Yeah son. Come on Marcus said. As he put my right arm around his neck. And grabbed my handbag. Oh! Wait Marcus. I have this cane. So I grabbed the cane and stood up out the car with it. I think I can use the cane to walk to the apartment. I said as I took my arm from around Marcus neck. I begin to walk with the cane and Marcus carried my handbag and Mia locked the car and ran up to Marcus. And started telling him about the creepy lady that was starring at me in the window of the psychic reader's shop across the street from Cole's Coffee Shop. What. Marcus said. Yeah! It was crazy. I didn't say nothing. I just walked slowly up the stairs on the cane. So Marcus walked up in front of me to open the front door. You got it Mom. Yeah. I said. Marcus walked in and said the basketball game will be starting in fifteen minutes. As he went t my bedroom and set my handbag on my dresser. Okay that will give me time to change into some sweat pants after spilling my coffee in my lap. Okay. Marcus said. And I'll start making us those sandwiches I promised. Okay. I said. Mom I'll be in my bedroom getting my clothes together for school this week. Mia said. Okay I said. So I went into my bedroom to change my pant's as soon as I sat down on my bed there was some kind of loud tapping sound on the sun beam outside in the bathroom. While changing my pants the noise got louder and louder! Damn what the fuck is that noise! I yelled. Marcus! Yeah! Mom! What is that loud noise coming from the roof. I don't know maybe their doing some kind of work on the roof. You think so? I said. Maybe. Marcus said. I'll go check mom. Okay. I said. So Marcus went out the front door and up the stairs to the roof to checkout that loud noise. I could hear Marcus walking around up there. Then the noise stopped. Finally! I said. So Marcus came back in and closed the front door locked it and walked back into the kitchen. And turned the water on. Marcus! Yeah! I'm washing my hands mom. Oh! I said I'm bringing our food in now. Okay. I said as I sat on my bed. Hurry up Marcus the game is starting! Coming mom! Marcus walked in with both of our plates with those big delicious sandwiches he promised to make. Marcus gave me my plate and set his on my dresser. Oh! Let me go get our drinks! Hey Marcus! What was that loud noise on the roof? I asked. Oh! That. Hold on mom. Let me get some cups and ice and the sodas. Marcus grabbed everything then he came back in my bedroom and said that noise was a big crow on the roof tapping it's foot and hitting it's beak on our sun beam. What! Now that's creepy! I said. Here I go thinking once again about that damn psychic. Kwana! I know that was creepy. Marcus said. When I seen the crow, it was looking down in the sunbeam like it was looking for somebody. Marcus said. What? I said. So the basketball game started. We yelled, we ate, and watched the first then the second quarter. Then it was halftime. I finished eating so Marcus took my plate to the kitchen. I laid back in my bed. Then all of a sudden! My left leg felt like someone started whipping it with a whip. It was burning so bad! I pulled my sweat pant up to my left knee and when I did. I had four wepts on the lower part of my leg and a bruise also in the lower part of my leg by y ankle. That look like a face! Kwana's face! I screamed! Marcus and Mia ran into my room! What's wrong! Mom. Mia said. Look at my fucking leg! I screamed. What is that? Marcus said. Did you cut yourself? Mia said. Let me get a picture of that Mia said. No! I didn't do nothing to myself. Click! Click! Stop taking pictures of it Mia! I yelled. Just one more Click! Stop it I'm serious! Okay. Okay. Mia said. Wait! Mom look at this. When I took the pictures you don't see the swelling or the bruise and there's no wepts! What! Let me see that! Marcus said. Mom! Mia is right. Look at this! I looked at the pictures Mia took and it wasn't showing anything wrong with my leg. This is so creepy! What is happening to me! I screamed. As I took the blanket and covered my left leg. I am going to just lay down. Marcus you can finish watching the basketball game in your bedroom. I said. Okay mom. Are you going to be okay? Marcus asked. Yeah. Son. So Marcus grabbed his plate and soda and went to his bedroom. Are you sure mom? Mia asked. Yes. Mia. As soon as you go get me two pain pills and a glass of water. So I can sleep through this pain. I said. Okay Mom. Mia said. While going to get me some pain pills from the medicine cabinet. Now I know that I have to tell my kids the truth, that I had a real bad argument with a psychic reader and she said she put a curse on me. I am convinced that there is a curse on me. Mom. Here you go your glass of water and your pain pills. Okay. Thank you Mia. Your welcome. If you need me mom. I will be in my bedroom. Okay. Mia. Should I tell her what happen now! Or just wait. Tell her Latrice tell her. Mia stepped out of my bedroom. Oh! Mia! I said. As I popped each pain pill in my mouth and drank the water in my glass up. Yes! Mom! I got scared. I! Um! Um! Just wanted to say thank you again. Fuck I couldn't tell her. Oh. Okay Mom. Mia said. Well I'm going to get some rest. Hopefully those pain pills kick in soon. I'll watch alittle tv. I said. I will tell Mia and Marcus tomorrow. I said while flicking through the tv. channels. I started to feel real drowsy. Oh. My leg hurts is what I said. Then I fell asleep.

The next day. Mom! Mom! Huh. I said. With my face in the pillow as I laid on my stomach. You over slept. Mia said. What. What time is it I said while trying to lift my face from the pillow. It felt so heavy. It's 12:30 pm. What! Where's Marcus? He left already. Don't worry he made it to school on time. He left early. He walked. Mia said. Oh. Good. I said as I lifted my head up. What is this on my pillow. Oh my god! My hair and alot of it all over my pillow. What the hell is going on with my hair. I said. Mom why is your face so swollen! What do you mean! I said as I touched it. Go look in the mirror mom! What is happening to you! Your face look twenty years older than what you are. Mia said. I got up and grabbed my cane and limped into the bathroom. I turned the bathroom light on and my god! It look like I was looking at something that was straight out the grave or a got damn scare movie! A fucking monster, in the mirror. I screamed! And I begin to cry. I could barely open my left eye. What happen to me! I leaned against the sink dropping my cane to the floor. Touching my face! Screaming and crying! My elbows had turned black. And my hair was falling out the back of my head in patches all over the bathroom floor. Mia! Mia! I yelled. She didn't answer she just walked into the bathroom and stood next to me just looking at me in the mirror. Mia I have something to tell you. I said. What is it. Mom. She said just starring at me. She then stood behind me and put her head on my right shoulder. And said you knew that lady didn't you? That lady that was starring at you through that window at that pyschic reader's shop. Yes. I got into a serious argument with that lady. Who is she? Mia asked. She was the psychic reader I did the voodoo with. For the coco. Oh! No! Mom! Why! Why! Did you do that! Mia said as she started to cry. And reach into the bathroom draw and took a hair scarf out and helped me put it around my head. So what happen? Mia asked. Well it was about the coco. Then one thing led to another. Then she said. Fuck your wish! I curse you bitch! I said as I cried telling Mia. I just wanted a better life for us. I said. Mom! Then you should of prayed and asked God! Mom! God! Not turn to voodoo! Just Look at you! I told you it could become dangerous and deadly! And I also said be careful what you wish for! Mia whispered in my ear just before she ran out the bathroom crying. Mia! Wait! What to do! I yelled. Call a witch doctor mom! Call a fucking witch doctor! A witch doctor I said to myself as I picked up my cane. And limped back into my bedroom. I grabbed my handbag. And sat on my bed. I then took that card out my handbag that the fat lady left on the table for me that day.

I reached over and grabbed my cellphone from my nightstand. And begin to dialed the phone number on the card I held in my hand.

As the phone rung. Ring! Ring! Ring! Ring!

Hello Carmen's Spiritual Cleansing

We remove all curses.

Hello! Hello! The lady said. Um. Yes. Hi. I said. How may I help you? The lady said. Well. Um. I um.

Yes tell me. She said. What's your name sweetie?

Um. My name is Latrice. Latrice Baldwin. I said as I begin to cry. Please dear don't cry. I am here to help you. I stop crying immediately! I got quiet. Now what seems to be the problem? She asked. I still was quiet. Hello! Are you still there? She asked. Yes. I am. Okay. She said. I um have a curse on me. And I'm scared? Please help me. I said. I can help you Latrice Baldwin. Now you come see me tomorrow at 1:00pm okay. Ask for me. I'm Carmen. Here's the address 20111 Warlock Lane. Come alone and wear white. She said. Okay thank you Carmen your welcome. Latrice Baldwin I will see you tomorrow. Yes tomorrow. I said. Bye bye now. She said. Bye.

Wondering what will be Latrice Baldwin's next move?
Stay tuned for the sequel, "Searching for the Cure".

Printed in the United States
By Bookmasters